Champagne Book Group

Presents

Love Songs

Opposites Attract, Book 2

By

DK Marie

This is a work of fiction. The characters, incidents and dialogues in this book are of the author's imagination and are not to be construed as real. Any resemblance to actual events or persons, living or dead, is completely coincidental.

Champagne Book Group
www.champagnebooks.com

ISBN 978-1-897261-01-9
October 2019
Cover Art by Robyn Hart
Produced in the United States of America

Champagne Book Group
2373 NE Evergreen Avenue
Albany OR 97321
USA

Other Books by DK Marie

Opposites Attract

Love Songs, 2
Fairy Tale Lies, 1

Dedication

This book is dedicated to my husband. His support and belief in me since the beginning of this journey means the world to me. Thank you, and I love you.

Acknowledgement

There are so many people to thank as this book came into being. First, my family, who've supported and understood my need to disappear into my stories for weeks on end. My agent, Dawn, who saw potential in my writing. Champagne Book Group, for picking up my *Opposites Attract* series. My wonderful writer friends on Twitter. Inappropriate Acres and Haven, you keep me going and make me laugh. You all are the best! Also, the excellent people in GDRWA. Your advice and support are priceless.

Dear Readers,

Whether you're a returning reader or new to my series, I want to thank you for choosing my book. It was a dream to write, like listening to my favorite song, one I can't wait to share with you. I sincerely hope you enjoyed reading it, as much as I loved writing this story.

DK

Chapter One

"We'll let you know," Maggie Preswyck told the last auditioner of the night. He snapped shut the case to his guitar, nodding goodbye. She couldn't even manage a half-hearted wave as he headed for the stairs.

She'd never call him, or any of the others who'd tried out.

The urge to kick Lincoln's bass drum or scream like a banshee was hard to resist. Detroit overflowed with musical talent. Apparently, those people weren't auditioning for her band. Most who tried out were adequate, yet none had a spark, the thing that would set ThreePence apart from the million other Indie bands fighting for recognition.

Every member needed to be unique. Extraordinary. Like her current lead guitarist.

The one who'd gotten knocked up.

Sure, Scarlett and her husband wanted a baby for years, but their precious bundle was messing with Maggie's future. Her dreams.

Scarlett's high blood pressure had her doctor demanding she stay off her feet whenever possible. Complete bedrest was in her near future.

Crossing off the name of the guy who'd just left, Maggie tapped her pen in annoyance, looking from her drummer, Lincoln, to her bassist, Jayce. "Please tell me there's others we've forgotten to add to the list. Anyone else trying out?"

Both stared back, offering nothing. Their discouragement matched hers.

"We should get Scarlett a hospital bed. Roll her on stage," Lincoln grumbled. "Finding a temporary replacement isn't working."

Jayce snorted, leaning his bass against a stool. "It's what we get for having a chick guitarist."

Irritation climbed along Maggie's spine. "Shut up, Jayce. If it weren't for 'chicks,' ThreePence wouldn't exist."

At times like this she wondered how she'd ever found him attractive.

Sure, she'd always preferred unconventional men like Jayce. His messy black hair, tattoo-covered arms, and tight jeans fit her preference perfectly. His attitude was unattractive.

None if it mattered now.

They'd never been anything more than a few sweaty nights together, which ended the day he joined ThreePence.

Once he became their bass player, they were done. She never slept with anyone in her band. That was one rule she never broke.

It hadn't been a big loss. The sex was decent, nothing spectacular. Plus, when he said stupid shit like now, there was nothing worth missing.

Jayce exhaled loudly, gripping the neck of his guitar and leaning back, extracting a pack of cigarettes from his front pocket. "Yeah, yeah, Maggie, we know. You found me, created the band, write most of the songs. Without you, we'd be nothing."

Damn straight.

"Don't smoke in here." Lincoln tossed a drumstick half-heartedly at Jayce. "What you say is true. She writes our songs, sings all of them."

"I own the house. Most of the equipment too," Jayce retorted.

He did love to remind them of this, daily.

"It is your parents who loaned us the money for the instruments and this place, not you," Maggie argued.

"Same difference."

She shrugged, there was no sense arguing about it. Who knew, maybe he could convince his parents to confiscate the instruments they'd purchased for the band and to kick her and Lincoln out onto the streets.

They'd saved half the money to pay off Jayce's parents. Maggie couldn't wait for the day they gave them the check. The day he could no longer hold so much ownership over the band.

Footsteps thumped overhead, and they glanced up. It was late, well after ten.

Oh hell, maybe the music gods heard her pleas, sending her the next Thurston Moore or Jack White.

"Must be Zia," said Lincoln. "She texted me a while ago, said she was stopping by. She'd sounded excited. Let's hope our manager found us a guitarist."

That would be fantastic. I love Zia, but I need a Carrie Brownstein.

Seconds later, Zia strode across the basement rehearsal area, a pleased smile on her lips and satisfaction oozing from her. A spark of hope ignited in Maggie's chest. Maybe Zia found someone.

"Where are you coming from? Can you take us next time?" Maggie asked. "From your smile, this place must be spectacular. We could use a little."

Zia perched herself on the edge of the couch, her gaze flicking excitedly from one band member to the next. "I was with my accounting tutor, Tanner," she said, dousing Maggie's small flame of hope.

"He gave you that smile?" Jayce smirked. "What exactly is he teaching you? Sex Ed? With hands-on demonstrations?"

Zia's dark eyes narrowed. "Do you always have your mind in the gutter?"

He shrugged. "Pretty much."

"Anyway, I do have some spectacular news." She jumped up, clapping her hands, her euphoric smile back. "I've found us a guitarist."

Maggie's hopes rocketed from the slimy pit where they'd been resting. She stood, pulling Zia into a tight hug. The woman had a nose for talent. She'd found Lincoln.

"That's fantastic news," Maggie exclaimed. "When can we hear this person play?"

"Soon. He's on his way. It's my tutor, Tanner."

Maggie's brows rose, a little of her excitement deflating. She could almost hear it, a little like air released from a small slit in a balloon. "Your tutor? Some professor?"

She did *not* need some sixty-year-old dude in corduroy pants, sporting a tweed jacket in her band.

No way. I'm not that desperate. Yet.

"Don't be so quick to judge," Zia snapped. "He's good. I'm telling you, the guy is incredibly talented"

"At what?" Jayce mocked. "Spreadsheets and grading papers?"

Lincoln waved a hand at Jayce, as if shooing away his dumbass comment. "Accounting to music? I don't get it. How'd he end up playing a guitar for you?"

"By accident. After tutoring, we always leave together. Today my damn car decided to die. I called James to get me, but he was at work, wouldn't be leaving for another hour. Roasting Bean was closing. Tanner invited me to wait for James at his place. When we arrived, his roommate was playing, badly I might add, on a guitar. Tanner took it away, complaining about broken strings and ear drums.

"I asked him to play a song. Guys, I was blown away."

There was no doubt Zia could spot talent, still…

"Do you honestly think he'll be a fit for ThreePence? If you say he's good, I believe you." She couldn't help picturing an old dude with liver spots and a pipe.

She glared at Maggie. "Stop picturing our high school math teacher, Mr. Blackson."

Busted.

Her lips quirked, and Zia smirked, her hostility seeming to fade. "And he's not a teacher. He's an accountant, soon to be CPA."

"Oh, so much better," Maggie mocked.

"Shut up, Ms. Judgie. Second," Zia wiggled two fingers, "Tanner's around our age, not some geriatric with a walker and a guitar. In fact, he is quite cute."

Maggie didn't give a shit how the guy looked. Band members weren't to play *with*; they were to play *music* with. Plus, Zia liked the clean-cut boring boys. Maggie was certain the guy was bland, dry as plain toast.

Lincoln shrugged. "What could it hurt? It's not like we've found anyone else."

"You better give him a chance," Zia huffed, slipping back onto the couch's edge. "Convincing him to stop by wasn't easy."

Indignation left a bad taste in Maggie's mouth. "If you needed to convince him, why'd you bother? We have plenty willing to audition. People who'd love to join the band."

Too bad they all sucked, none even a fraction of what ThreePence needed.

"You mean all the ones you've hated? We're running out of options. Hey, at least with Tanner, we know he doesn't have a problem with being temporary. He wouldn't even consider coming by today until I assured him this gig was for less than a year. He's not a big fan of bars and nightclubs. He doesn't want to do something like this long-term. Tanner wants to be a CPA. He's studying for the exam. After he passes it, he wants to quit tutoring, and begin working full time at an accounting firm."

"Who doesn't like the nightlife?" Jayce cut in. "He doesn't sound like a good fit for us."

Maggie rolled her eyes. Of course, that was his worry, not if this Tanner could play their music, but if he was willing to party and get high.

"The way he plays *is* perfect for us," Zia insisted, her gaze swinging between Jayce and Maggie. "Please don't be assholes when he gets here."

"Whatever you say. Bring the Prof by." Jayce snickered. "Should be at least good for a laugh."

"Assholes," Zia muttered.

Maggie patted Zia's shoulder. "You haven't let me down

before. I'm hoping you struck gold again. Otherwise, we're screwed. Scarlett's always sick. Hell, she's in the bathroom now puking out her guts. She told us her doctor is already hinting she'll probably be on bed rest by the end of this month."

~ * ~

Tanner shut off his car and stared at the 1950s style ranch. The house was on a corner lot, set far back from the road. He double-checked the address, wondering why he'd agreed to audition.

He was a CPA, well, hopefully by next year. He just needed to pass the damn test. What he wasn't was a musician.

Sure, he'd grown up around music, along with all the chaos surrounding it. His childhood was filled with late nights and selfish musicians. He had no desire to revisit it as an adult.

Or risk becoming someone like his father, a man who loved music and partying more than his family. Before Tanner had even reached his double-digit birthdays, his father had left, never looking back.

Shit. I'm thinking way too much into this practice session. If they want me, I'll just say no.

He got out of his car. Grabbing his guitar case and amp from the back seat, an unexpected zing of anticipation raced through his blood.

Making him acknowledge some aspects of music were pretty damn sweet. Even after his dad left, Mom couldn't seem to kick the musician habit. As a result, he'd learned from the best and worst and taken to playing multiple instruments better than kids way older than him. Hell, he'd surpassed most of his teachers.

He found music soothed him, gave him peace in his chaotic life. When he entered his teenage years, it filled his wallet with cash. In high school and college, he'd made a ton of money as a roadie or fill-in musician for his mom's old and current boyfriends.

Last year, while fulfilling his required hours under a CPA, he'd lost most of his music gigs. He could've gotten in contact with them but decided to pass.

Now, damn it, he missed it.

Sure, tutoring was more stable, but there was magic in creating music, watching it come together. When he could block out the crowds and let the music flow through him, there was nothing quite like it.

Zia's suggestion to audition arrived during a weak, nostalgic moment. She'd asked, and his stupid pulse jumped. Then he'd opened his damn mouth, agreeing.

However, standing outside her house, he recalled the

overcrowded clubs. The drunk, aggressive people. The heavy, oppressive mobs. These memories filled him with self-loathing, anxiety churning in his stomach.

Dumb ass.

He slammed the car door shut with the heel of his boot, cutting off less-than-pleasant childhood memories and his screaming doubts. Time to stop overanalyzing and making a big deal out of nothing. He'd play a couple of songs, then leave. He was a good musician, but they'd see he didn't have the rocker mentality.

Plus, it wasn't like Zia was asking him to throw away his years of studying or all his hard work to start traveling the world with some local college band. Even if she offered him the job, it was temporary. Less than a year. No touring.

Heaving an exhausted sigh, he hunched his shoulders against the cold drizzle. It might be May, but spring and summer were still in a tug-of-war in Michigan. Gripping his guitar and amp, he dashed to the front door.

His finger barely touched the doorbell when it whipped open. Zia appeared surprised he'd actually come.

"There you are," she said. "I was beginning to think you changed your mind."

I did. About twenty times.

"No. I got lost," he half lied. "I didn't know there were houses this far back in this neighborhood."

"Yeah, it's an old area. Perfect for us. Not many homes. We figured fewer neighbors, fewer complaints." Zia led him through a small living room stuffed with worn furniture, into an even smaller, outdated kitchen. They didn't stop. She headed to the other side, opening a closed door he hadn't noticed.

"And there is always music. Besides Scarlett, the guitarist who needs to take a temporary leave, the whole band lives here. Plus, there are constantly people from other bands crashing. Like I said, lots of music." She shrugged, glancing at him before twisting the knob.

He smiled. Probably came off more like a grimace. The house, the chaos, and music reminded Tanner of his childhood. It filled him with nostalgia and loathing.

Zia started down the stairs. "Come on. Everyone is in the basement."

Trepidation was running under her efficient business tone. Was she nervous he'd choke, embarrassing her for suggesting him?

She need not worry. His mom began teaching him the piano around the time he learned to walk. Others schooled him in different instruments, including the guitar, well before kindergarten. Music was as natural to him as breathing.

He considered telling Zia this, hoping it'd help calm her, but she was already at the bottom of the stairs. Following, Tanner discovered this was where all the money went.

The conversion from what he was sure had been a creepy cinder block basement to this top-notch practice studio was impressive. The soundproof foam and acoustic panels covering the walls screamed serious intentions.

It was also the cleanest he'd ever seen. Most were dirtier than a dive bar's bathroom at closing time.

They stepped onto gray carpet he was certain was there to protect instruments, more than to offer comfort. He saw a circular table piled with a mess of notebooks and play sheets; past it was a huge black leather sectional almost butted against one of the table's chairs. His gaze rested on the most important space in the basement: the makeshift stage.

His heart picked up its pace. He saw a drum set, a couple different guitars, amps, speakers, and the four people milling around. A mixture of anticipation and dread flowed through him. He was drawn to a tall woman, facing away from him who was messing with a speaker.

Her cropped black hair was pin-straight with purple streaks threaded throughout. Her willowy neck was bare, revealing a treble clef tattooed at the center, followed by a mixture of notes dancing along her spine, disappearing under her fitted white shirt.

Tanner didn't understand why he was entranced. He usually preferred more conservative women.

He shifted his focus to the blond man tapping absently on a snare drum while talking on a cellphone. Damn, the guy could be Kurt Cobain's twin. He smiled, waving a drumstick in greeting. Tanner nodded his hello.

Next to the drummer was a woman studying sheet music. She appeared ready to vomit. Tanner took an involuntary step back. She had the same crazy mismatch color-thing going on with her hair as the other woman except hers was longer with a riot of blonde and blues.

To her right was the typical rocker guy. Complete with septum ring in the nose, gauged ears, and sleeve tattoos on both arms. He studied Tanner with distaste.

Tanner stared back, willing to bet he and this dude wouldn't be best buds.

This is such a mistake.

If only his fingers didn't itch to touch the strings on his

Telecaster. To hear it sing with a full band. If not for that, he'd be up the stairs and out the front door.

Still, everything about it screamed upheaval and chaos. He didn't need it, not even temporarily. He could make extra money some other way.

As if sensing his desire to flee, Zia spoke before he could run. "Hey, guys. Stop messing around. This is Tanner. He's here to audition."

All thoughts of escape scattered from his mind.

The raven-haired woman studying him was stunning. She had stormy gray eyes with the sexiest mouth he'd ever seen; full and sinful.

She seemed less taken, returning her attention to the paper in her hands. She was dismissing him.

It pissed him off. He wasn't covered in tattoos or piercings, so she wrote him off before he'd strung a single note.

Her sensual looks or his need to escape was forgotten as his pride shouted to be vindicated. To prove this woman wrong.

Tanner mentally cataloged the most difficult songs he knew by heart. He may not look the rocker, but he could damn well play the guitar.

"This is the accountant?" drawled the guy who fit the want-to-be-rock-star to perfection. "This should be interesting."

"Jayce," Zia hissed.

Irritated, Tanner gripped his amp and guitar case. "If this is a bad time, I'll leave."

Screw proving himself to these assholes. He didn't need or want their scorn. Hell, he didn't even want to be here.

Liar.

The blond drummer stood, pocketing his cell. "No, it's not a bad time. Thanks for stopping by. Zia told us you'd needed some convincing. I'm Lincoln. The smart-ass is our bass player, Jayce. Scarlett is our lead guitarist who's left us scrambling for a temporary replacement." She smiled, waving. Lincoln pointed to the sexy dark-haired woman. "This is Maggie. She sings and writes nearly all of our songs."

She met Tanner's gaze, held it for a couple beats before nodding, then glancing at the bass player Lincoln had called Jayce.

Tanner wasn't sure if she was waiting for the guy's approval or for him to apologize for being a douche. Tanner knew the type. Guys like him were never sorry.

Jayce smirked at Tanner before turning to his bass and messing with it.

"What are you going to play for us?" Lincoln asked, moving back behind his drums.

Tanner got the impression Lincoln was most comfortable there. Not out front, in the limelight. Tanner understood the sentiment.

"I don't know." He dropped to his haunches, opening his guitar case. "What kind of music do you play?"

"Seriously, you don't even know who we are?" Jayce spat.

"Nope."

Zia groaned, and Lincoln chuckled.

Tanner was lying, enjoying the immature kick of pissing off the bassist. He'd heard of the band from the students he tutored. After Zia mentioned she was their manager, he searched for them online. Watched a couple grainy videos taken by fans at local shows. Even from the crappy cell videos, he could tell they were good.

His gaze shot to Maggie, then away. The videos had failed to show her beauty.

Plugging in his amp, he stood, holding his guitar. He shrugged off his jacket, sat on the nearest stool then began tuning his Telecaster. "Zia tells me you guys play rock music. Is it alternative, blues, or something else?"

"Don't worry about the genre. Play something difficult. Impress me," said a voice dipped in sex and honey, with a shot of whiskey.

Tanner turned, wanting to discover who'd spoken. Found it belonged to the stunning woman with the raven and purple hair. Damn. Her full lips were hot, matching her voice.

She tilted her head, her eyes asking if he was going to stare at her like the village idiot or play a song.

He shook his head, trying to shatter his unexpected attraction. It confused him. He didn't go for wild women. And this one oozed volatility.

He played the first song that came to mind.

Her lips twitched, but her voice was bland when she said, "*Maggie May*. Cute. Not bad either. What else do you have?"

~ * ~

Damn, the accountant could play.

Maggie had taken in the guy's gray slacks, white and navy striped sweater, and wrote him off. Well, until he held his guitar and made it sing like an angel, switching flawlessly from one difficult song to the next.

Tanner most definitely had that something the band needed. He was the best she'd heard. Judging by Zia's smug expression, she knew it too.

Even so, he might not be a good fit.

For one, he looked like a librarian more than a musician. Albeit an attractive one, all academia, not an edgy rocker. Would their fans accept him? Image mattered.

Second, Jayce worried her. His dislike was apparent, though anyone's guess to why.

Maybe he felt threatened because Tanner made it past the tenth grade, or, if she were honest, because his talented matched Jayce's. Hell, might even be better.

Not that Scarlett wasn't also a great guitarist. It was more as if Jayce's chauvinist attitude deluded him into believing he was better merely because he was a man.

To hell with Jayce's ego. Maggie wanted Tanner.

For the band.

She wanted him for the band.

Watching his long, agile fingers as they made love to the guitar, her gaze then traveled to the body of the instrument resting on a firm thigh. Following the edges of the sleek Tele she stopped on the zipper of his slacks.

Maggie blinked.

What the hell is my problem?

"Okay," she said, cutting into Tanner's playing along with her crazy thoughts. "Zia was right. You are good." Even though she already knew what they'd say, she asked, "What do you guys think?"

Lincoln and Scarlett's smiles told her they'd back her, and of course, Zia had Tanner's vote.

Not surprising, Jayce was the hold-out. "We should wait," he said. "Listen to more people."

"Like who?" asked Lincoln.

"I don't know. We have time."

"Not really." Scarlett wrinkled her nose. "Forget morning sickness. I have all day sickness. And you remember what I told you? What my doctor said? My diabetes makes me a high-risk pregnancy. No stress. I'll end up on bed rest, sooner than later."

"Whatever." Jayce sulked. "You just want to lay around eating pickles and ice cream, growing fat."

"What I want to do is stab you with Lincoln's drumstick." At this, Lincoln offered it to her. She laughed, keeping her focus on Jayce. "Your massive ego doesn't want to admit he plays better than you."

Ouch. Truth hurts.

"The fuck he does," growled Jayce.

Through all this, Tanner had remained silent. He'd unplugged his amp and was removing the strap on his guitar, seeming oblivious to the arguing around him.

She studied him, clicking the piercing in her tongue. If they could get him to switch the sweater for a T-shirt, lose the khakis for jeans…maybe grow out his hair a tad, he could work. He's so damn plain.

Tanner bent, placing the guitar in its case.

Damn.

Okay. He could keep the slacks. His long firm legs and ass looked really nice in them.

She quickly glanced away from his butt to his broad back. The last thing she needed was to give Jayce another reason to dislike Tanner.

She cleared her throat, asking, "You interested?"

His gaze seemed to taste her. "Possibly."

His single, innocent word sounded loaded, like a forbidden caress in the dark, waiting to be accepted or rejected.

Jayce placed an arm around her waist, making her jump. She didn't notice him move next to her, and he had no right to such a territorial gesture.

She gave him a what-the-hell look and stepped away.

"I'm going to smoke." He gave her a swift kiss on the cheek, taking off for the stairs before she could slap him.

What the actual fuck?

Had she step into an alternate dimension? She's checking out boring accountants, and Jayce is playing the attentive lover. Which was something they hadn't been since he joined ThreePence.

Shaking her head, she focused her attention back to Tanner. She didn't like the amusement shining in his eyes. Was it aimed at her or Jayce?

Assholes.

Both of them. All men.

Well, except for Lincoln and her brother, Levi.

Maggie took a deep breath, letting it out through her nose. Men and their childish games.

Why couldn't the man with magic fingers have been a girl? Would've made life easier.

"What's holding you back?" she asked Tanner.

"Are your shows local?" He matched her serious tone.

Good. If Tanner couldn't take ThreePence serious, it didn't matter how good he played. She wouldn't offer him the job.

"Most are in or around the Metro Detroit area. In September we're booked for a weekend in Chicago. Would any of this be a problem?"

Tanner slid onto a stool, propping one foot on a bottom rung, gripping the seat. He stared at the ceiling as if mentally checking his calendar. The movement pulled his thin sweater tight against him, showing off a spectacularly fit chest.

Shit! Stop noticing. He's not even my type.

"Are the majority of the shows on the weekend?"

"Yes."

"Shouldn't be a problem since most of my tutoring sessions take place during the week." He turned to Zia. "How long do you need me?"

She shrugged, tipping her head toward Scarlett. "Depends on her. When she wants to come back after having the baby. And listen, we'll pay you enough where tutoring won't be necessary."

"Let's play together first. See how it feels," he said to Maggie.

Why did everything this guy say sound like a double entendre? Maggie stood, hoping it'd alleviate the heat beginning to stir where it shouldn't.

It's because I haven't gotten laid in a while. That's all. Nothing to do with him.

After Jayce returned, she told him to play her favorite song by Matt Maeson, Lincoln followed on the drums. She said to Scarlett, "Give him the sheet music for this one. Let's see how we sound together. If we mesh, we'll start on our songs. Try a few shows. How's that work?"

Tanner nodded, taking out his guitar. Scarlett handed him the music. He ignored the proffered sheet, breaking into the song flawlessly.

Maggie glanced at her bandmates. She'd been friends with Lincoln, Zia, and Scarlett for many years. They were close as family. A discussion wasn't needed.

They'd found their lead guitarist.

Chapter Two

"What's wrong? You're scowling so hard at your notebook it might burst into flames."

Maggie's head shot up, frustration zinging through her veins, settling heavy in her chest. She probably did look like some crazy witch ready to cast a spell. It drove her nuts when the words wouldn't come. When she couldn't hear the music forming in her mind.

Tanner halted at the kitchen's entrance, as if reluctant to come all the way inside. She waved him in. "Don't mind me."

I'm just feeling like a talentless hack.

He strode to the counter, grabbed an orange from a bowl to his right. His calloused fingers dexterously peeled away the fruit's skin. She was riveted.

She'd learned over the passing weeks his hands were pure magic.

On the guitar.

He popped an orange slice in his mouth. Chewed, then swallowed, licking a drop of juice from his thumb. The gesture was oddly sensual. Watching his full, wide mouth was way more enjoyable than trying to write a shitty love song.

Tanner cleared his throat. She dragged her gaze from his mouth. He was waiting expectantly. Shit. His lips were moving because he was *talking* to her.

She wanted to laugh. Besides discovering the man was wildly talented, she found herself with a mild crush. His conventional looks somehow worked, especially combined with his easy-going manner and wicked sense of humor.

Get it together, woman. He's in ThreePence, therefore off limits.

"Sorry, um, what did you say?"

"I asked, what has your notebook done to offend you?"

She pushed it way in disgust. "I'm working on a song. It's total shit. Everything reads like a shallow cliché."

"What's it about? Maybe I can help." He shoved from the counter, sitting in the chair next to her.

She gratefully pushed the papers toward him. Sure, he was

studying accounting or some other numbers thing, but she was desperate. She'd take any help.

"It's a stupid love song. I'm no good at them," Maggie admitted.

"Why not?" He began reading her words.

He was close enough she caught a whiff of aftershave mixed with oranges. Ignoring the pleasant buzz it gave her, she said, "Hell if I know. Maybe because I've never been in love."

His bourbon eyes pinned her, making her steady pulse jump and quicken.

"Never?"

"Nope. It's no loss. I don't want to love anyone. Women are expected to be the selfless ones in any relationship, to abandon their dreams or fit them around their man. I'm not willing." She shrugged. "So, no love."

He leaned back, crossing his arms over his broad chest, studying her. She steeled herself. He was going to lecture. Tell her she was wrong, or too harsh. Something to defend his gender.

Instead, he agreed. "Yup. There are lots of assholes."

Her brows rose. "That's it? No speech on how great you men are?"

"Believe me, I learned early on how shitty and indifferent men can be. Still, not all of us are scourges born to make women unhappy." He smirked, patting his chest. "I, for one, am a great guy. Top-shelf, right here."

Maggie laughed, shoving his shoulder. "With a typical male ego, too."

She wanted to ask who'd wronged him. However, before she could, Tanner said, "Anyway, I understand why writing a love song is difficult for you. Hard to write what you don't believe in. You're like an atheist trying to write a poem about God."

She chuckled. "That's an apt analogy. So, tell me, Cupid, have you ever been in love?"

"Once or twice," he said vaguely, reading the few words she'd written.

Like that'd end her questions, he'd soon learn.

She poked his bicep. "Come on. Give it up." She used the universal hand-it-over gesture. "Maybe it'll help with my shitty song."

He gave an easy, enticing grin. She also couldn't help noticing how his amusement reached his eyes, crinkling the corners and pulling his thick brows closer. She'd be willing to bet her first hit song under Tanner's serious exterior was a man who loved to laugh and play.

He tapped the pen he'd taken from her against his lip. She couldn't help zeroing in on them, wondering if they were that heady combination of soft and firm.

"Fine," he grinned. "Anything for the band. Let's see. I was pretty smitten with the first girl who let me have sex with her."

Maggie snorted. "That's lust. Not love."

"Hmm, maybe." He peered out the window across from them, the one overlooking the backyard. His smile slipped as he seemed to be considering her question seriously. "I loved my high school girlfriend."

She wrinkled her nose. "Wait. Your high school girlfriend. If she didn't take your virginity, when was your first? In middle school or college?"

He waved this off. "High school. I met Stacey the summer of my sophomore year. We were together until I started college."

Wow. This man clearly doesn't have commitment issues.

"What happened?" She was surprised by the slight pang of jealousy springing into her veins.

Tanner quirked one brow. "You sure don't mind digging into the personal stuff, huh?"

She clicked her tongue ring against her teeth, guilt slithering into her conscious. She was being nosy, knowing she'd never share her history. The recent teemed with shallow relationships and one-night stands. Going farther back was worse. That was before she'd learn to protect herself. Now she gave her body to a man but saved her heart for music.

Maggie didn't want Tanner's derision, or worse, his pity. Time to change the subject. "I'm being nosy," she apologized. "Occupational hazard. Sometimes songs spring from other people's stories. I didn't mean to make you uncomfortable."

He ran a hand through his hair, gripping the back of his neck. "No. It's fine. But I doubt you'll get a song from it. The breakup was typical, and about as interesting as a commercial for dentures." He twirled the pen. "I moved here for college. She didn't want to come with me. I wasn't able to visit often, and she wasn't happy with the long-distance thing. She broke up with me to date a guy she met at her job. Guess our love wasn't very deep."

His somewhat bitter tone bugged her.

"Why?" Maggie asked. "Because she didn't want to follow you? Why couldn't you stay with her, for her career?"

His head shot back like she'd slapped him. "Holding on to some baggage are you, Maggie May?"

A flush of heat warmed her neck. She was an ass. He'd

answered her highly personal questions, and to thank him, she damn near jumped down his throat.

She was about to apologize, when, to her surprise, he answered. "I came here because Eastern offered me a partial scholarship. I couldn't afford to pass it up." He gave her a droll look. "Stacey's *career* was as a bank teller. From what I understand, they have banks here too. Anyway, I meant our love wasn't deep because even though we dated for over three years, she replaced me in less than six months."

"Well, she's an idiot," she blurted. "You're a nice guy. Cute too. In a preppy-boy-next door kinda way."

"Gee, thanks," he said with a crooked smile. "It's no big deal. I'm no longer crying myself to sleep while clutching her old underwear."

Maggie let out a sharp, surprised bark of laughter. Damn, his unexpected dry humor was a treat. "Never mind. You're an idiot. Also, weird," she teased, clutching the notebook, not wanting to return to it.

Tanner slid the pages from her grasp. He was close enough that his warmth mixed with hers. Once again, she caught his unique scent. It warmed her in places it shouldn't.

It wasn't strong, nothing like the malodorous stink of cologne some men bathed in, making her want to gag. Tanner's scent made her think of sex outdoors, hot summer sun on her naked skin, and a man making her writhe in pleasure.

A man. She watched Tanner.

A small smile tugged at his lips as he read what she'd written so far. It cooled some of her growing treacherous warmth.

Oh, God. It's awful. He's trying not to laugh.

She went to rip her tattered old notebook from his grasp, then paused when he asked, "What is that noise?"

"W-what is what?" She stuttered, glancing around, not hearing anything except maybe a lone car with a bad muffler driving by.

"No, not outside. You. The clicking noise you're making?"

It took her a second to realize what he was talking about, then it hit her. She stuck out her tongue. "This."

His eyes widened, making her giggle.

I better not mention the one on my clit. The poor guy's straight-laced values might hemorrhage onto the damn floor.

He studied her with such concentration his forehead furrowed. "Did it hurt?"

"Not the actual process, though the first week sucked."

"Why? Why would you do it?"

She shrugged. "I wondered how it would feel, and I like how it looks."

"Looks?" A corner of his mouth lifted. "How often do you go around with your tongue hanging out?"

Laughter bubbled in her. She couldn't resist teasing him. "Listen, buddy, my tongue and its ring are *much* loved."

Confusion flicked over his features. She saw the moment he understood. His hazel eyes fully dilated, and he sucked in a sharp breath. They were so close his inhale stole her exhale. It was intimate as a kiss.

Maggie wanted more. Warmth and need pooled between her thighs.

The front door banged open, making them jerk back. Reality crashed onto her.

She blinked rapidly, shocked at her visceral reaction toward Tanner.

"Mags, you here?" Jayce's voice carried in the guilty silence.

She cleared her throat. "Yeah. I'm in the kitchen."

Aggravation passed over Tanner's face before it shifted to his usual impassive expression. He dragged the notebook closer while scooting his chair a little from hers. Scribbling in the margins, he ignored Jayce sauntering into the kitchen. The slight distance bothered her.

Jayce stopped short and sneered. "What are you two doing?"

"He's helping me with a song I'm having a hard time with." She hoped to cut off another squabble between the two men.

Whenever Tanner was around, Jayce acted like a territorial dog. Maggie half expected him to try to piss on her to mark his territory.

As if he had a claim.

"Sounds exciting," he replied, sounding bored. "Good thing you have the accountant to help."

Wearing a fake expression of innocence, Tanner looked at the other man. "Yes, it is. So, what have you been doing today? Off scaring small children and kicking puppies?"

"Piss off," Jayce scowled.

Annoyance saturated the small kitchen. Maggie was positive if she had a knife, she could cut the tension, making the space between the two men bleed.

Jayce and Tanner's mutual dislike was the only glitch in the temporary transition of lead guitarists. If Tanner needed to leave practice early or didn't learn a song in less than a day, Jayce would bitch they needed to dump him. For his part, Tanner would goad Jayce or treat him like he was a juvenile reprobate. Never mind they were both in their late twenties.

She hoped they'd work out their differences before the shows when they'd have to spend anywhere from twenty minutes to an hour driving to gigs. If not, she needed to invest in earplugs.

Tanner stood. "I'm going to take off, Maggie. I forgot I have something to do at the school. Tell Zia I'm sorry. Told her I'd double-check her homework. Oh." He slid the notebook to her. "I wrote some suggestions in the margins. Let me know if anything works."

Huh, apparently, he's going to ignore Jayce's dig. Good.

Stopping at the arch of the kitchen, Tanner knocked on the frame, twisting around to face her. "Or you could chuck the whole song. Write what you know." His gaze fell on Jayce. "Like dating assholes."

Or not.

"You pissed because I got a taste and you never will?" Jayce called after Tanner.

Annoyance shot through her veins. "Jayce, shut the hell up. I'm a woman, not a goddamn piece of candy."

Tanner seemed to ignore them both. Collecting his jacket from the back of the couch, he opened the front door and left without a backward glance.

Jayce opened the fridge, muttering about assholes. After snagging a beer, he slouched against the counter, drinking it while studying her.

"I'm right, you know. That preppy cocksucker wants you," he said after taking a hardy pull from the long neck then licked his upper lip.

She recalled Tanner's heated eyes and the way her body's needy response washed over her. She shoved it aside. "Oh please, you're delusional. Besides ThreePence, we have nothing in common. Plus, you know my rule."

He strode across the small kitchen. Standing behind her, he set his beer down. "Yes. I know it. But I'm here if you ever want to break it. We had a good time. We could again."

He rested his hands on her shoulder, wandering low, trying to get into her shirt. She slapped them away. "No. Some rules shouldn't be broken. This is one of them. I don't sleep with band members."

"Whatever. Does the accountant know your rule?" Jayce grabbed his beer and left, not bothering to see if she'd answer.

When he was gone, she dropped her pen, resting her head on

the table. The 'no dating, no fucking' rule was smart. It had never been an issue. Until now. Why did it suddenly bother her? Hadn't anything to do with Jayce's offer. He made it at least five times a week. It held no appeal.

Who was she kidding? Tanner was the man who popped in her mind, urging her to ignore her rule.

The question wasn't who, but why.

Tanner was too clean-cut for her. His interest in her was likely fleeting. He was probably into wholesome, boring girls. Plus, he was temporary, much like her strange, eccentric lust for him.

ThreePence was her life, her true love. Nothing else mattered.

Picking up her pen, she pushed Tanner and Jayce from her mind and focused on writing about an emotion she'd never experience outside her family; love.

~ * ~

Tanner yanked open his car door, chucking his jacket inside. He leaned against the side panel, focusing on the lazy rolling clouds against the blue sky. It was a vision of tranquility, the opposite of his racing heart and churning gut.

Back in the kitchen, he'd been two seconds away from kissing Maggie.

What he couldn't decide is if it would have been a mistake.

Granted, he found her attractive, and the more time with her, it intensified. Yet, the fact remained she wasn't the type of woman for him. He needed stability. Her drive was admirable, but she was a musician. Their lives were chaos. She'd be like all the ones he'd known growing up, including his dad. Their only desire to travel from show to show, either building up or burning out on the successes and failures of their music.

No thanks. He'd been on the receiving end of the consuming, obsessive lifestyle with his dad and mom. No way would he repeat it now.

He slid into the driver's seat, discontent rolling through him. Besides, all this conjecture was pointless. She wasn't even an option.

Maggie had her rule. She didn't mess around with people in her band. If she did, she'd probably be with Jayce. Lincoln had mentioned she and Jayce were together before he joined ThreePence.

It bugged the hell out of him, but that had little to do with Maggie. Jayce reminded Tanner of his father. Talented and an asshole. His primary goal in life seemed to be the pursuit of pleasure and his alone.

Tanner started the car. He needed to leave. Get back to his

place, maybe swing by the gym, burn off some steam. Forget Maggie, with her Mona Lisa smile, crappy dating choices and rules.

It's not like he was right for her either. She was fire, brimmed with a wild liveliness he didn't possess. He was better suited with someone more contained.

On that thought, he put the car back in park, then reached for his cell, phoning Colton. His roommate answered. "Hey, Colton. You busy tonight?"

"No. What's up?"

"Is your girlfriend's friend still interested in going on a double date?"

"Jane? Yeah, she's interested. 'Bout damn time, man."

"Yeah, Yeah. See when they're free."

"I'll call my girl now."

"Okay, I'll be at our place in twenty."

Tanner disconnected, then tossed his phone onto the passenger seat, before digging deep to find some enthusiasm for the date. He needed to forget the fierce woman with purple and raven hair, the knockout with full, lush lips hiding a pierced tongue.

Oh God, her piercing...

Shit!

He shook his head violently, trying to dislodge Maggie's image from his mind. He jammed his car into drive, then blasted the radio volume loud enough to obliterate all thoughts and fantasies of ThreePence's sexy singer.

Chapter Three

Tanner leaned forward, elbows on knees trying to find his breath. It hid somewhere behind his rapidly beating heart. The crowd's shouts and surrounding chaos reverberated through him, making his pulse race.

Blue Skies, the opening act, was almost finished with their set. He could swear with each passing song the walls were closing in on him.

What the hell have I gotten myself into?

The door to the small prep room opened. Maggie sauntered in, close behind her was Lincoln, twirling a drumstick, both appearing relaxed.

He glanced at Tanner. Stopped. Backtracked to him. "Don't sweat it, man. You've been spot-on at every practice. You've got this."

Tanner stood, rubbing the back of his neck. "It's not that…now's probably not a good time to mention I don't like crowds, right?"

Jayce muttered something. Tanner ignored him, glancing at Maggie.

She was studying him.

Lincoln snorted. "Yeah. Now isn't the best time. Haven't you done this before?"

Tanner managed a weak smile. "It has been a while. I thought I was over it. Plus, back then, I mostly helped set up for shows or assisted during practice sessions. The few times I played an actual gig, they put me in the back, hoping no one noticed the underage kid on stage. I forgot about the crowds until I heard them tonight. Everyone crammed together in a claustrophobic mob, ready to lose all inhibitions."

Talking about it caused unease to crawl under his skin, and he shuddered.

Lincoln tilted his head, the side of his mouth twitching with humor. "Um, we're playing at a bar, not an S&M club."

"And you won't be in the craziness," Maggie cut in, with surprising gentleness. "You'll be away from it on the stage. Focus on your instrument. The songs. The rest will fade away."

Tanner nodded. She was right. It had in the past.

He picked up his guitar, avoiding her eyes. Part of it was he feared letting her down tonight, but also because when he looked at her, he yearned for things he shouldn't want.

Going out with Jane hadn't cooled his growing infatuation with Maggie. Jane was a sweet woman, yet there was no spark. She wanted more than he had to give. In the end, he broke things off.

When he couldn't resist any longer, his gaze flicked back to Maggie. She was still watching him. A burst of loud applause snagged their attention. She glanced toward the hall leading to the stage. He studied his shoes, reminding himself to breathe, his chest tightening as his heart hammered.

Zia rushed in. "Blue Skies is finished. I need you guys on stage. You'll have fifteen minutes to set up."

"Shit," he groaned, following Jayce and Lincoln. Maggie stepped in behind Tanner.

Tanner focused on the dull gray cinderblock walls as they walked toward the stage, trying to convince himself it would be easier than taking the CPA test.

Hell, clubs are dark. I'll be off to the side, far from the crowds. Stop being a wuss. No one will even notice me.

Unless he fucked up. Freaked out on stage

Sweat trickled down his back. His palms were clammy, and he had to grip his guitar tighter to keep it from slipping from his grasp. Jayce strode through the back curtains to the stage, with Lincoln close behind.

Tanner froze. There was a reason after his internship at the accounting firm he'd refused his mom's offers to help with her most recent boyfriend's band. Why tutoring was a better idea. He should have remembered that when ThreePence asked him to join them.

I love music. I hate crowds. I hate clubs. I shouldn't be here.

A pair of hands gripped his waist, and he jerked in surprise, twisting around. Maggie stood before him. In his clawing panic, he'd forgotten she was behind him.

"Take a deep breath, Tanner." She pinned him with a steady, calm gaze. "Please don't pass out on me."

He released a shaky breath, not realizing he'd been holding it. "Sorry. I'm fine. Really."

"You don't look fine."

Her soft touch and kind voice made him forget about crowds and screw-ups. He found a bit of calm staring into her serene eyes. "I'm sure I will be once I get out there." He smirked. "And find my dark corner to hide in while playing

She returned his smile, rising on tiptoe, running her thumb along his damp brow.

The pounding of his heart picked up again, but this time had nothing to do with nerves, and everything to do with her nearness.

Her gaze fell to his mouth, and she licked her lips. He leaned closer. Close enough to swallow her breaths.

Someone cleared their throat. Loudly.

Maggie stumbled back. Zia came into view.

Her arms were folded across her chest. "Are you two going to stare into each other's eyes or get your asses out there?"

"Shut up, tramp. Tanner has stage fright. I was trying to calm him."

Zia snorted. "Well, honey, I think his mind is no longer on the stage."

Maggie let out a harsh breath. "Whatever, Zia." She huffed, pushing through the backstage curtain.

Seconds later, shouts from the audience rose. They were shouting Maggie's name and clapping. Tanner made to slip through after her before the suffocating fear returned, but Zia grasped his elbow.

He stopped.

"Tanner, please don't. You mess with Maggie, you mess with the band."

He blew out his cheeks, trying to release the simmering frustration and desire running through his veins. He and Maggie were playing a stupid game. There was no denying they had chemistry, yet it'd burn faster than a newspaper in a fire, and the last thing he wanted was to leave the band in worse condition than when he started.

"I know. Don't worry. I'm not her type. It's like she said, I'm a bag of nerves. She was talking me down. Nothing more." He stepped around Zia, ignoring the skepticism painted on her face.

Suddenly being in the pandemonium didn't seem terrible. It sure as shit beat staying there to hash out his feelings with Maggie's friend and manager.

Once on stage, he did his best to ignore the crowd. He found an empty stool and began tuning his Telecaster. He planned to focus on his instrument. Nothing else.

In the end, his curiosity was stronger than his anxiety. He scanned the club.

The Cleopatra looked more like a speakeasy from the 1920s than a bar reflecting the ancient Egyptian queen. The walls were exposed brick. The tables and booths clustered behind the dance floor were simple black iron. The coolest feature was the lights at the back of the bar. They were made from old wine and whiskey bottles and gave off the illusion of a colorful wave.

The stage was the only thing he didn't like. It sat maybe a foot off the main floor. Close enough for drunk or overzealous patrons to climb up with the band.

Maggie would be front and center, at the mercy of the crowd. The thought of some stranger mauling at her set Tanner's blood on fire.

She, however, appeared relaxed, ready to start the show. He checked the perimeter of the stage, saw three huge bouncers scanning the crowd. Their presence helped release the tension trying to crush him.

"You guys ready?" Maggie asked, bringing his attention back to her.

He nodded, heard Lincoln and Jayce agree. She faced her mic and spoke to the audience. After a few words to pump them up, she gave the signal to start the first song. It was a fast one with a good beat, meant to get people moving and dancing.

Watching her, Tanner understood. This was her calling. She was in her element, and the crowd adored her. She didn't seem to suffer from stage fright or the fear of getting dragged into the masses. She'd alternate between leaning down to grasp the hands of people near the stage to sing to those in the farthest reaches of the club.

The crowd was in her palm. She owned them. Floor lights alternated from red to blue, as people swayed to the music, losing themselves to the beat and her sweet, whiskey-rough voice.

She, in turn, gave her heart and soul to them. To the hypnotic melody. Tanner was a little jealous of her passion. He'd enjoyed his college classes, was content with his career choices. Yet he didn't have the enthusiasm for it like she did for music.

As ThreePence switched from one song to the next, Tanner was surprised to discover he was having fun. Back when he was a teenager, he never paid attention to the dynamics between the audience and musicians. The few times he was on stage he'd stayed off to the back, trying to fade into the shadows.

Maggie, however, was having none of it. She kept him up front.

He was stunned to discover that he didn't mind. He found the crowd and the atmosphere both thrilling, somehow calming.

He wasn't in the pressing bodies and chaos. Instead, he was above it. From his vantage point, everything was perfect. Even beautiful. There was no other way to describe it. The pleasure on each person's face, their enjoyment washed away his anxiety.

Strumming his guitar with ease, he rocked to the rhythm of the songs. His gaze moved from the crowd to Maggie.

She was mesmerizing. He couldn't help staring.

As if sensing his gaze, she looked at him, flashing him a smile full of joy, with a touch of fire. Zia's warning echoed in his mind, but it didn't stop him. He grinned, coming closer.

Her enthusiasm was infectious. He couldn't resist the pull.

Maggie sidled next to him never breaking from the song. She leaned in, inviting him to sing the end chorus with her.

He wasn't sure what possessed him to accept. Maybe he wasn't immune to the magical fervor music seemed to produce. Or perhaps it was the thrill of having Maggie near, mingled with her scent of fresh sweat and woman. Whatever the reason, he joined her in singing.

After the song concluded, the crowd clapped and hollered enthusiastically. Maggie covered the mic, whispering, "We need to talk."

Great. The most dreaded sentence known to man.

Chapter Four

Maggie watched Tanner scan the basement. A familiar mixture of relief and disappointment swept through her. Two months had passed since Tanner joined ThreePence. He fit with them like a perfect note from her favorite song.

The only hitch was she hadn't yet convinced him to sing with her. After hearing his deep, smooth baritone, she'd run off stage and written the perfect duet. Now she just needed to convince him they'd sound perfect together.

It was only a matter of time. She'd break him down.

Besides his stubborn refusal to sing, the rest was a dream. His stage fright from the first performance didn't make another appearance, and his help with writing new songs was a godsend.

She'd also found him to be an unlikely friend. Her first impression had been all wrong. Sure, he was serious and, for reasons she couldn't fathom, was dead-focused on becoming a CPA, but he was also a blast to be around. He was interesting to talk with, made her laugh, and challenged her to write better lyrics.

Plus, he seemed to respect her and her rule. She'd catch him watching her with more than friendly curiosity, but he kept things between them pleasant and cordial.

This should please her. Things were calm, easy with him. He made a great friend.

Instead, it drove her bat-shit crazy. She yearned to see desire pool in his warm eyes like the time at the kitchen table or on the first night before going on stage together.

Yup. I'm a dumb ass.

What she wanted was wrong. There was a reason for her rule, and really, what was the point? He was her opposite in every way. They wouldn't last more than a month. Hell, the wreckage of such a bad decision would long outlast the lust.

If only her stupid, reckless side would stop whispering to the horny devil resting on her shoulder. Telling her, it'd be such a fun time. Replaying those short, heated moments over and over in her mind.

The spark of desire that afternoon in the kitchen, when he helped her with that damn love song. Or the sexual tension crackling between them backstage the first night they'd performed together.

"Damn it," Tanner muttered, standing straight.

Maggie darted her attention back to her laptop, not wanting him to catch her staring. *Again.*

"What's wrong?" she asked.

"My mom's boyfriend let me borrow his guitar. I am thinking of buying one like it and wanted to try his out first. He dropped it off at my mom's. I must've forgotten to get it last time I was visiting. I don't see it here."

"Did you say she lives in Dexter?"

Tanner nodded.

"It's on the way to tonight's show." She pushed aside the bracelets covering her watch. "There's time to swing by, get it, then head straight to the show from your mom's."

"Good idea. I'm going to do that." He shoved his hands in his front pockets, smiling. "Better anyway. Lincoln's driving makes me carsick."

Damn. Dimples. Ignore them!

She clicked her laptop closed. "Well, it explains why you're always sleeping on the longer car rides. Here I thought you had mono."

Laughing, he replied, "I don't have mono. I'm exhausted. Between studying, tutoring, and gigs, there isn't much time to sleep." He shrugged. "Also, if I'm not awake, I don't get nauseous."

"Why haven't you said anything?"

"Right," Tanner scoffed. "Like it'd help. Lincoln would drive worse, wanting to see how many different shades of green I turn before I hurl. Plus, as I said, it's a good way to catch up on sleep."

"Have you considered quitting? The tutoring, I mean. What we're paying you—doesn't it cover your bills?"

His smile disappeared. "I have to think about when Scarlett comes back. If I drop tutoring, those students might not return. There is no guarantee I'll pass the CPA test. I might have to retake it. I don't want to work in an accounting firm until then. I want the freedom tutoring offers."

"What if she doesn't want to come back?" Guilt tugged at Maggie, asking the question. She should want her friend to come back, and part of her did, yet another foreign piece ached at the thought of Tanner leaving.

He shook his head. "Doesn't matter. I don't want this life."

Bitterness replaced her guilt.

Yes, that's right. Tanner wants his nine to five and a Stepford wife. The complete package for the white-picket-fence life.

Some of her derision must have shown because he held his hands, palms out, in a pleading gesture. “Maggie, I’m enjoying myself, here with you guys. But I did this growing up. I’ve lived this life. I have no desire to repeat it. Nor have kids and put them through it.”

She recalled what little Zia told her about his childhood. His mom was a bit of a music groupie. His early years were spent in bars and nightclubs.

To Maggie, it sounded like a great life. However, his stiff posture and tight-lipped expression said he didn’t agree. Nor did he want to discuss it.

She let it go. “Okay fine, but what happens if you burn out from exhaustion?”

“True. Maybe I should quit the band.” He winked to let her know he was teasing.

Thank Christ.

“Ha, ha. If you quit the band, you won’t have to worry about exhaustion because I’ll kill you.”

“You’re all heart, woman.” He chuckled, pulling his keys from his back pocket.

She walked to him. “I am. I’ll even prove it. I’m coming with you.” She snatched his keys. “You get your guitar, after I’ll drive. You can sleep on the way to the show.”

“If you’re serious I’d appreciate it. Last night I got maybe four hours of sleep. I could use a power nap,” Tanner finished as Lincoln strolled in, heading for his drums.

“Stop spending your evenings with the painted ladies, then you won’t be tired,” he said without slowing his stride.

“You’re right. If only your sister wasn’t so damn good at her job,” Tanner goaded.

Lincoln grabbed a drumstick, pretending to throw it at Tanner before asking, “What’s our lovely Maggie going to do that you’ll appreciate?”

“I need to swing by my mom’s place to pick up a guitar for tonight’s show. Maggie’s going to go with me. She’ll drive, I’ll sleep.”

Lincoln’s brows furrowed, and he spun a cymbal, watching it. When he spoke, his easygoing smile was back. “Probably for the best. After the crack about my sister, I’m liable to push your ass from the van while it’s moving.” He asked Maggie, “Are you going to work on him again? Get him to sing some backup with you?”

“Of course,” she said over Tanner’s protests.

She narrowed her eyes at him. *Sooner or later, I’ll wear you down.*

He snorted. "I can almost hear the wheels spinning in your head, Maggie. It's not happening." He waved to Lincoln before loping up the stairs.

She made to follow. Lincoln stopped her. "You know this is going to piss off Jayce."

She stopped and faced Lincoln. "Jayce isn't my keeper. We're in a band together. Nothing more."

"Yes, but you know he wants more. If he sees you get cozy with Tanner, Jayce will get pissy. Make life difficult."

Fuck him. He can leave for all I care. I'll make sure the next bassist isn't such an asshole.

"I get his parents own the house and equipment, but he doesn't own me," Maggie snapped.

Lincoln's remark annoyed her. Jayce's ego and the financial power he held over them did worry her. However, she didn't like the way Lincoln's words hinted she was doing something wrong. That there was more to her offer than her helping a fellow bandmate, some hidden plan.

"You're right. I'm sorry." He tapped one of his drums lightly. "We'll meet you two at the show."

She nodded, trying to shake her guilty conscience. Not about Jayce. His feelings for her ran as deep as the dried-up brook at the back of the house. No, her remorse was for worrying Lincoln, and also in her foolish pleasure at the idea of spending time alone with Tanner.

Business and pleasure shouldn't mix.

She pushed through the back door, leaving behind the house and her guilt. Tanner was waiting for her, leaning against the house, looking all sorts of divine.

When did he go from stuffy accountant to a man who made my pulse surge every time I caught sight of him?

She cleared her throat, tossing him back his keys. "You drive to your mom's. I'll drive to the club."

"Works for me."

After getting inside, Tanner started the car, then placed an arm on her headrest. Twisting around, he watched the road while backing out of the driveway.

He kept his focus on the traffic. She kept hers on him.

She took in the light stubble on his jaw to his lush mouth. His bottom lip was a touch fuller than the top. She wondered how it'd taste. He cleared his throat, swallowing. The up and down slide of his Adam's apple was fascinating.

Maggie shifted, moving closer, wondering if he still had that fresh, wild scent, like the outdoors.

He did.

His arm dropped from her headrest. He sat forward, shifting from reverse to drive. "Thanks again, for stopping at my mom's place with me. I could use the nap before the show."

He sounded a little hoarse. She tried to catch his eye, to get a read on him, but he stared straight ahead at the road.

Annoyance washed over her. Not at him, but herself. She needed to stop acting like a smitten idiot, searching for signs when there was none.

Hell, more than likely, those flashes of desire were merely a reflection of *her* cravings.

From the start, he was clear about what he wanted from life. Someone like her wasn't it.

Good. At least one of us has our priorities straight.

Seriously, in less than ten seconds, she'd grow bored with him.

Friendship was better for them. For ThreePence.

The undercurrents of disappointment playing along her conscious were merely misguided fascination at their differences. Some dumb opposites attract thing.

Chapter Five

Tanner parked in his mother's driveway, amazed he'd managed to drive all the way there without pulling over and seizing Maggie and kissing her until she melted into a puddle of need. The way she'd studied him when they first got into the car was like having her fingers trailing his skin. Or her lips exploring him.

How was he going to manage sitting next to her during the long ride to the gig? Could he even fall asleep?

Shutting off the car, he rubbed his palms into his eye sockets. Maggie shifted, making the old leather seat creak. She was watching him again. Her gaze, hot and full of promise, ran over him.

She said they could only be friends, but her gaze told him a different story.

Clearing his throat, he pointed with his chin. "Welcome to my mom's home."

He tried to see the place as Maggie might. Did she find it cozy? Or like he did, somewhat run down and sad, a home brimming with dilapidated dreams. Not a place a family stayed and made memories.

She tilted her head. "Her house, not yours? Did you not grow up here?"

Tanner shook his head. "Nah, we moved around a lot. After my dad left for good, my mom wanted a change of scenery. We've moved from one end of Michigan to the next. Even lived briefly in Ohio and Kentucky. Oh, and Florida. She bought this place after I came here for college. She wanted to be closer to me so I could check on the house. Mom likes to take lots of road trips."

"She sounds like fun."

He snorted, shutting off the car. "If you say so."

"I do. I was born and raised in the same house my entire life. My parents and younger siblings still live there. Boring."

Yeah, I got to experience the anxiety of always being the new kid, or feeling like no place was home because we never stayed long enough to make it one.

"You have a father who cares enough to stick around and raise his family. Parents who put down roots, so you have stability and memories."

"Whereas you got to travel, make new friends, experience different places," She countered.

He wasn't going to debate their different outlooks. "Guess the grass is always greener on the other side."

Maggie hummed her agreement, seeming distracted. She pointed at the carport. "What's under the tarp?"

Mom wasn't home. All Tanner saw was an old lawnmower and his covered motorcycle. "It's my bike."

A squeal of delight filled the car. Then Maggie was ripping open her door. "What kind? A cruiser or crotch-rocket?" She didn't wait for an answer, hurtling from the car, half skipping, half running to the bike.

He laughed, following her. "A *what*?"

She tore back the tarp, sighing, as if in love. "A Yamaha. Hell, what year is it?"

"Nineteen eighty-six. It's an xs650. A guy my mom is friends with was getting rid of it. I bought it off him for a couple hundred dollars. My friend Jacob is a wizard with anything mechanical. He helped me fix it."

"Damn, Tanner, it's June. The middle of summer. Why the hell are you driving around in some boring four-door?" She tilted her head in the direction of his car while settling herself on the bike.

He eyed his nondescript gray Ford. "Nothing wrong with my car," he muttered. "Normally I *am* using my bike by now, but with everything going on I haven't had time to renew the plates. Plus, it's a bitch to ride with a guitar and laptop strapped to my back."

"Understandable." She tightened her grip on the handlebars, wearing a smile so wicked and sinful it shot straight to his groin. "That's why you should loan it to me."

He cocked a brow. "When exactly are we going to have time for me to teach you to ride?"

"Teach me to ride?" Her lip curled, and he wanted to nip it. "Please. I know how."

He eyed her from head to toe. "Of course, soon to be rock legend and bona fide ballbuster Maggie May would know how to ride a bike."

"Damn straight." She winked.

He couldn't help laughing. Or wanting to close the distance between them to kiss those cocky lips.

The ride here already had him on edge. Now she was straddling his bike in black leather pants like an erotic fantasy come to life.

Heaven help me.

"Come on." He motioned to the side door. "I better find the guitar."

And I need to stop ogling like she's my next meal and I haven't eaten in a week.

Even if there was no doubt she'd taste delicious.

Maggie replaced the kickstand and swung her long leg off the bike. With a forlorn sigh, she placed the tarp back over the motorcycle. He couldn't stand the yearning in her eyes or the frown pushing at the corners of her mouth.

"Fine. I'll go this week to the DMV, have everything renewed. I'll bring the bike to your place. You can use it whenever you want."

When the hell he was going to find the time was beyond him, but when she threw her arms around him, the fifty million other things he needed to do vanished. Every nerve he had was too busy rushing to the places pressed against her.

Her hair brushing against his nose, the soft texture and enticing scent, made him crave more. He resisted, stepping away, not wanting her to notice his jeans were getting tighter around the zipper.

He was such a pervy creep. She hugged him in delight, and he got a hard-on, imagining her straddling him instead of the damn bike.

He cleared his throat. "Glad I made your day." Needing to fill the silence he asked, "If you know how to ride, why don't you have a bike?"

She ran her palms down the outer thighs of her leather slacks, searching his face and grinning. "Stupid deal I made with my parents. An old boyfriend taught me back when I was sixteen. I was smitten. With riding, not the guy. Anyway, I saved every penny, bought an old Shadow for my seventeenth birthday. My parents threw a fit. My oldest sister, Abigail, kept removing important wires. A little over a week later, my parents came home with a pretty purple two-year-old Ford Ranger. Paid in full." She shrugged her slim shoulders. "To keep it, they told me all I had to do was sell the bike and agree never to buy one again."

A bark of laughter escaped him. Moving to the side door, he unlocked it, saying, "I kinda pity your parents."

She shoved him playfully from behind. "Hey! It wasn't some nefarious plan I hatched to get a nice newer truck. It just worked out that way."

"I believe you. Though I bet your parents spent lots of time trying to halt some wild idea you'd devised."

Maggie muttered, pushing past him. The back entrance was a tight fit. Her front brushed his side, making him realize his whole left side was a freaking erogenous zone. Wherever she touched him was branded.

She waited for him inside the kitchen. After reminding himself repeatedly they were friends, he motioned for her to go farther into the house.

Okay. Time to get the guitar and head to the show.

He'd made it to the narrow hallway past the living room when he noticed Maggie wasn't following him. Backtracking, he found her running her fingertips along the keys of the old upright piano.

"You play," he asked.

She nodded. "What about you? Or is it your mom who plays?"

"Both." He stepped around Maggie, sitting on the piano's bench. "My mom learned when she was a kid, wanted the same for me. She was my teacher. Told me if I could play this, I could play anything."

"I like your mom." Maggie was behind him, standing close enough her body heat pressed against him. To his relief, she was oblivious to the effect she had on him and continued talking. "Well, she was right. You definitely can play the guitar. You might not look the part, but you play like a rock star."

He shrugged, though her compliment warmed him. Even if he wasn't attracted to her, she was a talented musician and valued her opinion.

"It must've been difficult dragging this piano to all your different homes."

He began keying his favorite Beethoven song. "We didn't. Whenever we moved, my mom would ask around. There's always someone wanting to get rid of a piano. It's not like a guitar or trumpet, something you can shove into some corner when the kids tire of lessons."

"True." She came around his side. Sliding onto the bench, she bumped him with her hip. He scooted down, making space for her. "I love *Moonlight*, but can you play anything modern?"

"You know this one?"

"Of course. My parents had such high hopes when they discovered my musical talent. They dreamed of me becoming a concert pianist or singing classical music. At the very least, a headliner on Broadway. To their utter disappointment, I fell in love with rock n' roll. It speaks to me in a way classical doesn't. I love spilling my emotions into lyrics. My parents don't understand it." She nudged his hand aside, taking over playing the keys nearest to her. "Lucky for my parents, my oldest sister Abigail is living up to their expectations."

"She's also a musician?"

"No, even better. She's a banker."

Tanner heard the wound in Maggie's voice and stopped playing, peering at her. "Oh, come on, I'm sure your parents are proud. You're in a nearly impossible business, making a good go at it."

A mixture of humor, gratitude, and happiness danced across her features. He looked away because the expressions made him yearn for something he had no business wanting. She'd made it clear. He was a friend. Nothing more.

He should be fine with it. She wasn't right for him. She was too wild, too volatile for someone like him.

Why do I have to keep reminding myself of this fact?

He ran his fingers over the keys a few times before he began playing a solo piece from a song he and Maggie composed a couple of days back. From the corner of his eyes, he caught her smile before she joined, singing the melody.

Her seductive voice filled the small house. He didn't doubt it would soon be all over the radio waves. Her vocals were a wonderful mixture of soul and heartbreaking sweetness.

The final notes were low, mixing perfectly with her poignant words. Tanner let his hands fall from the ivory keys. The echo of the melody fading along the walls of the quiet house, filling his soul with beauty. Creating music with her was such an unexpected reward, one that would hurt to give up when it was time for him to leave.

They sat in companionable silence. Eventually, he turned, taking in her stunning profile.

Her graceful neck and creamy skin left him yearning to run his lips from her collar to her ear. Once there, he'd bury his face in her hair, taking in her exotic scent of vanilla and cloves.

She didn't ask why the hell he was staring at her. Instead, she focused on his mouth while clicking that damn piercing.

Which, of course, made him think about all the things she could do with her tongue and the damn metal ball.

Though from the way her breaths were becoming shallower, the way she was devouring his mouth with her eyes, he wasn't the only one having wicked, immoral thoughts.

And damn. The struggle to not let his gaze drop to the quick rise and fall of her chest was difficult.

Hell, his erratic breath matched hers. His blood pulsed, thick and heavy. He needed to say something. Or move away. Find his guitar. Anything to create distance, to break this charged silence.

Instead, he gave into the near-constant craving. He leaned

forward, placing his lips softly against hers.

She tasted like heaven with a bite of sin.

She deepened the kiss with such vigor he couldn't stop the growl that escaped from deep in his throat. Wanting, no needing, more, he grasped her waist, slipping his hands under her shirt. Her warm skin against his calloused fingers was like an electric shock, but instead of wanting to pull away, he wished his flesh would melt to hers.

"Blair, is that you—"

His mom's voice rang out, slamming into him like a bucket of ice water. Thrown by a nun. He and Maggie shot apart, standing so fast the bench tilted back, crashing to the ground.

He righted it before facing his mom. She was standing in the archway between the kitchen and living room. Her head was tilted, her gaze bouncing between him and Maggie.

Did she see?

"Hi. You're not alone." His mom's eyes gleamed with amusement.

Shit. Yup.

He cleared his throat, coming closer to kiss her cheek. "Mom, this is my friend Maggie. She's the singer in the band I'm subbing for, ThreePence." He faced Maggie. "My mom, Carleen Reid."

"Nice to meet one of Blair's *friends*," she cooed, actually cooed, while shaking Maggie's hand.

"Mom. Tanner, not Blair." His mom knew he hated his birth name but loved to tease him.

Maggie appeared unruffled, even entertained. He wasn't sure if he should be relieved or annoyed.

"Sorry, Mom, we can't stay. We swung by to grab the guitar for tonight's show. Can't be late," he babbled, then forced his mouth shut.

"What a shame. I'd love to catch up with you." His mother turned her attention to Maggie, sighing. "I was beginning to worry. Afraid he'd spend his whole life in stuffy libraries or playing with numbers."

Tanner rubbed his forehead. "You know, Mom, most parents would be proud."

Maggie laughed. "I was placed in the wrong family. Would you be willing to adopt me, Ms. Reid?"

"Please call me Carleen. And I'd love to." A wicked smile spread on his mother's lips. *Great.* "Although if you were my daughter, it'd make what I just wandered into a tad awkward."

Tanner wanted to sink into the floor. Maggie burst out

laughing.

"Wow, look at the time. Sorry, Mom, we gotta go. Don't want to miss the show…"

~ * ~

Sauntering toward the car, Maggie swiveled around, walking backward. A huge smile lit her whole face. "Blair. Really?"

He flashed a dimple, before pulling in his smile. "Shut up."

She slowed, waiting for him. "Isn't it a girl's name?"

"No!" After a second, he shrugged in a who-knows gesture. "Guess it's both. My mom loves our Irish and Scottish background. My full name is Blair Tanner Reid. Each one is a surname from my family tree. Blair is my dad's last name. Maybe my mom thought he'd stay if he had a constant reminder I was his. Didn't work." Giving her the keys, he smiled, though his words held a bitter edge.

She wanted to know more, hell, wanted to know everything regarding Tanner. It wasn't any of her business, so she bit her tongue to stop from asking about his dad. Instead, said, "I think it's kinda cool." After opening the car door, she slid into the driver's seat.

"No, not at all. Please, don't ever call me Blair." His tone was light and easy, yet she caught the undercurrent of hurt and disappointment.

She hated to hear his sadness and decided to distract him with her own mortification. "Fine, only if you never call me Magdalene."

From the way he was gaping at her, she'd successfully diverted his mood.

"Are you serious? Like Mary Magdalene. The prostitute from the Bible?"

"Yes, well, my parents told me they chose the name because of her devotion and loyalty to Jesus. Not her career choices."

He smirked. "Do you believe them?"

"It's that, or they have a sick sense of humor." She shook her head. "Nope. My parents don't even have a funny bone."

"Okay. Maggie and Tanner, it is."

"Oh God, we sound like a bad sitcom." She laughed, starting the car and backing into the street. "Watch Mags and Tanner get into all sorts of zany trouble together, five nights a week…"

"I wouldn't mind getting into trouble with you any and every day of the week."

Damn it.

"Tanner…"

"Let me guess. What happened at the piano was a mistake." He exhaled and faced the passenger window. She didn't need to see him to know he was irritated. It resonated in his tone.

Still, she needed to be honest. And to put a stop to this before things spiraled out of control. "Yes."

Hadn't felt like a mistake. Tanner's lips were a heady mixture of sweetness and ruthlessness. She was almost willing to sell her soul simply to get another taste.

Hers yes, but not ThreePence's.

Her heart whispered she was safeguarding more than her band. Surrendering to this nearly consuming attraction might result in her giving him more than her body. There was something about him that had her wanting to know more than how many orgasms he could give her.

His gaze roamed over her skin, finding all her secrets. "Didn't feel wrong," he said.

She rubbed her forehead with one hand while guiding the car onto the freeway with the other. "It did to me," she lied. "And aren't you dating some girl named Jane?"

"No. She and I went on a few dates. Nothing serious. How do you even know about her?"

"Lincoln mentioned it." Maggie suspected he made the remark hoping it'd create some distance between her and Tanner. "Does she know you're not serious?"

"Yup. We haven't talked in weeks."

They were getting off topic. "Doesn't matter. What I did was wrong. I don't mess around with guys in my band. I have two rules. No heavy drugs and no fucking around with those in ThreePence."

"Is Jayce the exception to the rule?"

A spike of annoyance shot through her. "No. Why would think he is?"

"You slept with him. I also think he's using heavy drugs."

Both statements gave her pause. She decided to address the second part. "Why would you say Jayce is using?"

"A good friend of mine is a recovering addict. Some of Jayce's behavior reminded me of Will when he started using the heavier stuff."

A silence permeated the car as she worried on Jayce's drug use. Tanner broke it, repeating his earlier argument. "Back to the first part. Jayce. You had something going on with him…"

Maggie swallowed her annoyance, at both him and herself. She wanted him to drop it, but was also pissed at herself with her desire to toss out the "no-fucking" rule. She craved his lips. His touch.

"We hooked up before he joined. Nothing has happened since. Nothing will. With him or you," she finished firmly.

Tanner's lips pressed in a firm line, and he stared out the window. "Okay. I'm sorry I kissed you. I know your rule."

Great. Now she felt like total shit. It wasn't like she tried to stop him. More like devoured him. "It's fine. Forget it."

He nodded once, pushing his seat all the way back. "Mind if I take a short nap?"

"Go ahead. I'll wake you when we're close."

He laid an arm over his eyes. Within minutes his breathing evened in sleep. She merged onto I-94 and into rush hour traffic. For once, Maggie was happy for the congested freeway. It forced her to concentrate on the road. Instead of how sexy his forearm and bicep looked resting across his face, how it brought into focus lips slightly parted in sleep, appearing ready for another kiss. Or more dangerous, how she not only wanted to ravish his body but also cuddle and talk with him until the sun pushed over the horizon.

Chapter Six

"I gotta say, this is nice." Colton clinked his beer bottle against Tanner's. "I've known you for what, two years? All I've seen was you elbow deep in books and numbers. Tonight, I saw you rocking it on stage." He tilted his beer, pointing. "You've even managed to get a groupie."

Tanner followed Colton's gaze to a curvy woman with reddish-brown hair who was watching him. She smiled when she caught him looking.

He quickly turned back to his friend. "She's not a groupie. She's Scarlett's friend. They came together to hear us play. Dude. Stop staring at her. She'll come over."

Colton shrugged. "That's a problem?"

"She accosted me after the show. Telling me she wanted to know everything about Scarlett's temporary replacement." Tanner shuddered.

"Again. The problem?"

"By the way she was pawing at my jeans, I'd say she wasn't interested in my musical talents."

Her forwardness still shocked him. He'd dated bold women before, though none quite like her. Okay, some of the women he met after the ThreePence gigs were damn forward.

Colton chuckled low. "I'm still failing to see the problem."

The disbelief on Colton's face made Tanner laugh. "Not my style. Maybe I'm crazy, but I like to know someone's name before they have their hands on my dick."

"Standards," Colton huffed. "Okay, well, there's Jane. She's been asking after you..."

"Ah, she's nice, but we didn't hit it off." Tanner ran a palm down his face as if he could wipe away his restlessness. He knew damn well why things hadn't worked between them.

Maggie.

The woman consumed all of his thoughts and didn't leave room for anyone else. "Anyway," Tanner said, after taking another sip from his beer, "what's with you? Why is my love life so important to you?"

"I'm not worried. More like hoping a good lay will cheer up your irritable ass. I do have to live with you."

Tanner finished his drink. "Whatever, I'm barely home to annoy you. I'm either here, at the school, or at the coffee shop tutoring. I don't need sex. I need sleep."

Colton was right. Tanner was irritable. However, the lack of shut-eye was only half the problem. He scanned the after-party, searching for Maggie. She was deep in conversation with Zia. One hand held a glass half full of either water or vodka, while the other played with her bottom lip.

He wished it was his tongue teasing her full mouth instead of her fingers. The image had him a little drunk on lust.

Ever since last week's brief, heated kiss, he couldn't get Maggie out of his head and fantasies. He'd meet with ThreePence for practice or to play a show. He'd listen to her whiskey-soaked voice in his waking hours, then he'd go home and dream about her all night.

"Dude," Colton said, a millimeter from Tanner's ear, making him jolt back. "You with me, man? You're staring at your lead singer like a starving man and she's dinner."

"No. I'm not," Tanner said, trying to sound dismissive.

"Sure, man. Whatever. I'd say I've discovered your lack of interest in Jane and the red-headed hottie."

Tanner studied his empty beer bottle, refusing to look at Maggie or Colton. "What are you rambling on about?"

"At the show and here, there have been some *fine* women, all of them invisible to you. Well. Except for one." Colton pointed in Maggie's direction.

"Put your hand down, asshole. She and I are friends. Nothing more."

Colton, thankfully, did stop pointing. Unfortunately, he didn't stop talking. "Sure, she doesn't seem like a woman you'd be interested in. You go for the preppy ones. Now I wonder."

Tanner shrugged, repeating his mantra, "We're friends."

What could he say? He wanted Maggie, but she clung to her no-dating rule. And since their kiss, she'd kept him at arm's length.

Colton made a noise that said he wasn't buying it. Tanner ignored him, pretending to look for someone. He made sure his gaze didn't fall on Maggie. He caught Scarlett's friend watching him again. She smiled and stood.

"Ah, shit," he muttered. "I'm going to get another beer, head outside for some fresh air."

Colton followed Tanner's line of sight. The asshole started

laughing. "You want me to run interference? It's tough, but I'll do it to help a friend."

Tanner snorted, clapped Colton on the shoulder. "Don't get yourself in trouble with Katy on account of me."

~ * ~

"I need this." Maggie knocked back her drink. "Too many shows. Not enough rest."

"Oh please. I bet by tomorrow morning you'll be up early writing songs. Or working on the melody. Or harassing me to get you more gigs." Zia laughed.

Maggie saluted with her glass. "You're probably right."

A flash of red hair caught her attention. She clenched her jaw shut to hold in her insults. Scarlett's hussy friend was making her way toward Tanner. She'd eye-fucked him throughout the show and now was watching him like a bitch in heat.

Zia leaned in, blocking her view of Tanner. "Is there a reason you're giving Alecia the death glare?"

Maggie scrunched her nose as if smelling something rotten. "She's a sleaze. I'm afraid she'll give the men STDs just by smiling at them."

Her friend winced. "Wow. Slut shaming. That's not like you. Aren't you the one who says, 'Grab pleasure where you can find it and ride it'?"

"Yeah, sorry. It's been a while since I rode anything. It's making me moody."

Apparently petty too.

Zia laughed. "Maybe it's time you found a stallion to mount."

"Ah, please stop. No more innuendoes." Maggie covered her ears, sloshing a bit of her drink over the side of her cup.

"Okay, Okay. Deal. If you promise me one thing."

"Sure. What?"

"When you do decide to go for a 'ride,' don't have it be Tanner."

Her annoyance and guilt played tug-a-war. "Zia, it's not like that…Tanner and I are friends."

Zia tapped her beer bottle on Maggie's knee, lowering her voice. "I want to believe you, but we've been friends for too long. If you go after Tanner, it won't end well. It'll cause friction in the band. Hell, Jayce will throw a fit. You know he wants to get back into your pants. If you drop your rule and panties for someone else in the band…" She mimed an explosion. "I'm sure he'll have no qualms kicking us out of this house, leaving us homeless and without instruments."

"Don't you think I know?" Maggie didn't bother to refute her attraction to Tanner. She stood. The house, her life suddenly felt like a prison. "I need some air."

Not waiting for a response, she hurried to the patio door, putting all her energy into yanking on it. The damn thing always stuck. After a couple of hard tugs, it opened. She practically dove through it, needing peace and darkness.

The crisp night air teased her hair, lifting it and tickling her cheeks. She closed her eyes, listening to the crickets serenade the stars while a light breeze whispered secrets to the trees.

Moving to the edge of the patio, she inhaled deeply. The scent of dewy grass begged her to slip off her shoes, to run her bare feet through its thick, damp lawn.

Who was she to resist?

Maggie slid off her ballet flats. The cool blades tickled the soles of her feet. It helped calm her chaotic mind.

The house sat on half an acre, and she made her way to the center of the yard. The harsh lights and loud voices faded away. There were few trees in the open space, leaving a wide-open sky for her to admire. She loved it.

It was in the heart of summer, however even in the winter this was her haven. One she'd visit after a stressful rehearsal or bombed show.

Moving farther into the yard, she glanced at the sky. The stars were bright, showing off, overshadowing any beauty man could ever hope to create. Her plan was to melt into the constellations, remembering the old Greek and Roman myths her mother used to tell her when she was a child. Let the stars burn away her concerns.

A hand wrapped around her ankle. "Needed to get away from the crowd too?" asked a man, somewhere below her.

Maggie squeaked, her heart thumping. In the muted light from the house, she saw Tanner laying in the grass, propped on an elbow, watching her.

"Shit, you scared the hell out of me."

"Sorry." He let go of her foot, patting it. "I didn't want you to step on me."

She sat next to him, stretching her legs. "No worries. Yeah, I'm escaping the crowd. The smoke was getting thick and the bullshit deep."

He chuckled. The sound shivered down her spine. "Tends to happen when too many drinks have saturated the brain."

"So, why are you here, in the dark alone? I'm surprised you wanted to leave your newest number one fan."

Shut up, Maggie. Your jealousy is showing.

"Who?"

"Alecia," Maggie cooed all saccharin sweetness.

He studied her in the dim light. "Does it bother you?"

"No," she sputtered, wondering if he could hear the echo of yes in her denial.

From the way he smirked before shifting back and scanning the sky, she'd say he heard it loud and clear. Her gaze traveled to his heavy brows then his thick lashes, to eyes that brimmed with kindness that was no illusion. She moved to his straight, almost hooked nose, resting on his wonderful plump bottom lip. Loving how his mouth always seemed ready smile and laugh.

How had I ever considered him bland?

There was no doubt men with long, messy hair, multiple piercings, and tattoos were sexy. However, there was something to be said for a smooth-shaven face and trimmed, wavy hair. Plus, Maggie was quite sure she could stare at Tanner's tattoo-free flesh for hours and never grow bored.

He turned from the stars to her. "You're watching me in that way again."

"In what way?" she whispered.

"In a way that says you want to be more than friends." He shifted on to one elbow again, resting his face in his palm. His posture was relaxed, but the intensity etched on his handsome features made her flesh tingle and grow warm.

She should go back inside the house. She was, after all, the one who'd shoved them roughly into the friendship box. Instead, she remained frozen in a battle between responsibilities and desires. Her rule faded as she recalled his firm, searing kisses. The delicious memory sent a shiver along her spine, making goosebumps break out on her arms.

"Are you cold?" he asked, running a hand up and down her arm.

Lying, she nodded. His nearness had desire coursing through her veins.

He ran his hand up her arm, continuing to her neck. There, he brushed a fallen strand of hair behind her ear, increasing pressure before he trailed his fingers to the back of her head, digging lightly into her scalp.

She submitted to the pleasure of his touch. Her head fell back, and her eyes drifted shut. A moan escaped her lips.

"Jesus, Maggie," he murmured. There was an inferno in those two words, almost a plea.

The sounds she was making were obscene. She couldn't help it. The sensations were heaven. "Please don't stop."

He continued the steady movement with his strong, sure fingers. His breathing changed, becoming heavier and irregular.

When she touched his chest, his heart raced against her palm.

Her lids slid open. He stared at her with hooded eyes, desire rolling off him in waves. His greedy gaze devoured her.

Yet he made no move to come closer.

She didn't wait, crashing her lips to his. He tasted of beer and something sweeter, maybe licorice. His grip tightened, pulling a little at her hair.

His rough touch and hungry mouth made her desperate for more. Her body was stuck on a low simmer since their kiss on the piano bench. Now desire amped to a boil.

Her pent-up passion poured out, and she pushed him. He dropped onto his back, and she rolled onto him. Falling onto delicious, hard muscle. She wanted more, wanted every mouthwatering, delectable piece of him.

Her civility vanished. She became pure sensation. All lips, tongues, hands, and debauchery.

"You don't know how many times I've fantasized about this," he growled between kisses, slipping one hand under her shirt to caress her breast. "Jesus, Maggie, you're perfect."

She arched at his touch. They were moving too fast, but there was no slowing. Not when every part of him touching her was lighting her like a torch.

The familiar squeal of the patio door being forced opened pierced Maggie's, lust. A silhouette appeared against the backlights of the house.

Zia.

Shit.

"Maggie?" she heard her friend call out.

Zia's voice brought Maggie back to reality and the possible fallout from what they were doing. She tumbled off Tanner.

He exhaled and sat up. "Let me guess. Another mistake."

"Shh, it's complicated," she whispered, hoping Zia was too far to hear them.

Tanner didn't bother keeping his voice down. "What's complicated? Either you're attracted to me or not."

"There's more at stake than what I desire. I have the band to consider."

His mouth opened, as if ready to argue, but Zia was almost to them. "Can we talk about this later," Maggie begged.

"No. Forget it." He stood, brushing past Zia. "I need to get back inside."

Maggie rose, turning to her friend who was studying Tanner's retreating form. He didn't have a problem opening the patio door. He yanked it with such brutal force it damn near ripped off its tracks.

Once he slammed it shut, Zia faced Maggie. "Everything okay?"

She brushed non-existent dirt and grass from her ass. "Don't say a word, Zia. I don't need a lecture to know I've fucked up."

Zia straightened. "You wish. Less than an hour ago you told me everything was under control. Then I come outside to see you rolling off him. That's under control?"

"Shut up. I don't need a sermon."

"Yes, Mags, maybe you do." Zia sounded more concerned than angry. For some reason that was worse than yelling. "Listen, I don't know what's going on between you and Tanner, but you better figure it out. Quick. While keeping in mind the collateral damage."

Maggie groaned, rubbing her forehead. "I know. It was a moment of weakness. Blame it on the vodka. It won't happen again. I'll stay away from Tanner."

Chapter Seven

Maggie stepped from the bathroom, shutting the door behind her and paused to listen. The house was silent, except for someone moving around in the kitchen. She padded down the narrow hallway. Found Tanner at the counter.

She stopped and stared. He was in black sweatpants. Nothing else.

His back was to her, and he was humming to some song filtering through his wireless headphones. His arms were moving in the circular motion indicating he was stirring something.

He reached for an egg, cracked it then began stirring. She was fascinated with the way his back muscles flexed and bunched. His body was solid and sweet under her last night. However, in the morning light, he was downright delectable

Hot damn. The man should be on the cover of magazines.

Suddenly his voice rang out in the silent kitchen as he sang the chorus from whatever song he was listening to on his headphones. His deep, rusty baritone made her want to weep.

This man needed to be center stage. Singing duets with her. Hell, solos.

She stood on tiptoes, close to his ear. "What are you singing?"

Tanner whipped around with a startled grunt, bringing the dripping spoon with him. He stared at her, breakfast goop dripping onto his bare toes.

Even the man's feet were sexy.

"Shit, Maggie. You trying to give me a heart attack to go with my hangover?" Placing the spoon in the bowl, he yanked out his headphones, setting them on the counter before grabbing a washcloth to clean his toes and floor.

Tanner hungover. That was new. It explained why he was there in clothes she assumed were Lincoln's. At least he didn't go home with Alecia. The two were rather cozy after he stomped in from the backyard.

Pushing aside her irrelevant and unfair jealousy, Maggie asked, "If you're not feeling good, why in the hell are you awake at the butt-ass crack of dawn cooking?"

He tossed the washcloth into the sink, returning to whatever he was making. "Once I woke I couldn't go back to sleep. Thought I'd make something since I probably won't be the only one waking up with a hangover."

"Want some help?"

He gave a curt shake of his head. Maggie stood next to him, resting two fingertips on his bare arm, trying to ignore his enticing warm skin along with the spectacular view of his muscular arms and flat stomach. Seriously, what the hell's an accountant doing with a six pack?

"Tanner, please don't trash our friendship because of yesterday."

His lips thinned into a hard line. "Friendship? Damn, Maggie, I don't want to be your friend. I want more. You do, too."

She glanced over her shoulder. A handful partygoers were passed out in the living room, including his friend Colton. "You know my rule. I don't mess around with guys in my band," she whispered.

"I'm not a true member of ThreePence. I'm temporary."

His point was valid, and oh, how she'd like to run with it.

"That's not how Jayce would see it. If I started something with you, he'd cause problems."

"Fuck his ego. Fuck his problems," Tanner hissed.

"Don't you get it! He'll make it ThreePence's problem. It might not matter much to you since you plan on leaving us." Her voice cracked at the sudden rise of her emotions. She didn't know if it stemmed from frustration at Tanner's inability to understand, or at the thought of him leaving.

Maybe he did understand somewhat because the tension around his eyes and mouth softened. When he spoke again, anger no longer traced his words.

"Okay, fine. Friend." He said the last word like it tasted bad, yet he seemed resigned. He motioned toward an empty casserole dish. "I'd love your help. I found some frozen fruit. Do you have oatmeal?"

Relief spilled into her. She peered at him, smiling. "Only instant."

"Any kind'll work."

She grabbed the oatmeal from the cupboard behind them. He sliced a banana, telling her what he was making. The recipe was simple, and soon they were working side by side, talking and laughing like old friends. Or lovers.

While pouring the egg batter over her oatmeal and fruit mixture, she asked, "Do you have to leave right after breakfast?"

He shook his head, checking something in the casserole dish. “No, not really. Why?”

After he placed it in the oven, she said, “I’d liked to practice for the next gig. Zia told me a guy from a big nightclub in Chicago will be at our show. We need to be in top form.”

“Staying today won’t be a problem if Lincoln doesn’t mind me stealing more of his clothes.” Tanner wrinkled his nose in the most adorable way. “Someone spilled beer on me last night. I found these in the dryer.” He indicated the mouth-watering sweats sitting low on his hips.

Maggie took in Tanner’s naked torso. “Couldn’t find a shirt?”

He rubbed his forehead, then fidgeted with his ear as red crawled up his neck, staining his cheeks. He was so freaking cute.

“I ask this in the most platonic way possible. Why are you in such good shape?”

“What? Because I like books, I have to be scrawny?” Amusement crinkled the corners of his eyes.

“Hey, I have nothing against skinny men or books.” She ogled him from head to toe. Hell, a shirtless Tanner was downright delightful. “It’s just I don’t remember my parents’ accountant looking like you.”

He shrugged, his blush deepening. “I like to move. I meet with friends for drop-in basketball or tennis. If I can’t, there’s always running or my old weights.”

She wanted to keep teasing him to see how red he’d get. However, she resisted. Wouldn’t help with their friendship status. “Last year we printed some shirts with the band’s logo. I’ll get you one.”

Shortly after returning with a T-shirt for Tanner, the sleepy and hungover began trickling into the kitchen. Okay, people would be a kind description. They were more like zombies than actual living, breathing humans. A few made a beeline for the coffeepot. Others collapsed at the table, vocalizing nothing coherent.

“Hope you guys are hungry,” Maggie said, strangely delighted to have a proper sit down with everyone.

She loved having the whole band sitting at the table together. Their extra guests were a bonus. The gathering was loud and chaotic. She adored it.

Plus, cooking with Tanner was fun. She couldn’t remember a time when she’d laughed so much. The other members in her band hated to cook, which left them either eating takeout or Maggie making meals alone. Now she had a cooking companion, and a fun one.

Scarlett walked in, stopped then smelled the air. “Wow. It smells delicious in here.”

Alecia trailed in behind her. Maggie's good mood deflated.

"Of course, it does," Tanner called from the fridge. He closed the door, carrying a jug of orange juice to the table. "I made it."

Maggie cleared her throat.

"With my lovely assistant," he amended.

She was sure to take the empty seat next to Alecia. Not from a desire to make a new friend, more to ensure he didn't sit there. Alecia was eyeing him with way more hunger than her food.

Yeah, yeah, I'm not supposed to care. Whatever.

Someone tapped Maggie's shoulder. She found Scarlett tilted back. "Tanner's working out, huh?" She asked. "From what Lincoln told me he's a quick study and is even helping you with some new songs."

"Yup. He's great."

Scarlett leaned in closer, lowering her voice further. "You two seem to get along really well."

"He's easy to get along with," Maggie replied evenly.

"Easy to look at too."

"I guess. If you're into preppy guys."

Turns out, I am.

Alecia pushed her chair back, glancing at Tanner before returning her gaze to Scarlett. "He's my type. And after last night, I think I'm his."

The mouthful of eggs Maggie had shoveled in suddenly tasted like ash. She choked them down, causing her to cough.

Zia, on Maggie's other side, rubbed her back while leaning over, asking Alicia, "Did you sleep with him?"

Before she could answer, Jayce sauntered in, asking Maggie why she cooked. His arrival sidetracked her thoughts as she studied him.

Worry wiggled in the pit of her stomach souring what was left of her appetite. Last night, Jayce was high as a kite. Again. If he continued partying at this pace, he'd end up in trouble.

Now wasn't the time to discuss his bad habits. So instead, Maggie said pleasantly, "Tanner's the cook. I just helped."

At the mention of Tanner's name, Jayce expression darkened and turned to Lincoln. For his part, Tanner ignored Jayce's arrival, talking with his friend, Colton.

Scarlett frowned. "Guess not everyone likes Tanner."

"That's because Jayce is feeling territorial," Zia whispered loud enough for Scarlett to hear.

"Territorial over what?" she asked.

"Maggie, of course."

"What's new? Everyone wants Maggie. Hell, *I'd* switch teams if she were interested," Scarlett joked, making everyone laugh. She leaned forward, tapping Maggie. "Is Zia wrong? About Tanner and Maggie? Did you two hook up?"

Alecia glanced at Maggie with eyes that said she wanted to stab her with her fork. She focused on Scarlett. "No. We talked some. I gave him my number…I…umm…forgot to get his."

Relief flooded Maggie, and she tried to hold in an unfair smirk. It didn't work. She stared at her plate, hoping no one noticed.

"I hope he calls you," Zia said. "Maggie and Tanner get along a little too well. Him dating someone would be convenient."

"Would you stop talking like I'm not even here," Maggie grumbled, pretending the idea of Tanner with another woman didn't form an ugly jealous beast inside her. "He and I are friends. Nothing more."

"I'm not," Zia said tightly. "I want you to hear this. Back off. Stick to your rule. You're friends, all right. Friends who want to fuck."

"Zia!" Maggie choked on a strangled whisper, glancing around. Thankfully no one was paying them any attention.

"Oh my God, it's true," Scarlett exclaimed over Alecia's annoyed huff.

Tanner was visible from where he stood leaning against the frame of the kitchen's archway. He was watching them, his forehead creased.

He was probably wondering why they were staring at him. Scarlett gave him a quick wave before saying to Maggie. "Umm, he has no tattoos or piercings."

Hell. First, she was some errant child. Now they insinuate she was shallow. Nice friends.

"Please, bitches. I can be attracted to more than one type of guy." She caught both women's skepticism. *Assholes*. "Whatever. Shut up. It doesn't matter. I won't be hooking up with Tanner."

"Why not?" Scarlett was never one to mince words. Alecia squeaked in indignation. Scarlett shrugged. "Sorry. I didn't mean you can't have a go at him too. May the best lady win."

"No. Maggie can't have a 'go' at him," Zia cut in. "She's not risking ThreePence's current momentum for some stupid, fleeting opposites attract infatuation that is destined to crash and burn. We were lucky to find Tanner. We can't take any chances with Jayce or Tanner quitting because of bruised egos."

"Still sitting here. I can hear you," Maggie groused, knowing

Zia was right.

She needed to put this crazy crush aside and remember ThreePence was her passion. Nothing comes before the music, not even a sexy-hot guitarist.

Chapter Eight

"Come on, hurry," Maggie exclaimed, bouncing on the balls of her feet. The intoxicating pre-show jitters were swirling, mixing with the excitement at seeing her little brother. "If we don't hurry Levi will arrive before us, and he can't get in without us."

Jayce walked past her, sliding his guitar case under the middle seat of the van. "Oh, now there's a tragedy," he groused. "First, we played at Tanner's friend's barbeque on Labor Day, like a crappy high school band. Now we have to rush to our gig for a teenager."

"Shut up, Jayce. That was over a month ago and playing those new songs at Jacob's party was good practice. The feedback was helpful. It let us know what to play in Chicago. And after those rave reviews, clubs are begging for us. I'm positive finding the right songs at the BBQ is what got us the New Year's gig at the Oriole Terrace."

Maggie pressed her lips together, staring at his back. He didn't acknowledge her lecture, just kept fiddling with something in the van. She should stop talking. Ignore his cranky ass.

He'd been so damn irritable lately. Chicago had been a pressure cooker, brimming with stress and anger. Jayce partied, hooked up with any girl who looked his way and was an all-around asshole to everyone, though most particularly to Tanner. There were a few times Maggie was sure he was going to punch Jayce.

Chicago was weeks ago, yet his attitude was the same. Jayce clung to his hostility and late-night parties like a lifejacket as if his vices would save him.

Tanner came into view, asking, "Who's Levi?"

"Maggie's twerpy little brother," Jayce said before hopping inside, taking a seat in the second row. "I'm surprised he'd want to come. Doesn't he have chess club or something?"

She pushed off the side of the van, wrenching open the passenger door. No way was she going to sit in the back, next to Jayce's moody ass for the next hour and a half. "He's not a twerp, and he isn't in chess club," Maggie huffed, lying about the second half of her statement.

"What's wrong with chess?" Tanner asked, sitting in the driver's seat. He must've sprinted around the van to beat Lincoln to the spot.

"You play chess," Jayce replied caustically.

No surprise *he* didn't play the game. Strategy and patience didn't seem to rank high on his list. "I'm sure you and Levi would be pals. Two geeks."

Of course, Tanner played chess. Maggie found it oddly attractive. What wasn't cute was Jayce acting like a petulant, pissy teenager.

"Jayce," she gritted out, not even trying to keep the irritation from her voice. "There's nothing wrong with using your brain for more than guitar riffs. You just don't like my brother because he told me to stay away from you."

"Smart kid," Tanner muttered.

Maggie stifled a giggle, glancing back at Jayce. His scowl said he wanted to argue, but Lincoln barreled in next to him, complaining loudly about Tanner driving, effectively cutting off Jayce.

Good.

The constant snipping was getting old. She believed a small part came from her and Tanner's friendship. Jayce didn't like it. However, she worried something else was going on with him.

Most times she saw him, his eyes were bloodshot, and there was a stagger in his step. Even more troubling was the frequent trips to the bathroom, where he returned sniffing, twitchy, but in a better mood.

For now, she brushed off her difficulties with Jayce and focused on a different sort of trouble.

Tanner.

She kept circling back to the party. To them on the lawn. They'd spent less than ten minutes together, barely explored each other, yet his touch branded her.

Besides those stolen, heated moments, Maggie also liked being around him as a friend. He made her laugh, challenged her to write better songs, and impressed her with the way he juggled the band and his other responsibilities.

Shit. I'm staring at him again.

Giving herself a quick shake, she said to Tanner, "Anyway, Levi is twenty. I want to get there before him. He can slide in with us. Then the bouncers won't give him a hard time."

"Does he go to many of your shows?"

"No. He's going to an out-of-state college. I haven't seen him in months."

"Is he your youngest sibling?"

She shook her head. "My sister Lydia is the youngest. She is seventeen. The oldest is Abigail. She's the one I told you about, the perfect daughter. She has two years on me, but acts like she's a decade older."

"Wow. Big family. You're lucky. I've always wished there was more than just me and my mom."

She could hear the envy in his voice but didn't understand it. All the fighting, disappointing each other. The vying for attention was exhausting. "Abigail and I have never gotten along. Lydia is not only much younger than me, but also big into sports. Most of the time, we live in different worlds. Levi is the only one I'm close with. We may have seven years between us, yet it never seems to matter. We always have a great time together."

Tanner smiled. "Sounds cool to me."

"It is. Levi's a great kid. Super smart. He's able to speak German and Dutch fluently."

"Wow, impressive. How did he manage three languages? I can barely speak English."

Maggie laughed. "He took German in high school. Liked the process of learning languages so much he signed up for Dutch classes online. He made friends from both countries in those chat groups. They have video chats, each practicing the other's language. Levi hopes to live abroad for a while after college."

Lincoln tapped Tanner's headrest, leaning between the seats. "Don't get her started on her brother. She'll never stop singing his praises."

Maggie shifted to face Lincoln, her smile widening. "Oh, shut up. You only wish I'd talk about Abigail." She smiled at Tanner. "Our drummer has a crush on my big sister."

"It's those business suits. All strict, stern, and perfect. Ready to crack the whip. I want to be the man to tousle the facade." Lincoln swooned, causing the guys to laugh. Maggie made gagging noises.

Tanner smirked. "Sounds more like you have a small S&M fantasy. What'd ya say, Maggie? Think your sister's a dominatrix?"

"Probably." She shuddered, then covered her ears. "Now, stop! New conversation. I do not want to picture my sister in a corset holding a cat o' nine tails."

"Oh, I could…" Lincoln groaned, leaning back into his seat.

Tanner cut a sideways glance at her. "You seem to know your whips. You have a side job you'd like to share with us?"

"Like I have the time." She laughed. "I'm a voracious reader, including erotica. That's how I know about the cat. Though do tell me, how do you know what it is? Are you the one with a secret?" She leaned in, playfully stage-whispering, "Please tell me your secrets. All your secret desires."

His gaze, brimming with sinful promises, met hers. "You sure?"

Lust tugged at her stomach and pooled between her thighs. She found herself leaning toward him.

Lincoln popped up between the console, again, startling her. "I liked picturing Abigail, hell even you Mags, in a corset and thigh-high boots, but dude, Tanner, if it's your secret desire…keep it to yourself."

The way Lincoln shot forward, she wondered if he sensed the sexual heat crackling between her and Tanner. Was her attraction obvious?

She checked the rearview mirror, wanting to gauge Jayce's reaction. Thankfully he was wearing headphones and facing the window.

Tanner gave a slight shake of his head. "Oh, come on. If I'm going to be a rock star, I need to have a fetish."

Lincoln laughed, settling back into his seat. "That's wrong. So wrong, man."

The rest of the ride passed with idle talk about famous people and their reported fetishes. While amusing, it couldn't erase the memory of Tanner's hungry looks or her yearning to taste him.

Maggie didn't doubt it would be fun, but destructive. For ThreePence and her heart. Her love life was a path littered with regret and deceit. She'd built a fortress around her, only allowing it to beat for music.

However, she suspected Tanner could knock down those walls. Then he'd leave it in ruins when he left the band and disappeared from her life.

She turned up the radio. The loud, hard beat and strong lyrics chased away her depressing musings.

Two accidents added an extra forty-five minutes to their drive. By the time they arrived at the club, Maggie was a bundle of stress. They'd barely have time to set up, plus she was worried about her brother. She'd tried texting and calling Levi. He responded to neither.

Climbing from the van and opening the side door, she rechecked her phone. Still nothing.

"I wondered when you'd get here," said a familiar voice.

She spun around, and her brother wrapped her in a bear hug. "Levi," she whooped. "Sorry we're late. We hit some traffic. Were you waiting long? And why don't you answer your damn phone?"

She stepped back, taking in her little brother. Though he wasn't so little anymore. He was a head taller than her. On the tipping point of manhood, so handsome with his messy black hair and warm smile.

He waved away her barrage of questions. "Sorry. My cell was on silent. And I didn't mind waiting. Gave me time to double-check my homework that's due right after the break. Freaking math."

"You brought homework here? To a nightclub?" She grumbled. "Only you."

Tanner came around from the driver's side. Seeing him had her readjusting what she'd said. "Well, maybe not the only one. Levi, I'd like you to meet our newest member, Tanner. He's covering for Scarlett."

He offered Levi his hand. "Nice to meet you." After shaking hands, Tanner asked Maggie. "Not the only one, what? I have a feeling your statement was directed at me."

"Did you bring CPA notes to tonight's show? To study."

Looking sheepish and adorable, Tanner said, "Maybe…"

Laughing, Levi asked, "Are you a student or teacher?"

"Neither. Used to be a student, now I tutor accounting students while studying for the CPA exam."

Her brother's dark eyes flickered with delight. Her heart melted a little at Tanner and Levi's easy camaraderie. He usually hated the men she brought around.

Not that I'm bringing Tanner anywhere.

"Accounting. So. You're good at math. If you have a chance could you help me with a homework problem? I have this one, no matter how I work it, I keep getting the wrong answer."

"Sure." Tanner chuckled. "Guess Jayce was right."

"When has the douche ever been right?" her brother quipped.

"Levi…" Maggie warned.

His smirk was unrepentant. "Sorry, sis, but he is. Anyway, what's he right about?"

Tanner answered, "He said you and I would get along."

Maggie shoved him playfully on his shoulder. "Of course. You're both geeks."

"Proud of it," both men responded at the same time. They turned to each other, laughing.

"Oh God," she groaned with mirthful disbelief. "Jayce was right."

~ * ~

"That was damn cool. I'll never get tired of watching you guys perform," Levi said, claiming the barstool next to Maggie.

Tanner took the seat on Levi's other side, nodding in

agreement. They'd been perfect. The crowd was awesome. The combination sent euphoria rushing through Tanner's veins.

"You know what'll make the next set even better?" Maggie asked.

He grunted, not bothering to answer. He knew what was coming. The same thing she'd been demanding for weeks now, becoming more insistent since she overheard him singing last week. "It's not happening, Mags."

"What's not happening?" Levi's head swung back and forth like he was taking in a tennis match.

Maggie leaned across her brother, clutching Tanner's arm. "Come on. It's not too crowded tonight but big enough to see if it works."

Levi tilted back, focusing on Lincoln. "What works?"

"Your sister wants Tanner to sing a couple duets she wrote. He should."

For once, Tanner wished the narcissistic asshole was back from his smoke. Jayce was the only one in ThreePence who argued adding duets to the playlist was a stupid idea. In the past five months, it was the single thing they'd agreed on.

"Don't be a pussy," Lincoln continued. "I've heard you sing with Mags. You two sound good."

Tanner ignored Lincoln. His focus was on Maggie's pleading eyes. Ones that said only he was capable of making her happy.

Crap.

She got off her stool and stood in front of him. *Shit.* "We could sing *Love Songs*. It's mostly my vocals."

Damn it. I'm her prey. She seeks out and senses my weakness.

She inched closer, leaning her forehead against his. "Please, Tanner. For me."

The last of his resistance crumbled.

"Shit. Fine," he groaned.

"Yes!" She kissed both his cheeks before landing a firm one on his lips. Then she was off and running, shouting cheerfully over her shoulder. "I need to tell Zia. We need to make the changes before we get back on stage."

"Hell," he muttered, swinging around to face the bar, dropping his head on to it. Why in the fuck had he agreed?

"Dude. You don't know when the last time this counter was washed. Gross," Lincoln said oh-so-helpfully.

"Hey. I cleaned it. Last night," the bartender said.

Tanner shot back up, making Levi and Lincoln laugh. The

bartender looked pleased with herself, asking, "What can I get you to drink?"

"Vodka, neat. I need liquid courage."

When the bartender turned to her shelve of drinks, Levi spun on his stool and faced Tanner. "You've got it bad."

Tanner quirked a brow. "What are you talking about?"

"You aren't the first. Probably not the last," Levi continued, not unkindly. "You've been snared by Maggie." He shrugged. "I've seen it my entire life. She has something guys cannot resist. Age, race, education; doesn't matter. They're all enthralled."

He shouldn't ask. Did it anyway. "She ever drawn to them?"

Levi tilted his head, glancing to his left. "Sometimes. In a distracted sort of way. For her, the sole focus has always been her music."

That was the truth of it.

She told him the same thing. Repeatedly. So why couldn't he get the image of them together out of his mind?

Chapter Nine

Tanner splashed cold water on his face from the restroom's sink. Straightening, he studied his reflection in a scratched and dented mirror. Water dripped down his face and neck, clinging to his brows and lashes. His calm was an illusion. His pulse raced, his heart thundered fierce and sharp, like a summer squall.

Not from fear, from exhilaration.

When he'd first stepped on stage, after he stupidly agreed to sing with Maggie, panic and dread played tag in his stomach. When the first chords of *Love Songs* began, he'd closed his eyes, pictured the basement and pretended there was no crowd. He strummed his guitar and focused on her whiskey-drenched voice, losing himself in the melody.

His lyrics tumbled recklessly from him with a slight quiver, then his nervousness slipped away, and he found his stride. By the time the song ended, his anxiety had fled, replaced by euphoria.

The crowd loved it, demanding more. They ended up singing another two songs.

Tanner ripped some paper towel, using it to wipe his face and neck. The cold water didn't help. He was still hyped and didn't know what to do with his excess energy.

He tossed the towel into the garbage before opening the door. Then he halted in his tracks. A few feet from him was Maggie. The hallway was deserted, except for her.

She was alone. Her steps faltered at his sudden arrival. Her eyes held the same fevered glaze he'd just seen in the mirror.

She raced toward him. Tanner caught her as she tumbled into his arms.

"You were amazing," she breathed against his ear. Her heat lit him like a flame to gunpowder.

He captured her lips with his. She responded with equal force, deepening the kiss. The combination turned him from a rational man to a being of sensation and carnal cravings. Every part of her touching him begged for more.

He wanted all of her.

Tightening his arms around her, she grinded against his

growing hardness. His heart pounded in time with his thrumming desires.

A woman's laughter traveled down the hallway, piercing his lust-addled brain. Tanner broke their kiss, waiting to see if the echoing footsteps would come closer.

Maggie's breaths were short, needy bursts. He wanted to swallow them, make them grow in volume while she writhed against him, or with him in her.

Shit.

The voices were growing louder, and he stilled. Maggie grabbed his hand, pulling him to an unmarked door. She tested the knob. When it opened, she tugged him inside.

The scent of pine cleaner permeated the space. Through a small window, light from the parking lot filtered into the tiny room. He saw mops, buckets, and other cleaning stuff.

Maggie nearly flung herself against him. He stumbled back, landing against the door, the handle dug into the curve of his spine. He didn't care. All that mattered was the way she was running her lips and teeth from his neck to his jaw. The sensation shot straight to his dick.

He clicked the lock, then shifting to the side he brought Maggie with him. He slid his palms underneath her loose-fitting shirt, running them up her back, reveling in her warm, soft flesh.

"More," she demanded.

He recaptured her beautiful, hungry mouth, tugging the hem of her shirt. They broke away, and she quickly yanked it off, tossing it on a broken chair.

She reached for him.

"Wait. Let me take a minute. I want to take in *all* of you," he whispered.

She was exquisite. His gaze caressed her in places only moments ago, his hands had touched. Creamy skin, gorgeous breasts spilled from a low-cut purple bra. Curvy hips wrapped in a tight, short, black leather skirt. The Treble tattoo he'd spotted on the back of her neck, months ago, he now saw came around her shoulder in a mixture of music notes forming a melody he recognized.

Using his fingertips, he traced the lines and curves of the tattoo, from shoulder to lower rib. He wished there was enough light to read the lyrics.

Next time.

He made his way back up. When touched the side of her bra, he veered off track to the tops of her breasts where skin met satin.

Dipping his head, he shoved the material aside, capturing her budded nipple with his mouth. He swirled his tongue, feasting in her salty tang of clean sweat and woman.

If there's a heaven, it tastes like her.

Maggie shuddered, tugging at his shirt again. "Please, Tanner. I need your skin against mine."

He grunted an inarticulate agreement, pulling back and removing his shirt as she unsnapped her bra. She let it fall from her arms.

Holy hell, she's perfect.

He palmed her soft breasts, craving another taste. Before he could, she kissed him fiercely. It spoke of a need matching his own.

A guttural growl escaped deep from his throat. He sounded more animal than human. It fit, since his every sensation was primal. He'd never wanted someone this much. He gripped the bottom of her leather skirt, dragging it slowly over her ass and waist.

He paused to see if she wanted him to stop. She took his hand, slid it down her stomach, past where her panties should have been, and through tight, trim curls. If possible, he grew harder.

"Jesus. Maggie, you're killing me."

She laughed quietly against his throat, licking his Adam's apple. "I didn't want panty lines." Her laughter became a purr, and she rocked against his palm.

Unfastening his jeans, she pushed them and his boxers past his thighs. She gripped his erection, stroking from base to tip.

The pleasure of it had his head falling back, banging into the door. It should've hurt, but the only throbbing was centered around the hand stroking him.

She released him and demanded, "Lift me."

Shoving off from the door, he gripped her waist, doing as she demanded. She wrapped her legs around his hips. When her wet heat licked against his rock-hard erection, the sweet anticipation nearly killed him. He twisted around, pressing her back against the door.

She said something. He paused, asking, "What?"

He was having a difficult time understanding words.

"I'm on the pill," she repeated.

Yes. Right. Protection.

How'd he forgotten? He had a condom in his wallet. They should use it. His jeans weren't even past his knees.

"Okay?" she asked.

He nodded, breaking one of his rules as well tonight.

Then her heat engulfed him, and consequences were forgotten.

Oh hell, she was perfect. The tight pleasure made it impossible not to move, and he thrust.

She devoured his mouth with her lips and tongue while riding him in a way that was neither gentle nor tame, taking what she needed. Damn, it was hot. He lifted her, slamming her back onto him, guessing she didn't want it slow and tender.

Her moan grew loud, and she dug her nails into his neck, dragging them down his shoulders. He wanted this to last forever. Her warm desire engulfing him was pure bliss.

She felt so fucking good.

Her moans became whimpers, and her legs tightened vise-like while the rest of her body began to stiffen as she pulsed around him. The combination sent him over the edge with her, his powerful release mixing with the tightening clench of hers.

~ * ~

Maggie kissed Tanner's neck, whispering, "I'm afraid to unwrap myself from you. I might melt like a puddle to the floor."

His chuckle was low and deep. "My knees are locked. If I release them, we'd be there now."

With regret, she disentangled herself from him, shimming her skirt over her ass and thighs. She glanced around for her bra and shirt as he zipped his jeans.

What a shame. She could have stared at him for hours. Her man had one hell of a body.

Her man?

No. She needed to banish that thought. She didn't want or need a boyfriend. Especially one who planned on walking away from her and the band in less than a year.

After putting on her clothes, she cleared her throat. "We should probably get back before someone comes searching for us. I'll leave first."

His relaxed smile became into a scowl. "Why can't we leave together?"

"Because people will know," she stammered.

Shit. I should've known better. A man like Tanner wants more than a quickie in the dark.

He let out a harsh breath. "Who gives a fuck? Neither of us is married or dating someone else."

Irritation flared in her chest. "Damn it, Tanner. We are not going to start dating now. The band—"

He ignored her angry words, talking right over her. "Oh, I see. This is a one-off. A 'thank you' screw. For me giving in and singing."

Anger thundered through her. "Seriously, Tanner? You fucker.

You know my rule for ThreePence."

He crossed his arms over his naked chest. "Yeah. You broke it."

"I never, I mean, never break it. Do you know what a shit-storm this would cause if we strolled into the bar holding hands like some happy couple."

Some of the fight seemed to fall from his tense shoulders.

Good.

He whipped his T-shirt up from the floor, yanking it on with such force the collar stretched. He frowned. "You don't want more?"

Yes.

No.

Maggie's stomach dropped. The consequences of her actions rushed at her, crushing her glow. No matter how good he'd felt, what they'd done was wrong.

They were too different. One of them would quickly grow bored with the other. In the end, it'd fuck up their friendship. More importantly was the disastrous fallout it'd cause with the band. Jayce barely tolerated her friendship with Tanner. If there was more, Jayce might quit.

Then what? ThreePence would lose their bass player, house, and equipment. Sure, they'd nearly paid off his parents for the instruments, but there was the house. Would he kick them out? They'd lose the money they'd sunk into their practice studio.

Meanwhile, Tanner was counting his days until Scarlett returned. Which Maggie was positive would also be the end to whatever this was between her and him. If they even managed to last more than a month.

All this flashed through her mind while he waited for her answer. Impatience rolled off him, crashing into her. She wanted to shut him down, to let him believe she wanted nothing from him. Only his body. Too bad she'd always been a shitty liar.

"I don't know what I want. I like you. A lot. But we won't last, and I can't risk pissing off Jayce. I don't want him to start shit with the band, or worse, quit."

"So the fuck what? You want to ignore how good we might be because it might upset Jayce?" Tanner ran a hand through his already mussed hair. "Jesus, Maggie, Jayce is a whore. I've seen him go off with some groupie after almost every show. He's not worried about your feelings, so why do you give a fuck when it comes to his? Why is he important to you?"

"It's not him. It's what he owns. He could take so much from me. Not to mention, if he decided to up and leave, it'd fuck with ThreePence's upward momentum. All this proves is fucking was a mistake. I shouldn't have broken my own rule. I haven't even wiped your sweat from my skin, and what we did is already causing problems." She touched his bicep, making him stiffen. Maybe now wasn't the best time, but she had to try. "We could continue, like this. You know, keep it separate. I need to put the band first."

"In secret? Meeting in broom closets when you have an itch to scratch." Tanner spat, clearly insulted. "I'm fucking stupid. Why do I lose all reason around you?"

Maggie stumbled back, surprised by his venom. "Why are you so angry?"

"Because to you I'm nothing more than a tool. Something to help you release excess energy."

She heaved a heavy sigh. "What the hell is wrong with enjoying each other's bodies? What? Because we screwed, I have to be your girlfriend and who cares if it fucks with the band? Not happening, Tanner."

Her words hurt a small secret place in her heart. The part that whispered that she wanted so much more with him.

He cocked his head, eyes cold as ice. "Is that what you do? Fuck with no emotion?"

No. Not this time. Right now, she felt too damn much. That was part of the problem.

Not only was she worried about the strife it'd cause within the band, but what would happen when Scarlett returned. He'd leave, quite possibly taking her heart with him. Maggie needed to protect herself.

She said none of this instead waited to see what he'd say next. Hoping it be something to harden her heart toward him.

He didn't let her down.

"Should I feel special because you broke your precious rule? Tell me, not using a condom. Is it another rule you broke? A gift just for me?"

His hypocrisy was sharp claws against her flesh. She'd never had sex without protection. Plus, he sure as hell didn't ask her to stop to get something.

Her fury swelled, flying from her mouth. "Fuck you, Tanner! Don't get all holier than thou with me. You were willing and ready. You know what—" She shoved past him, unlocked the door, whipping it open. "Forget this shit!"

Hurrying down the hallway, she tried running from his words, along with her stupid disappointment. She'd been delusional to believe he'd be any different.

"Wait," he shouted.

His footsteps pounded after her. She picked up speed.

Fuck him.

No way was she talking to him. Asshole.

Tanner called her name again. She was half tempted to march back, just to slap him. Maybe it'd help relieve the pain coursing through her.

Why had she expected more from him?

She didn't stop. Instead, she rounded the corner, slamming out a side exit. She needed time to compose herself. To let go of her disappointment.

Chapter Ten

Soon as Tanner slid onto the stool next to Lincoln, he asked, “Where’ve you been?”

Trying to find Maggie.

She’d taken off around the corner and vanished. Damnit. He’d been such an asshole.

“In the back.” He slumped, placing his elbows on his knees. No way was he going to share what happened, especially not with someone in the band. Or with Maggie’s little brother sitting one stool over from Lincoln.

Why had he opened his mouth and spewed shit everywhere? He’d insulted her for something he’d wanted just as much. Them together was incredible, but shit, he wanted more than a quick, secret tumble.

So, like a dipshit, I lashed out.

Lincoln choked on his drink, bringing Tanner back from his self-flagellating. He turned, finding his friend staring at him, mouth hanging slightly open.

He sat up, trying to see if he’d done something stupid like put his shirt on backward. Nope. “What?”

Lincoln yanked at Tanner’s collar. “What the hell happened to your neck?”

Shit. Now that he mentioned it, Tanner could feel the scratches across his neck and down his back. The ones made by Maggie.

Shrugging, he leaned back into the bar. “I don’t know.”

“How could you not? Looks like a panther attacked you.” Lincoln cocked a blond brow and smiled. “Was it Scarlett’s friend? Did she finally get to you?”

“Um. No. Drop it.” His gaze shot past Lincoln, landing on Levi. Tanner whipped back, sitting up straight and staring ahead, hoping Lincoln didn’t notice.

He did.

“Ah shit,” Lincoln choked. “Maggie disappeared right after the show too. Were you and her, you know…”?

Ah, crap.

“No. Jesus, Lincoln. Shut up.” Tanner swung around, trying to catch the bartender's attention.

He didn't want or need a drink. He needed a diversion.

Levi covered his ears. "Eww. Stop. Please. I don't want to hear any more. I want to pretend my siblings don't have sex lives." His hands fell to his sides as he stood. "I'm leaving. I'm going to ask the lady who keeps checking me out if she wants to dance. Go ahead, have your manly gossip session."

"There's nothing to talk about." Or at least nothing Tanner was willing to share. He wasn't a kiss-and-tell kind of guy.

Levi pulled a face. "Yeah, right."

Damn, I need to work on my poker face.

"Hey, don't try to get her to buy you alcohol," Lincoln called after Levi.

Levi snorted. "I'm not some sixteen-year-old trying to sneak a drink. I'm fine with pop."

"Dude, it's not 'pop'. It's soda."

"*Dude,* you're living in Michigan now. It's pop," Levi shouted over his shoulder before disappearing into the crowded dancefloor.

"Smart ass," Lincoln groused without any malice, turning his knowing gaze back on Tanner.

Before he could ask any more awkward questions, Tanner spoke. "You're not from Michigan?"

Lincoln arched a brow, but thankfully let it go. "Nope, I'm originally from Maine. Moved here in the seventh grade."

Moving was something Tanner understood. "Man, that sucks. Why'd you come here?"

"Work. My dad took a job at Ford's as an automotive engineer."

Lincoln told stories about his adolescence in a small town in northern Maine. Talked about the cultural shift to Dearborn, Michigan, finishing with how he met Maggie and joined ThreePence.

He was a great talker. He even managed to make Tanner laugh, allowing him to temporarily push the mess between him and Maggie to the back of his mind.

Sure, later tonight it'd keep him awake, but at least for now, he could hold it together. The last thing Maggie would want was a confrontation with the band there to witness it. He needed to either find her and fix this or at the very least, get his shit together before they all piled into the van.

~ * ~

After a brief stop at the restroom, Maggie went to find her friends. She hoped no one noticed the ugly mood wrapping itself around her.

Doubtful. She was a mess. Angry, with herself and Tanner. She should've resisted her attraction.

It didn't matter she craved him like a perfect melody. His words after had proved her original opinion. Men were pricks.

Yet, damn it, lust simmered on the surface. Something she couldn't seem to smother. Because hell, Tanner was a good lover.

Right about now, she'd have liked him to have been a shitty lay. It'd match his attitude.

To heap more crap on her chaotic emotions, guilt began to nag at the recesses of her mind. Not because she had sex, more because she had it with him.

She liked sex, and while she didn't throw herself at every man who caught her attention, she wouldn't be shamed for her desires. Men sure weren't, why should she?

Maggie raked a hand roughly through her cropped hair while pushing through the door next to the stage with her other. Scanning the club, she spotted her brother dancing with a leggy brunette. Behind them, at the bar, was Lincoln. Next to him was Tanner. Her traitorous pulse jumped.

His gaze snagged onto hers, before she turned away, spotting Zia in the middle of the packed dance floor. She made her way toward her friend, ignoring Tanner's heavy stare following her.

Why did he have to bring up a relationship? What a stupid idea. They'd either grow bored or resentful for holding the other back. He hated the life of a musician, and she sure as hell didn't want to quit and move to the suburbs.

Fuck Tanner and his outdated ideals. Fuck her too because a small part was still tempted.

Swaying her hips in time with the music, she leaned in close to Zia, asking, "Where are Scarlett and her friend?"

"They went home right after the show. Scarlett wasn't feeling well." She paused, seeming to study Maggie a little too closely. "Are you okay?"

"Fine." She closed her eyes, swaying as if caught up in the music. Hoping it'd end Zia's questions.

The pressing bodies and pulsing beat gave Maggie comfort. She let her toxic brew of emotions fall from her mind.

Her serenity was short-lived, shattered when a man came up from behind and placed a large hand on her shoulder. She sighed. The last thing she wanted was some guy bothering her.

Intent on telling the stranger to get lost, she faced him. The words died in her throat when she saw Tanner's hazel eyes.

Did she see remorse in them?

He leaned close to her ear. "Can we talk?"

She stepped back. Not from unease, but more because she needed space between him and her nonexistent restraint. Even now, when she shouldn't, she craved him close.

The heat coming off his body sang to her, and she swore she could smell the scent of their sex on him. It shouted at her. The combination made her want him naked again, whispering dark, wicked things in her ear.

She needed to get away. Shaking her head, she started to leave. He caught her before she could bolt. The song switched, the melody making it impossible to hear anyone, but she could read the single word he spoke. "Please."

"Why?" she mouthed back.

He crowded into her personal space. "We need to talk. I need to apologize. Profusely."

Surprise stilled her. The men in her life didn't ask for forgiveness. They either acted like bigger dickheads or pretended the wrong never happened.

He seemed to take her hesitation as assent and grasped her elbow, probably to lead her off the dance floor. Her first thought was to refuse then she caught Zia staring at them. Curiosity oozed from her.

Shit.

Now Maggie's choice was either a crappy apology from Tanner or interrogation from her friend.

She'd take the apology and allowed him to lead her away. They cleared the dance floor and the tables, heading for the main exit. Once outside, she steered them to the left. They'd played here before, and Maggie remembered there was outdoor seating. She hoped Jayce wouldn't be there.

He wasn't. In fact, there weren't more than a scattering of partygoers, even though the club was packed.

She swung around to face Tanner. Letting her hurt and humiliation spill, she sneered, "I don't need your apology. I want to forget tonight happened."

"I don't. Please don't let my stupid words ruin it."

"Ruin what, Tanner?" She folded her arms around her, trying to freeze the warmth his words gave her. "We had sex. Nothing more. An itch we've both wanted to scratch for a while now. We didn't make love."

He winced. "It doesn't excuse my words. I was wrong. I'm

sorry."

"Fine. Forgiven," she said tightly, not meaning it.

She turned to go back inside. He stopped her with a gentle grasp on her upper arms. "Really?"

The regret in his voice softened her anger. She sighed. "I don't know. You said some pretty shitty things."

"I'm sorry," he whispered. His expression was so damn earnest. "Give me another chance."

Now she growled in frustration. "A chance at what?"

"I get you don't want a relationship, a boyfriend, but I don't want to go back to how things were. I don't want to be…"

"What, Tanner? *What* do you want?"

"Hell if I know." He released her, running both hands over his face and through his hair. "No, that's not true. *I want you.*"

His words were a balm to her wounds. Still, she wasn't letting him off easy. Hurt at his callous words scrapped her heart. "Once you *have* me again, will you call me a heartless slut right after?"

"No. Shit, Maggie. I really am sorry for my stupid mouth." His lips quirked. "Listen, if I ever say anything like that again you have my permission to kick me in the balls."

She couldn't help smiling back. "I don't need your permission. And I will."

He reached for her. She stepped back, swallowing the impulsive words trying to claw from her throat, the ones wanting to shout, "I want you, too. Right now. For as long as you'll have me."

She closed her eyes, focusing on the noise from nearby traffic, searching for her restraint. When she found it, she opened her eyes and said, "I like you as a friend and lover. But I'm not willing to risk losing the momentum we've built surrounding ThreePence for a man. Especially not for one who plans on resuming to his regularly programmed life in less than a year."

He studied her like he was genuinely considering her worries. Then asked, "Is that why you won't take a chance on me? On us? Because I don't want this life?"

"It's one reason. You want a normal job, a normal life. I don't fit into your equation. Once Scarlett comes back, hell, even if she doesn't, you'll leave us."

She said us, meant her.

He gripped her waist, bringing her closer. "Mags, I have no idea what'll happen six months or a year from now. All I know is what I want right now. That is you."

She withdrew from his embrace. "I'm sorry, Tanner, I want

you too, but this crazy attraction could ruin, or at least slow down my dreams. I'm sorry, great sex isn't worth having my band break up."

"Damn it, Maggie," Tanner growled. "Fine. Be with me outside the band. Outside your dream."

"What do you mean?" Hope sparked insider her. She ignored it, waiting for him to explain.

"During practices and shows, we're nothing more than band members. Away from it all, we're together."

She raised her chin. "In what way?"

He dug his fingers into her waist, bringing her flush against him. "In whatever way you'll give me. My lover. A friend. Both or one, you choose."

"I want that, too." She kissed him, reminding herself this was about pleasure, nothing more. Why, then, did his lips feel like arriving home?

Chapter Eleven

Maggie woke, and still half asleep, she padded around the other side of the bed. Finding it cold and empty, she squinted open her eyes.

She saw a bookshelf jam-packed with textbooks, biographies, and a hodgepodge of fiction. Leaning against the shelf, on the floor, was a framed print she recognized by Dali.

Maggie wondered if Tanner chose it because the print was popular and cool looking, or if the melting clocks and barren landscape meant something to him. For her, it spoke of apathy. Of letting life pass by and merely existing in it, half asleep, afraid to take risks.

The sound of a pen scratching across paper snagged her attention. She rolled over in the full-size bed, spotting the man she wanted with her in the bed. Tanner was sitting at a scarred wooden desk shoved into the corner.

Damn. He was stunning in only a pair of faded jeans, twirling a highlighter between two fingers. He was peering at a binder.

The window on his right filtered in the weak early winter's morning light, spreading it across his spectacular back. She'd love to design a tattoo for him. Have it permanently etched on all his delectable skin. They'd been sleeping together for more than three months, and she still thrilled at watching him. She loved the way his body moved.

He dropped his pen, stretching his arms above his head before taking a sip from a mug. His muscles bunched and shifted, unobstructed by ink, making her reconsider tattooing him.

After pushing aside the gray comforter the chilly morning air brushed over her naked flesh, giving her goosebumps, but she didn't bother getting dressed. Instead, she tiptoed toward Tanner.

He jumped when she tweaked his nipple. It puckered at her touch, and she thrilled at his responsive body.

"Damn, woman, you're stealthy." He scooted back, settling her on his lap. The chair didn't have arms, allowing her to sit astride on him. "You'd have a bright future as a cat-burglar."

"Nah, you're just focused on whatever you were studying."

"Not anymore." He nuzzled her neck while palming a breast,

playing with her nipple. The man was a master at multitasking. "Your naked body is way more interesting."

And the way he made it sing was magical. She leaned back, to give him more access, her elbow knocking into his mug.

She grabbed it, taking a sip. He liked his coffee the same as her. Piping hot with a splash of cream.

"Was the whimper for coffee or what I'm doing?" he asked, his attentions moving to her neck, inching toward her lips.

She set the cup down with a heavy clunk, raising her chin to give him more access. "I don't know," Maggie teased. "I *do* love coffee."

"Ouch. You wound my ego." He shifted, tilting her against the desk. Then he nipped the underside of her breast before rubbing his stubble across her chest. The abrasion across her hardened nipples was paradise. "I should make you pay," he finished.

Digging her fingers into his hair, she pressed him against her. If this was his retaliation, she'd offend him more often.

He sat back suddenly. Her nails dragged across his scalp as dissatisfaction flooded her.

Smirking, he reached for his mug. "You're right. Coffee in the morning is tempting. So delicious." His sip was slow and relaxed as if he had all the time in the world and nothing else on his mind except his morning java.

Two could play at this game.

Taking the cup from him, she sipped leisurely, moving a little farther down his lap. With her free hand, she slipped it between them, palming him through the front of his jeans.

He shifted into her touch, his breath hitching.

She toyed with his zipper, making like she was going to release him. Instead, she removed her hand, wrapping it around the mug. Tanner grunted, sounding displeased.

"Why'd you leave me alone in bed? Was it for this delicious coffee," Maggie asked, pretending the answer mattered to her when in reality, she wanted to know what he'd do next.

His hungry gaze traveled over her breasts, making her nipples tighten in anticipation. His perusal moved farther south, stopping between her naked thighs. Need thrummed through her, settling heavy and warm right at the area he studied with intent, hooded eyes.

"I left because you were snoring," he teased without glancing up.

She slapped his shoulder. "I don't snore."

He smiled. "No, you weren't. You were sleeping so peacefully,

I didn't want to wake you." He skimmed his hand between her legs, cupping her and using his thumb to find her favorite spot. "I figured I'd read over the study guide. I'm trying to decide if I should take the CPA test during the fall window or wait until Scarlett returns."

When he left.

Her good mood dimmed a little. Well, it did until he twirled is thumb and slid a finger inside her.

Oh, God.

"Can…" She paused, trying to remember what he said. "Can I help?"

"Studying, or," he tilted his chin, indicating his busy, magnificent hand, "this?"

She shifted, giving him more access. He took it.

"Ah, baby, you don't need any help. You're magic all on your own," she panted, finding it difficult to form words, yet somehow managed to get out what was probably her last coherent sentence. "I meant your studying. I could quiz you."

He stilled, a softness mixed with the desire held in his expression. "Really? You'd do that?"

His shock wounded her. Did he think she was so selfish she didn't give a shit he was drowning in his workload?

Instead of revealing her hurt, she gave him a sultry smile. "I won't if you don't finish what you've started. *And* do me a favor."

Okay, maybe she was selfish. Tanner repeatedly offered his help without asking for anything.

"Yes, madam." He began his marvelous ministrations again, as he nibbled from her shoulder to her ear.

"Um, hmm," she gasped. His talented tongue sent more rivets of heat between her legs.

He stopped again. Damn it.

"*What,*" she huffed.

The bastard chuckled. "Tell me your favor. Is it some new experiment you want to try?" He hummed, kissing her shoulder. "I'm up for it."

She wiggled against his erection. "I bet you are, but no, sorry to disappoint, my favor was more mundane."

"What is it?"

"I'll tell you later. I'm focused on other things right now." She undulated her hips, smooth and slow, listening to his rough exhale.

"Come on. I need to know."

Damn persistent, stubborn man.

"Will you come with me to my parents' house tonight?" she

blurted, oddly nervous. "They'd love you. A dream boyfriend. A 'real' job. No piercings."

She was babbling. Stupid nerves. She wasn't even sure why she wanted him there.

I'm such a liar.

Seemed she always wanted him around, and not just for sex. Their downtime was as much fun as their "naked" times.

She'd expected a purely physical relationship with Tanner. However, as one month slipped into another, they'd begun to do more than indulge in each other's bodies. She'd discovered an entirely different kind of pleasure with him.

They'd gone out to eat, visited live performances ranging from poetry to theater. Taken long rides together on his motorcycle. Tanner even let her drive with him on the back. They'd gotten odd looks, making them laugh. All those outings were a blast. She craved the way his eyes heated with desire but also adored the glint of merriment flashing in them when she amused him.

He touched her cheek. "Will I be introduced as your boyfriend?" Tanner asked, his expression guarded.

Guilt shattered the glow brought on by their play. Unlike most men, his unhappy bearing wasn't from a feared commitment.

The opposite. He was keeping things casual between them for her.

Sometimes I'm an asshole. Why did I say boyfriend?

"Um. Would you mind if I introduced you as a friend?" She ran a palm over his light stubble, trying to soften her words.

A muscle in his jaw twitched as if he held in angry words. Then, after a moment, his mischievousness smile returned. Maggie wanted to dance with joy. She suppressed the emotion. Barely.

"A friend with benefits?" he asked, gripping her hip.

"Definitely," she purred, leaning in to lick his neck. He tasted wonderful, like morning and virile man.

She shifted on his lap, straddled him, running her tongue from his clavicle to his nipple. Once there, she bit gently. His heart pounded against her lips, in a rapid staccato beat.

Maggie slipped from his lap, kneeling between his thighs. Dragging down his zipper, she was immensely pleased to discover he hadn't bothered with underwear. His erection sprang free, thick and generous, making her mouth water. Pushing the jeans from his hips, she watched him through her lashes.

"You wreck me," he groaned, as she took him into her mouth.

Chapter Twelve

"Which house is it?" Tanner asked, trying not to gawk at the neighborhood.

Two-story upper-middle class homes lined the street. He couldn't believe Maggie had grown up in this suburbia heaven.

It made him wonder what she thought when they visited his mother's rundown track house. Glancing at Maggie, he doubted she cared. She'd never complained about the dated home she shared with her bandmates. Material things didn't seem to matter to her.

"Right there. The one with the blue slate roof." She pointed at a brick house with a massive front porch. It reached around both sides of the house. "Park in the street. I don't want to get boxed in."

"Scoping a quick exit?" Tanner teased.

She offered her crooked smile that never failed to warm him. "Maybe."

He parked at the curb, and Maggie was out before he could come around to open her door. She'd probably done it on purpose. She kept telling him she was perfectly capable of opening her door.

Whatever. His mom might be flighty, but she taught him that small details matter. A little respect went a long way with any woman.

Coming around the car, he studied Maggie. She waited for him on the sidewalk, a nervous smile tugging at her lips.

She was a stark contrast against the old, traditional neighborhood. The streets were lined with conventional homes and perfect lawns, all fading, going dormant as fall slid into winter. Everything was grays and browns. She was a riot of colors and energy.

The wind tugged at her blood red, knee-length coat while also making strands of purple and black hair peeking from her vibrant hat dance wildly. Stepping closer, he noticed her nose was pink from the cold, accentuating the small diamond stud in it.

He tucked her into his side, trying to block the wind's fury. At the front door, Tanner dropped his arm, putting distance between them. Remembering, to the outside world, they were only friends.

He shoved down the bitterness threatening to rise up and rebel. He didn't have the right to demand more. He couldn't ask her to risk ThreePence. Not when he wouldn't be around for the consequences.

Granted, Tanner enjoyed his time with the band, more than he dreamed possible. However, maintaining his life outside ThreePence was becoming tricky. He couldn't keep doing both, and even though the thought of leaving saddened him, knowing next year life wouldn't be bursting with late nights and constant travel filled him with relief.

Would he also lose Maggie? Did she plan on ending things with him when his time with the band was over?

He forced his worries aside. They made his chest hurt as if a fist wrapped around his heart and tugged.

She didn't seem to mind or notice the absence of his arm as she pushed through the door of her childhood home. She called out a greeting, and a woman appeared from Tanner's left, striding through a formal dining room.

There was no doubt the lady was Maggie's mom. Her chin length hair was lighter than Maggie's, but she had the same wide full mouth and dark, expressive eyes.

"Hello, dear." She pecked Maggie on the cheek before shaking Tanner's hand. "You must be Tanner. I'm Barbara Prestwick, Magdalene's mother."

Maggie groaned, probably at the mention of her birth name. Her mother either didn't hear it or chose to ignore it. Probably the former, because her focus was entirely on him. She was scrutinizing him in a way that made him feel like a bug under a microscope.

"You're in her *band*?" Barbara asked, breaking the increasingly awkward silence. She said 'band' like the word tasted bad.

Tanner was starting to understand Maggie's need for a speedy escape route. His mom used the same tone when he talked about accounting. Drove him mad.

"Yes, ma'am. To both." He handed her the wine he insisted they bring. Tanner wasn't comfortable arriving to dinner without a gift for the hosts.

Barbara accepted the bottle, her brows shooting up. "Wow. Polite, no tattoos, or looking like a pincushion with so many piercings. Where did you find him?"

Maggie's mouth was pinched tight, as if holding in the fire she wanted to spew. Before she could, Levi arrived, moving around his mother to hug Maggie.

"I've missed you." Releasing his sister, he fist-pumped Tanner. "How've you been?"

When she focused on her younger brother Maggie's shoulders lost their rigidness. He must be the family peacekeeper.

"I'm good," Tanner said. "I'm surprised you're here. Is your semester already finished? The JC where I tutor at has another week."

"Nah, mine ends next week too. I finished all my classes early except one and the teacher is letting me email my final paper."

"You're in college?" Mrs. Prestwick cut in, her surprise ringing clear.

"No. Not anymore. I tutor." He kept it simple, not wanting to give the speech on his life outside ThreePence. Maggie's mother seemed the type who'd use it for fuel against her daughter's career choices.

It bothered him. Made him want to defend his girlfriend. Wait. Was she his girlfriend?

"Hey, Mags," Levi stepped in again, "I hear you guys are playing at the Oriole Terrace for New Year's. That's so cool. The hottest nightclub in Detroit. Could you sneak me in?"

"Levi. No," Mrs. Prestwick said firmly before turning to Maggie. "Why don't you show Tanner to the family room, introduce him to your sisters? Your father ran to his office before stopping at the store for me. He'll be back at any moment. Now, I have to go check on the roast." She left, making her way through the formal dining area, calling over her shoulder, "Come on, Levi. I need your help."

He saluted his mother's back, gave Tanner and Maggie a tight-lipped smile before following his mother.

Maggie stopped him, leaning in, "I'll get you into the New Year's show."

Levi's grin became genuine, and he mouthed, "Thanks."

"Right this way." She motioned with her head down the hall. "Let's see if the rest of the family is as smitten with you as my mom."

"You have doubts, what's not to love?" he quipped, hoping to make her smile.

It worked, while earning him a playful swat to the stomach. "Come on, Mr. Perfect." She led him down a carpeted hallway, past a staircase, to a spacious family room.

The first thing Tanner noticed was a cozy fire blazing in the hearth off to his right. Movement from the couch near the back snagged his attention. Two women sat there, leaning in close and talking. Neither noticed him or Maggie enter.

Maggie cleared her throat. "Hi, Abby. Hey, Lydia."

Both girls' heads shot up. For a beat, their gazes swiveled between him and Maggie like they were trying to figure out an impossible puzzle. Made him wonder if Maggie did have a specific set type for her friends and lovers.

Were they all carbon copies of Jayce?

The younger one recovered first. She stood, making her way to them. After hugging Maggie, she introduced herself to Tanner. She was the little sister, Lydia.

The other one rose, staying by the couch. Tanner figured this woman was Abigail. The one Maggie didn't get along with. This sister's resemblance to Kate Middleton was uncanny, right down to the tailored skirt and striped shirt.

"Are you really the newest guitarist?"

Tanner realized Lydia was talking to him. "Yup." He grinned. "Why do you sound unsure?"

She studied him from head to toe, taking in his dark brown boots, black slacks, white collared shirt under a brown sweater, and navy pea coat. "You look more like one of Abigail's boyfriends," she said, cocking a thumb over her shoulder, smiling with a wicked gleam in her eyes, "than a *friend* of Maggie's."

He wasn't sure what to say, so he shrugged.

"Don't mind her. She likes to start trouble." Maggie stuck her tongue out at her sister. "I have conservative friends, Lydia. Remember Zia?"

Maggie sat in one of two chairs kitty-corner to the couch. Tanner took the seat next to her. Abigail sat on the couch next to him, shifting to face him, speaking for the first time. "Tanner, were you in another band before joining Maggie's?"

"No. I left the music scene when I started college. Now I tutor students."

"In what?"

"Accounting. I'm studying to become a CPA." He was beginning to wonder if he should've brought a resume. Dinner with Maggie's family was starting to feel like a job interview.

Before Abigail could respond, an older man came in, already talking. "Sorry girls, I meant to be here when you arrived, but I needed to stop by the office. Then your mother phoned me, asking me to pick up something at the store." He focused on Tanner. "Oh, hello. I didn't realize Abigail was bringing a guest. I'm her father, Dr. Jefferson Preswyck. Call me Jeff."

"Dad, he's *my* friend. Tanner. Remember I told you I was bringing him with me to dinner."

Jefferson's brows drew together, forming a deep line. "You don't know Abigail?" Confusion tugged at each word.

"Met her for the first time ten minutes ago," Tanner replied, before smirking at Maggie. "No tattoo. No piercing. No friendship. Is this another rule of yours?"

Lydia's giggles morphed into loud laughter, yet she somehow managed to answer for her sister. "Yeah. Usually."

"No. Obviously," Maggie growled, gesturing at him as if saying, 'You're here, aren't you?'

"Well, it's nice to meet you." Jeff backtracked to the hallway, obviously wanting to sidestep his daughters' bickering. "I'm going to head to the kitchen, see if your mother needs any help."

Levi strode in as his father left, and they almost plowed into each other. Levi steadied the other man before saying, "Dinner's ready."

Tanner followed the Preswyck family, wondering if they were going to have him sit next to Abigail or Maggie.

He ended up between them.

After everyone was seated and eating, Levi asked Maggie, "Did Scarlett have her baby?"

"No, it's too early. Her due date's December twenty-seventh," Maggie replied.

Abigail rested a hand on Tanner's arm. "Does she plan on returning? Or are you permanent?"

He shifted, hoping she'd take the hint. She didn't, and Maggie's gaze reflected murder. *Could this get any more uncomfortable?*

Before the food was even on the plates, Abigail made it clear she was interested in him. He couldn't deny she was easy to talk with; friendly and her career in banking gave them lots to talk about. Heck, she even looked like a woman he usually dated: reserved in both style and attitude.

None of this mattered. He was hooked on Maggie.

Too bad she wasn't as invested in him.

He barely understood reasons for hiding their relationship, or whatever this was, to the band. Though why her family? It made no sense, and it chaffed him.

It sure as hell would help with the current awkward situation. Maggie's furious gaze burned where Abigail's hand rested.

Tanner reached for his wine, and her light grip fell away. "No, I'm not permanent."

Maggie stared at her empty plate, looking like someone had stolen her muse. Her unhappiness confused him. Zia told him he was temporary, a year, tops. Didn't she want her old friend back?

He nudged her shoulder. She offered him a weak smile.

"Yes, right. Maggie mentioned you're an accountant, studying for the CPA test, right?" Jefferson asked.

Tanner nodded.

"I bet it's a relief, being temporary, I mean," Barbara said, seemingly oblivious to her daughter's mood. "I'm sure you're ready to get back to a more respectable occupation."

Tanner cocked a brow. That was harsh. The backhanded compliment aimed at her daughter made him want to protect Maggie's dream. "Respectable? What I do with the band is respectable."

"I suppose. Though you can't claim it's more important than what you will be doing."

"I disagree. Yes, a good accountant is important. However, a world without music would be awful. It's not an easy career. I admire Maggie for going after her dream."

Under the table, Maggie grasped his thigh. He peered at her and was relieved to find the sadness and anger was gone from her eyes. Instead, they glowed, filling him with warmth.

"If you hold music in such high regard, why don't you stay with ThreePence?" Lydia asked bluntly.

Maggie's fingers traveled higher, and the current spreading warmth had nothing to do with happiness. When she found the fly of his jeans, he jumped a little, then clasped her roaming hand with his.

Tanner hoped like hell her parents didn't notice the blush creeping up his neck. Or discover its cause.

He swallowed, trying to center himself. *Okay, answer Lydia's question. Start there*. "One, Scarlett wants to come back. Two, a musician's lifestyle isn't—"

"I'm not sure she does," Maggie cut in.

Thrown, Tanner halted. "What?"

"Every time I visit she tells me how traveling worries her. Once her baby is born, Scarlett doesn't want to leave him or her. At the same time, she isn't sure taking an infant on the road will work. I have to agree. It could be difficult." Maggie shifted in her seat, letting her hand fall from his thigh. She appeared to be studying him.

Tanner didn't know how to respond. He loved performing with ThreePence, but did he want to give up a stable career as a CPA? Did he want the chaotic life of a musician? Hell, did they even want him permanently?

Too many questions and what-ifs.

His turmoil must've shown because she offered a carefree smile and shrugged. "I wouldn't worry. I'm sure it's her pregnancy hormones talking. Scarlett loves ThreePence. She'll miss performing and will soon be begging to get back on stage with her guitar."

Maggie pushed from the table and started gathering the dishes.

"Levi, you helped with dinner. I'll clean up and get the desserts."

Her sisters began helping.

Tanner tried to take the dishes from Maggie. "Let me help."

She waved him away. "No. We've got it. Go play chess or some other nerdy thing with my brother."

"I'll play winner," Jefferson added.

Tanner laughed. "I wonder if we were switched at birth. You were meant for my mom. I was supposed to be placed with your family."

Maggie gave her trademark husky laugh. The one that made him a little lighter when he was the cause. It also made him want to pull her into his arms and turn it into a needy moan.

"I was wondering the same thing." She made a shooing away gesture. "Anyway, have fun. We'll be in shortly to cheer you geeks on."

He raised his hands in defeat. "Okay. If you insist, I'll let my nerdy side out to play. First, will you point me in the direction of the bathroom?"

"Do you ever put the geeky side away?" Maggie teased, setting the dishes down and moving around the table. "Come on I'll show you where the bathroom is."

~ * ~

"You needed to walk me here? Afraid I couldn't find it on my own?" Tanner said, drolly from behind Maggie.

Okay, the half bath was a sharp left from the dining room. It wasn't rocket science to find. Her motives weren't because she was worried he'd get lost.

Nope, nothing so innocent.

She pushed him inside, shutting the door with the heel of her boot and wrapping her arms around his waist. "Shut up. I'm feeling possessive. I need to touch you. Mark you." She stood on tiptoe, biting him lightly on the slope between his neck and shoulder, reveling in his warm flesh and sweet taste. "Maybe then my family will stop thinking you're freaking perfect for my sister. Abigail will stop thinking it."

He drew her closer, running his nose and lips across her jaw. "Mark me. I'm okay with it." He pressed his lips gently against hers.

Her answer wasn't verbal or tender, but he didn't seem to mind. She loved how Tanner responded so readily to her touch. Craving it, like her.

Their tongues tangled in an erotic dance, yet when she reached between them, he stepped back. It hurt her. He was usually always ready for her.

"We need to stop unless you're serious about wanting your family to know we're together. Someone's going to notice our absence. Plus, me strolling in with a hard-on would be a giveaway." He kissed her nose. "And awkward."

Maggie peeked down between them. Too late.

She ran her hand up the front of his slacks, palming him. Standing on her toes, she teased his bottom lip with her tongue.

He hummed in appreciation before he stepped away. "Leave, you wicked woman, before I peel those tight jeans to your knees and bend you over this counter, marking *you*."

The vision sent desire rushing between her legs. "Oh, how so?"

"You'll have the telltale signs of an explosive orgasm." He ran his fingertips along her cheek to her collarbone. "You turn a lovely shade of pink like you were in the wind or kissed by the sun."

He grabbed her ass, hauling her flush against him and captured her in a rough kiss. One that would leave her lips swollen long after they parted.

Tanner might look conservative, though Maggie soon discovered he had an incredibly hot reckless side. He was willing and ready to have sex anywhere. It made for some thrilling, fun times.

Good thing too, since keeping their relationship a secret required them to be creative. They'd christened many unusual places. However, her favorite would always be their first time together at the club in Detroit.

"Mags, where are you?"

Shit. Lydia.

Thankfully her voice sounded far away. However, Lydia wouldn't stop until she found Maggie. She hoped her sister hadn't been looking very long.

Resting her head against Tanner's chest, she waited for her pulse to slow. "I'd better step out."

He sucked in a lung full of air. "Yeah. Okay. You should go. I need to picture eating live bugs or necrophilia. Anything to get rid of this hard-on."

A peal of loud laughter escaped from her. She covered her mouth. Someone was going to hear her. "Please don't have your dick and sex with dead people in the same sentence," she whispered.

"Hey, a man's gotta do what a man's gotta do."

Damn, she loved the way he made her laugh. There was much she loved about him.

That thought was both thrilling and scary, so she set it aside for now. Pecking his cheek, she slipped out.

She'd barely closed the door behind her when Lydia came around the corner.

"There you are. The coffee's finished. We're ready to take the dessert to the study." Lydia cocked her head, studying Maggie. "Where were you?"

"Upstairs." She hoped the lie wasn't written on her swollen lips and flushed cheeks.

"I didn't hear you coming down the stairs."

"So? Maybe you weren't paying attention." Maggie strode past her sister. "Come on. I'll help carry the stuff."

"Something's up," Lydia said to Maggie's back. "Are you and Tanner friends? Or more?"

Maggie stopped, peering at her sister. "What makes you say that?"

"For starters, the white-knuckled grip on your knife every time Abigail flirted with Tanner at dinner."

Maggie put her hands on her hips. "I bring a friend to dinner, and she's on him like catnip. Talk about desperate."

And he's mine.

Lydia shrugged a shoulder, continuing with her reasons. "He watches you like you're more than a friend…and I didn't hear you on the stairs."

Damn. Girl's too observant.

Maggie sighed. "Leave it alone, will you? It's complicated."

"It's your life." Lydia tossed an arm across Maggie's shoulders. When they got closer to the kitchen, she said, "Though you may want to clue in Abigail. She's smitten with him. Probably already picking out a wedding venue and china patterns."

The two laughed, strolling into the kitchen. Abigail set down the carafe of coffee she'd been pouring, giving them an annoyed scowl. "Where the hell have you two been?" she asked while placing mugs on the serving tray. "First, Maggie disappeared. Then you, Lydia. Leaving me to do everything. Nothing new there."

"Don't get your panties in a twist." Maggie exhaled, smothering her growing annoyance. She stomped to the fridge, snatching the cream, she said, "We're here now."

By the time they made their way to the family room, the chessboard was out. Dad and Levi were playing, while Mother watched from her spot on the couch.

Observing others playing games put Maggie to sleep faster than sleeping pills. She thought about joining Tanner. He was scanning the different titles on the floor to ceiling bookshelves.

She set the tray on an end table at the same time he turned from the books. She glanced at the front of his slacks then back up. Guess the bugs and dead people worked.

He smirked. She swallowed a smile, giving him a small shrug. What woman wouldn't look?

After giving everyone their coffees, she sat next to Tanner. Unfortunately, Abigail took the spot on his other side. Lydia settled across from them, her gaze dancing between her sisters. She was clearly amused

Annoying girl.

Ignoring them both, Maggie shifted her focus to Tanner. He was back to talking with Abigail about economics. Maggie took a sip of her coffee.

Between the chess and finance talk, she was going to need something stronger to stay awake. Stifling a yawn, she tuned into the conversation between Abigail and Tanner. Her lethargy fled.

"...would you be interested?" Abigail finished.

She was asking him out. As in, on a *date*.

Fury shot through Maggie's veins. Enough was enough.

She set the delicate coffee cup on the elegant glass end table and placed a hand on Tanner's thigh. Leaning forward to face her older sister, Maggie said, "No, he wouldn't. We're dating."

The back and forth between everyone died. His eyes widened, and a small smile playing at the corners of his mouth encouraged her to continue.

"Since when?" Abigail scoffed. "You said he was your friend. Not your boyfriend."

Maggie shrugged. She didn't want to get into the complexities of her relationship with Tanner.

Lydia's mouth curved into a mischievous grin, but she didn't mention their recent conversation. She might've just knocked Levi from favorite sibling status.

"What could you two possibly have in common?" Abigail spat.

That's rude.

Maggie sipped her coffee, swallowing a mean retort. "Gee, I don't know. We're in a band together. Write songs together. We love to go riding together—"

"Oh, Magdalene, don't tell me you're riding those damn motorcycles again."

Maggie waved off her mother's concern when Levi practically shouted, "I knew it! Did you two hook up the night at the bar? Or before?"

Their dad's brows furrowed together, making a deep crease between them. "Hooked up?"

Maggie's stomach plummeted to somewhere around her ankles. She peeked at Tanner. He looked as if he'd swallowed a chess piece.

"What night?" Their mother's mouth flattened into a thin line. "When were you at a bar, Levi?"

Maggie wasn't sure who to answer first. She'd like to ignore both her parents' disapproving glares. She stared hard at Levi, silently demanding he help. He'd started the shit-storm.

He appeared lost in his thoughts. Shit. That was never a good thing.

Levi sat in the chair kitty-corner from Tanner, yet he spoke loud enough for everyone to hear. Hell, the neighbors probably heard him. "You were gone for a long time, and came back with those marks—"

Jesus, Levi! Shut up!

"I think you're mistaken," Tanner cut in loudly, his eyes the size of saucer plates.

She almost dropped her cup, alarm bursting like fireworks in her brain. Was her brother actually going to mention the scratches she left on Tanner? Shit, she'd never be able to face her parents again.

Tanner's sharp tone seemed to register with Levi. His cheeks flushed red, and he stuttered, "Oh, wait. My mistake. I was thinking of someone else…"

"What is going on? What are you talking about, Levi?" asked their confused, clueless mother. "Mistaken about what? *And again,* when were you at a bar?"

Maggie grabbed onto the topic that didn't mention wild hookups. "He came to hear ThreePence, a while back. No big deal. You know Levi is too responsible to get smashed. He only wanted to hear the band."

"Yeah. They were great," he was quick to add, probably trying to atone for his big freakin' mouth. *Asshat.*

Abigail stood and walked stiffly to the fireplace. "Thanks for making a fool of me, Maggie."

In her opinion, the way her sister had thrown herself at Tanner is what made her appear foolish. Maggie was smart enough to keep this thought to herself.

"You still haven't told us why you made us think he was a friend, *not* a boyfriend," Abigail continued, keeping her gaze locked on the flames.

A small dose of guilt ate at Maggie. They might not be close, but it didn't mean she wanted to humiliate her sister. "We're trying to keep it quiet because we don't want it to get back to Jayce. The fewer people who knew, the better."

Tanner nodded like he agreed. She appreciated the gesture. It made her appear less neurotic in front of her family.

Although in hindsight, said aloud, it was ridiculous.

From the way Abigail rolled her eyes, she agreed.

I mean really, what did her family care about her "no-dating" rule? They wouldn't understand her reasoning or give two-shits about the complications it might cause with Jayce.

Hell, besides Levi, none of them bothered to come to her shows. The two worlds never would've met.

Then again, the way he nearly announced her first time with Tanner, maybe keeping things from her brother wasn't such a bad idea.

She glanced at him. Tanner and her dad stared fixedly at the chessboard, though she doubted they were planning their next move, more than likely, they were devising a way to escape the stifling awkwardness.

She could help. The need to bolt was fierce. Pulling her cellphone from her back pocket, she said, "Oh, wow. Sure is getting late."

The time was a little after eight.

"We better go." She focused on Tanner, hoping he'd get the hint. "Don't you have a thing tomorrow?"

Bless his heart, he played along. He thanked her parents for dinner and said a hasty goodbye to her siblings.

Once on the front porch, they both took a deep breath. Maggie tried to hide her discomfiture with a smile. "That was interesting."

He let out a sharp bark of laughter. "Yeah. That's one word for it." He laced their fingers together, starting for the car.

The simple gesture made her anxiety crumple and float away with the dead leaves tumbling at her feet. She wasn't a hundred percent sure declaring their relationship had pleased him, especially since her confession came from jealousy.

Also, a little demon in her mind kept whispering that hearts were fickle. Someday soon he'd grow bored and leave for a woman more like Abigail. A woman more his type.

Damn, that landed like a physical blow. Maggie wanted to be his type.

No, she didn't want to leave behind music to live the suburbia dream, commuting into the city for an office job. She just wanted to be enough for Tanner.

Forever.

She wondered if such a thing was even possible. The men in her past had always been reckless with her affection. Would Tanner be different?

At the car, Maggie tried to let go, but he held tight.

"You got quiet," he said. "Everything okay?"

I think I'm falling in love with you, and I don't know what to do about it.

She needed more time before admitting such a thing, so she threw on a sardonic smile and jerked her thumb back toward the house. "Yeah. I'm just wondering if my siblings are explaining to my parents the many vague meanings of a hookup."

Tanner let go, opening the passenger side door for her. "Shit. Let's hope they stick with the innocent one, meaning when did we start dating and not the one insinuating we screwed like over-sexed rabbits in a janitor's closet."

Maggie choked on a laugh. "I'll have to ask Levi next time we talk. That is, if I don't strangle him first."

Tanner groaned, rubbing his temples. "Yeah, I almost pissed myself when he practically announced to your family about the scratches you'd given me." He dropped his hands. "Hell, Maggie, forget bugs and dead people. If I ever need to get rid of a hard-on, I'll replay Levi almost announcing to your parents about me having wild sex with their daughter. Shit, just the thought makes my balls crawl up inside me."

Chapter Thirteen

Maggie woke in her bed, satiated and euphoric. Yesterday's New Year's performance was a huge success. The glow of triumph still surrounded her like sunshine.

To add whipped frosting to her already cake of a night, Tanner was able to stay over. At this very moment, he was naked, pressed against her back with an arm draped loosely on her waist.

Snuggling in closer to his warmth, she played back, dissecting every small nuance of the past evening. The crowd had been fantastic, a dream. They'd enthusiastically danced, applauding every song they performed. Also, the duets with her and Tanner were again, a hit. The partygoers seemed to adore them.

After the show, the manager of Oriole Terrace asked ThreePence to stay, to celebrate with close friends and select fans who'd won some contest the club had held. Even better, they asked Zia if ThreePence would like to perform at the club on a set schedule.

She accepted without hesitation. It would be a *massive* boost in publicity. Just thinking about it gave her a jolt of delight and anticipation for the future.

The only gray cloud in a flawless night was a few female fans. They'd paid way too much attention to Tanner.

Maggie tried to bury her ugly jealousy. The look wasn't pretty on her. Plus, Tanner shouldn't have to pay for the mistakes of her past boyfriends. Yet, it was damn near impossible to keep the green-eyed bitch at bay. She found it hard to hold back from marching to him and sticking her tongue down his throat, letting those bitches know he was going home with her.

It was ridiculous. Tanner never encouraged the women. He'd kindly rebuffed the more forward ones. He seemed content to spend his time with her, joking around with Lincoln or catching up with his friend Jacob and his girlfriend Greta.

Maggie rolled over to face Tanner. She cuddled in closer, needing to assure herself he was with her. He hummed his approval, placing her leg between his warm thighs.

On mornings like this, she almost wished he wasn't in the band. There'd be no need for the stupid charade. The secret dating.

Keeping their relationship under wraps was starting to wear thin. Five months was a long time to sneak around.

Would they even care? Maybe not Lincoln and Scarlett, however she could easily picture Zia shaking her head in worry and disappointment. Then there was Jayce.

Jayce and his threats.

Whatever, too many thoughts before coffee.

Maggie lazily extricated herself from Tanner's delicious embrace. She didn't get far before his arm around her waist tightened. He mumbled something about her staying.

"Sleep," she whispered, scooting off the bed. "I'm going to make some coffee and breakfast. I'll wake you when it's done."

He shifted onto his stomach, his reply lost in the pillow. She learned early on he was slow to wake. Her empty stomach couldn't wait for him.

She stepped over the sexy black leather dress and lace undergarments she'd worn to the New Year's show. Recalling the way he peeled off those pieces of clothing with his busy hands and mouth in those early morning hours sent a delightful shiver through her, running all the way to her toes.

They'd arrived home exhausted, until his fingers, tongue, and other magnificent body parts managed to push past her fatigue, keeping her up for hours. The man was good at strumming her body as he was with his guitar.

The sweet memory almost sent her right back to bed for a repeat performance. If she didn't fear her stomach would start eating itself from the lack of food, she'd already be under the covers.

Besides a couple crackers and too much champagne, she'd not eaten since breakfast the previous morning. If they had sex right now, she'd probably pass out from a lack of calories.

After finding clean underwear, Maggie found one of Tanner's discarded T-shirts and pulled it on as she padded quietly down the hall toward the kitchen.

Her thoughts drifted back to her relationship status.

Again.

It's becoming a vicious circle of uncertainty.

Dropping the secret dating crap held more appeal with each passing day. She just needed to put on her big-girl panties, deal with the mutterings and disappointment at her lack of impulse control.

As for Jayce, with each passing day, she was more certain he wouldn't give two shits about her and Tanner. Nor would he leave the band, taking the house and equipment with him because his ego got a little bruised.

Passing Lincoln's and Jayce's bedrooms, she nearly skipped with happiness. An empty house. That never happened. After the show, Jayce left with some platinum blonde, and Lincoln decided to stay the night at a friend's who lived by Oriole Terrace. Now she'd have the whole afternoon alone with Tanner. She was willing to bet a Benjamin everyone would be too tired or hungover to practice.

Although, at some point, she'd have to leave her self-imposed house arrest with Tanner to visit Scarlett and her adorable baby girl, Noella. A fitting name, given she was born on Christmas Eve.

Maggie was never one to go crazy when it came to babies, but damn, Noella was precious. All those tiny toes and sleepy eyes. For the first time in Maggie's life, she was baby smitten. She'd wanted to hang around the hospital for the entire day watching Noella's delicate movements.

Then life got in the way.

The craziness of preparing for the big New Year's show ruled her life, and Maggie only visited Scarlett once at her house, and for less than an hour. Now, without any other pressing plans, Maggie wanted to spend an afternoon with her friend and her new baby.

After getting the coffee machine started, she rummaged through the fridge, grabbing the eggs and milk. Cracking the first egg, she decided to ask Tanner to come with her to Scarlett's.

Like a couple. Sort of.

Arms wrapped around her in a hug from behind, startling her. She dropped the egg. It made a soft 'thunk,' the shell cracking.

Tanner's sleepy scent caressed her, slowing her pulse. She sighed, relaxing into his embrace while picking broken shells from the bowl.

He kissed her neck. "Sorry. Didn't mean to startle you."

She turned, resting her hands on his bare shoulders. He was glorious in last night's black jeans and nothing else, sporting major bedhead hair.

Standing on her tiptoes, she kissed him on the lips. He smelled of minty toothpaste and drowsy male.

He ran his tongue along the seam of her lips, opening them and deepening the kiss. He shifted slightly, and she heard the click of the flame shutting off on the stovetop, the bowl scraping the countertop as he moved it aside. Grasping her bottom, he lifted her onto the counter, nudging open her legs with his hips. He settled between her thighs, humming into her neck and pressing his erection against her, making his intentions clear.

Counter sex worked for her.

Running his hands under the T-shirt, he stopped at her underwear. "Why are you wearing these? We have the whole day to ourselves. Seriously. Why bother dressing?"

"My mistake. Please, don't let a small piece of cotton get in your way," she breathed, wrapping her legs around his waist when he was flush against her, she rocked. The heated contact made them moan.

She didn't need foreplay, just hot, ravenous sex. Maggie unsnapped the top button of his jeans.

"Is your New Year's resolution to break old rules, Maggie?"

Jayce sarcastic voice popped her lust like an over-inflated balloon.

She gasped, looking over Tanner's now tense shoulders. Jayce's molten glare stared back.

Tanner gave a heavy sigh, resting his forehead briefly against hers before facing the other man. She slid off the counter, pushing down the oversized T-shirt.

He stood with his arms crossed, his face blank. He was going to let her decide how to handle Jayce.

She appreciated Tanner's confidence that she could handle her mess. She never liked it when men jumped to her rescue without prompting, treating her like some weak damsel in distress, incapable of solving her problems.

"What are you doing here, Jayce? Did your 'friend' from last night already tire of you?"

Jayce ignored her questions, spitting out his own in rapid succession. "Don't you only fuck band members *before* they join? What, are you taking one for the team, Maggie? Did he threaten to leave? Is this your way of distracting him?"

This is how he's going to play it.

"Don't be an ass, Jayce."

His clenched jaw, and he balled fists until his knuckles strained. She started a silent countdown, giving him ten seconds before his massive ego was going to explode all over them.

It took five.

"Hey, I'm just trying to understand this. You told me your golden rule when I joined. Seems it's being tossed aside." He licked his lips in a way that made her want to smack him. "I wouldn't mind another taste of you."

Tanner lunged forward. She placed a hand on his chest. He stilled.

She glared at Jayce. "Please, you don't miss me. You've found plenty of women to replace me."

"Jealous?" Jayce asked, still leering.

Not at all.

"Is it because I lost interest in you?" he asked, continuing his tirade. "You needed someone, *anyone*, to keep you warm at night? You could've at least looked outside the band. Stuck to your rule. Too much effort, now that we are playing more shows? So, you're taking whatever's around, right?"

Maggie found it funny how he twisted things in his little mind. Acting like he made the call to stop sleeping together. Whatever. Hell, good. Maybe if he convinced himself, he wouldn't cause trouble.

Jayce's face darkened as if he read her thoughts and didn't like them.

Damnit. He's going to lash out.

"Tell me, is it only him or is Lincoln also helping? You know, when Tanner can't finish the job." His sneer grew, and his gaze flickered to Tanner. "Which I am sure is often."

There's the first lash from his whip.

To Maggie's surprise, Tanner laughed.

Not helping.

Jayce's head jerked back like he'd been slapped. His nostrils flared, and he yanked on the cuffs of his Henley. "Whatever. Keep the whore."

Tanner sprang forward, slamming his hands into Jayce's chest. Hard. He crashed into the opposite counter.

"Shut your mouth, asshole," Tanner growled, taking another menacing step.

Indecision played over Jayce's features as he tried to remain standing. Pride demanded retaliation, although he probably suspected he'd lose. Even without knowing Tanner had grown up in rough bars and could fight, it was obvious he was the stronger man.

Jayce's wiry frame was of a man who doesn't relish physical activity. Meanwhile, Tanner's thick arms and muscled chest told a different story.

Jayce cricked his neck, rolling his shoulders before giving them his back. "Whatever. She's not worth it."

"Yes. She is," Tanner shot back.

"Shush," Maggie said quietly. "Don't make it worse."

Though honestly, part of her thrilled at Tanner's quick defense. Having a man willing to defend her honor was nice even if logic told her letting Jayce get the last word would be better. Let him think he was the winner.

Jayce kept walking, giving them the middle finger before banging open the door his room, then hurling it closed.

She faced Tanner. “You should have kept quiet.”

His eyes sparked. “Why? Why would you let him speak to you that way?” He rubbed his temples. “Please don’t tell me because it’s better for the band. Is even your self-respect worth less than the band?”

“ThreePence has nothing to do with it. And what do I care what he says about me? His words don’t make it true.” She gave him a frosty look. “Does it?”

“No. Of course not,” Tanner muttered.

“Then why fight with him? I’m stuck sharing this house with Jayce, working with him and his attitude, day in and day out. Why create more problems?”

Before Tanner could respond with something equally reasonable, she changed the subject. “Let’s go to the breakfast place around the corner. I can’t eat here now. Not with Jayce’s hostility blanketing the house.” She pointed with her chin toward the door. “Come on, after we can visit Scarlett.”

“If we go together, she’s going to start asking questions.”

Maggie shrugged. “Let her ask.”

“Wow,” he said with a small smile. “Jayce walking in on us practically having sex on the counter puts an end to this whole secret dating crap. I should’ve molested you in front of him months ago.”

She smacked Tanner’s arm. “Oh, shut up. I planned on asking you to come with me to Scarlett’s before Jayce came home, ruining our morning romp on the counter.”

His expression said he didn’t believe her, but Tanner didn’t argue. “Yeah. I’ll go with you to Scarlett’s. I need to stop by my mom’s place first. I have something there I want to show you. I bought it back around Christmas. With everything going on I haven’t been able to show you.”

Maggie rested her hands on her hips. “It’s for you, right?”

They’d agreed, no Christmas gifts. Made things seem serious. Too official. She didn’t have boyfriends. She had lovers, and that was what Tanner was, even if her heart screamed something else.

She chose to ignore it. They didn’t share the same dreams. Hell, his dream was her nightmare.

“Well, it’s for both of us,” Tanner said, jolting Maggie to the present. “Kind of like what you did on Christmas. You know after we left the hospital.” He looked her up and down with a playful leer. “Thanks to you, whenever I hear *Santa Baby*, I’ll get a hard-on.”

Maggie laughed. “Believe me. The gift was mutual.”

On Christmas, before all the chaos and boredom of sitting around in the hospital waiting area, she sauntered into his bedroom wearing the sexiest red lingerie. She serenaded him with carols while stripping, teasing him.

She'd only made it through one song before he made her forget all the words. He'd made love to her, giving her the spectacular gift of three orgasms.

Which was another thing she didn't do with the men in her life. She had sex. She didn't make love.

What was with her this morning? She couldn't seem to stop the sentimentality when it came to Tanner.

She pushed aside her unexpected sappiness, saying, "Tell me, what did you get?"

He smiled. "I found a bike on Craigslist. An old Triumph. It needs some work, but Jacob said he'd help me with it. I should have it running by spring. I was going to let you pick which bike you wanted. The Yamaha or Triumph."

Oh. My. God. He's a man after my heart!

Maggie clapped and did a little skip dance, making him laugh. "I'll take whichever is cheaper. Let me know the cost."

"I got a great deal on both, almost free. I'll give you one." He glanced down, rubbing the back of his neck. "Um, don't tell your parents where you got it from."

She laughed, hugging him. "Or my brother, since he has a big mouth."

"Yes. He does." Tanner kissed her forehead. "Let's go. Laying around all morning in this house has lost its appeal."

Too true.

Maggie nodded, turning away. She didn't want him to see how much his kindheartedness touched her. It reached into a secret place she didn't often acknowledge, the one that yearned for love, for her own happily-ever-after.

She'd never imagined the day she first met him in his slacks and preppy sweater, sporting a severe frown, he'd become something like her other half.

Even with his constant tardiness because of tutoring lessons, working with him was a dream. Their personal side was pretty awesome too. Not only did he screw like a freaking sex god, he also treated her with respect outside the bedroom.

He was fast becoming her best friend. If she wasn't careful, she'd fall for him.

The secret side whispered it had already happened.

Maggie pushed the notion into the deep recesses of her heart, locking it away with chains and deadbolts.

Falling in love would be a disaster.

Sooner or later, he'd want his old life back. When that happened, he'd leave her. Therefore, she needed to prepare her heart for it.

Chapter Fourteen

Maggie pulled her cell from her coat pocket, scanning Scarlett's small house. It looked deserted. "I hope this wasn't a wasted trip," she said to Tanner, scrolling through numbers in her phone's address book. Finding Scarlett's, Maggie hit send.

"Yeah. We should've tried before leaving my mom's place."

They decided to stop there first, wanting to mess around with the bikes while visiting Carleen. Maggie adored his mom and lost track of time chatting with her. When Tanner mentioned the time, she rushed them out the door, forgetting to call beforehand.

Scarlett answered on the second ring. "What's up, Mags?

"Where are you?"

"Um. My neighbor's, why?"

"Tanner and I are outside your house."

"Oh, cool. I'll be right there. Give me five minutes."

"Okay. We'll wait." Maggie disconnected.

Tanner was already at her car door, opening it. It didn't matter how many times she told him she could do it her own damn self, he always tried.

Okay, fine. A small part of her loved it.

As they strolled toward the house, she leaned into his warmth. However, it was no match for a strong gust of wind greeting them at Scarlett's door. It blew snow around them, managing to bite at her covered flesh, chilling her bone deep. On cue, her teeth started to chatter.

Winter sucked.

Come January, the urge to pack and move south was fierce.

"Come here." He opened his heavy wool coat.

Okay, maybe there were some benefits to winter.

She slipped her arms around him, under his coat. Snuggling into his warmth, she skated her fingers under his sweater, running them up his back.

"Jesus, Maggie!" he yelped. "Are those icicles?"

"Sorry, your warmth is heaven." She stood on her toes. "Come here. Share some more."

His mouth met hers, and the cold was forgotten while he

expertly heated her from the inside out. His lips teased hers open, sliding his tongue inside and tangling with hers in an erotic dance. She could kiss him for hours and never grow bored.

"Glad you two found a way to keep yourselves busy while you waited."

Startled, she jerked away from Tanner. She'd forgotten about Scarlett.

Guess today was the day to let everyone in ThreePence learn she and Tanner were together. Hell, maybe after leaving here, they could stop by Zia's or find Lincoln. Start making out in front of them too.

Maggie cleared her throat. "Hey, Scarlett."

"Hey, Maggie." Scarlett cocked her head, apparently waiting for an explanation.

"What?" Maggie smirked, acting like it were no big deal. "It's cold. We needed to do something to keep from freezing to death."

Scarlett's eyes glistened with amusement. "Glad you both are resourceful. Now, come on, let's get inside before the fire coming off you two melts my beautiful snow." Cradling a bundle of blankets Maggie assumed was Noella, Scarlett unlocked the door and went inside.

Maggie glanced at Tanner, wanting to get a read on him. He appeared ready to burst into laughter. She elbowed him before taking his hand and following Scarlett.

Maggie shoved the sturdy wood door closed, then caught Scarlett eyeing her and Tanner's physical connection. She waited.

Scarlett looked between them. "You two are together?"

"Yes." Maggie raised her chin, daring Scarlett to say something negative.

Instead, she shrugged a shoulder. "It's about time you found a man worthy of you." She motioned them farther inside.

Uh. That's it? Nice.

Her friend's unexpected approval lightened Maggie's spirits. Scarlett knew something about committed relationships. She'd been with Neal since high school. If Maggie didn't see Tanner and her as such an odd couple, destined for failure, maybe they'd last past the lust.

Besides her dickhead high school boyfriend, the one who taken her virginity then broke her heart all on the same night, this was her longest relationship. She hoped Tanner wouldn't cause her the same pain, because unlike the guys from her past, she wasn't antsy to move on.

She and Tanner sat on the couch. Scarlett settled into the easy chair across from them, resting Noella on her lap. Maggie eyed the bundle. "I'm surprised you left the house. Are you feeling better?" Scarlett's doctor's prediction had come true. Most of her pregnancy was spent in bed.

"Yes, I'm on the mend." She fidgeted with baby and the blanket. "I know I shouldn't go out with Noella, but I'm going crazy cooped in the house with Neal fretting over us. So, um, when he left to pick up some groceries, I took the two-second walk to Pam's house."

Maggie shrugged. She didn't know the newborn protocol. "I won't tell."

"I might," Tanner teased, and she gave him a playful push.

Scarlett smiled. "Tell me about the East Coast tour. Zia started to, but I was rude and went into labor." She said this last part with good-natured humor, kissing her baby's head.

The reminder of the *Cabin Fever* tour made Maggie's heart skip with anticipation. The drummer from the extremely popular band, J.Hoffa, happened to be at a club ThreePence was playing shortly after Thanksgiving. He'd been blown away and mentioned them to his bandmates.

Then like kismet, well for ThreePence anyway, J.Hoffa's opening act unexpectedly canceled. They contacted Zia, asking if Three Pence wanted to audition as the replacement band.

And, holy shit! They got the gig!

The publicity would be extraordinary. The bigger venues would be magnificent. Her dream was coming true.

The only holdout had been Tanner.

The tour would start on Valentine's Day in Grand Rapids, finishing Memorial Day in New York. He might have to put off taking his CPA test, and he feared losing tutoring students during his long absence.

It bothered Maggie the tour caused Tanner added stress. However, there was no way ThreePence could let pass such a fantastic opportunity. Thankfully, he seemed to understand this and agreed to go with them.

In the end, the fallout wasn't too bad. Most of his students stayed with him, deciding they'd communicate via emails and video chats.

She grinned at Scarlett. "We leave next month. Our first show is here." She let go of Tanner to count off the cities on her fingertips. "Then we go to Chicago, Cleveland, Philadelphia, D.C., Richmond, and ending in New York. We'll spend a couple of weeks in each city, playing various venues in the surrounding area. Zia also booked us with some smaller places we'll play separately from J.Hoffa. We're hoping it'll give us a following outside of the Midwest."

"That's wonderful," Scarlett said, excitement ringing in her voice. "Oh, I wish I could be there with you guys. And not just because I'd probably get more sleep on the road than with my little girl here."

As if Noella understood her mother was talking about her, she stretched and opened her mouth, letting out a healthy squeal, making them laugh. Scarlett cooed at her lovely daughter.

They were so damn touching even Maggie felt a twinge of longing.

"Do you know when you want to come back?" Tanner asked Scarlett, effectively crushing the sweet moment.

She looked away from Noella with obvious reluctance, facing Tanner. "I don't know. I've been a mom for around a week and have slept maybe five hours. I can barely remember to shower, let alone consider something months away." She tilted her head. "Why? You ready to quit?"

"No, just curious," he mumbled, suddenly seeming to find the decor fascinating.

Huh.

She'd thought he was enjoying his time with ThreePence—with her. Was maybe even hoping Scarlett wouldn't come back.

Apparently, I've been assuming wrong. Seems the opposite is true.

Hell, maybe he was counting the days until he left, craving his normal old life with his well-mannered, docile women.

The possibility cut like a knife.

An uncomfortable silence started to spread. Before it could suffocate them, the sound of the garage door opening broke it.

"Neal's home. He probably needs help with the groceries. I better go open the side door for him." Scarlett clutched her baby, jumping up like her ass was on fire. "Would you mind holding Noella?"

Maggie started to freak, until Tanner stood, accepting the small bundle. When he sat back down, she arched a brow, studying him.

"What?" He smiled sheepishly. "I like babies."

She shrugged in an I'm-not-judging-manner. In fact, Maggie found it adorable.

She was glad he offered. She found Noella gorgeous, a freaking angel disguised as a human, but holding such a little human made Maggie nervous.

He didn't have the same problem and held Noella with

complete ease. The two of them appeared equally smitten with each other.

Maggie scooted closer, dipping to run her nose over the baby's black peach-fuzz hair. It was soft as silk and smelled like a dream.

Tentatively, she ran her fingertips across Noella's belly. She farted, loud and proud, kicking her feet excitedly, quite pleased with herself.

Maggie and Tanner laughed. She poked Noella gently in the stomach again. "Feel better?"

"From her triumphant kicks, I'd say so." Tanner smiled.

Noella gave Maggie an excuse to forget his earlier questions about Scarlett's return. By the time she and Neal came in carrying a tray with coffee, only a small bit of sadness tugged at Maggie's heart.

Chapter Fifteen

"Come on, people, get your asses in here," Lincoln shouted from the kitchen. "We're running out of time. We need to figure out what to do with the damn hotels."

Maggie cursed, and Tanner agreed. Not one bone in his body wanted to move. He'd happily sit slumped on the couch with her and Zia. Plus, the best part of *Pulp Fiction* was coming up.

"I've got Baileys to go with the coffee," Lincoln tempted.

Zia pushed the old afghan off from her lap, standing. "I'm sold." She looked from Tanner to Maggie. "Up, lazy bums. This is more important to you than me. I'm managing my stuff from here, so it makes no difference to me where you all sleep."

"Wow. Nice manager," Maggie groused.

Zia laughed, giving a half shrug on her way to the kitchen. Tanner didn't stand, stretching his arms and legs from his spot on the couch. The movement pulled up his T-shirt. Maggie admired his sexy, exposed stomach.

He cleared his throat, waggling his brows, running his index finger along the waist of his jeans to his stomach, lifting his shirt higher. Leaning closer, he whispered, "Want to skip the band powwow? I can warm you better than Baileys."

She laughed, following the trail he was mapping.

"Tanner! Maggie! Get your asses in here," Zia shouted.

Damn it. Duty calls.

Maggie sighed. "Come on. If we skip, Lincoln and Zia will have us sleeping in a tub or the halls." She grabbed his wrist and stood, heaving him up.

"Are you going to tell them?" Tanner whispered.

Maggie nodded.

About damn time.

Satisfaction seeped into his veins. Smiling, he took proud possession of her hand.

He'd said the truth about them dating should come from her, not Jayce or Scarlett.

She agreed, then did nothing. Only asked Scarlett to keep quiet until she talked to the rest of the band. To his and Maggie's surprise,

Jayce hadn't said a word. It wouldn't last.

Tanner understood her nervousness. He'd witness many groups fall apart when members decided to sleep together. However, they already crossed that line. Repeatedly. He believed the longer they kept it from Lincoln and Zia, the more friction it could cause within ThreePence.

Right before entering the kitchen, Maggie let go. He clamped his jaw tight, annoyed. *Still with this shit?*

She leaned close to him. "Be patient. I'm trying to find the right way to tell them."

Tanner resisted the urge to roll his eyes like a teenager, even if Maggie was acting like one. What's done was done. The band will learn to deal with it.

Hell, if Jayce could handle it without being a total asshole, Lincoln and Zia would be fine. Then Tanner recalled his first show with ThreePence, the one when Zia warned him to not mess with the dynamics of the band. Okay, that made him feel a bit shitty.

Still. Maybe at first Zia wouldn't be happy. However, she'd soon see he and Maggie were magic together. Inside and outside of the band.

"I'm going to get a beer. You want one?" she asked, clearly trying to smooth things.

Unable to let his annoyance go, he gave a curt shake of his head before sitting at the kitchen table.

After grabbing her drink, she sat at the empty chair next to him. "Where's Jayce?" She seemed to be asking no one in particular.

Lincoln shrugged. "Probably sleeping off his hangover." He leaned his chair back on two legs, peering down the hallway. "Hey! Jayce get your ass out here. Or we'll have you sleeping in the tub."

Maggie grinned at Tanner, giving him an I-told-you-so smirk. He couldn't help but return it.

Jayce stumbled in a couple minutes later, taking the empty seat across from Tanner. Studying the other man, Tanner's unease grew. Jayce looked rather rough.

He reminded Tanner of his friend Will when his partying was becoming a habit, the addiction digging its claws in deep.

Before Tanner could decide if he should voice his concern, Zia spoke. "Okay, it has dawned on J.Hoffa the rooms their manager booked for the original opening act might not work for us since our lead singer is a woman. I've checked out a bunch of hotels. There's nothing available on the first couple legs of the tour. We can get two in D.C., Richmond, and New York." She turned to Maggie. "Will you survive sharing with the guys until then? You can sleep on the couch. The dudes will share the beds."

"I don't mind sharing for the whole trip. Why waste the money?"

"Screw that," Jayce cut in. "Lincoln and I will have our own bed. She can cuddle with Tanner."

The world halted. Everyone's gaze flew to Maggie.

Shit.

He'd never understood the term *the silence was thick.* Tanner sure-as-hell did now.

"Excuse me?" Zia's glare bore into Maggie, hot enough to leave scorch marks.

"She's been fucking him for who knows how long. Behind our backs," Jayce spat.

"Jesus Christ," Tanner muttered, resting an elbow on the table, rubbing the bridge of his nose.

So much for easing the news in gradually. Thanks, Jayce. Asshole.

Maggie leaned back, linking an arm over her chair, as if relaxed. The tightness around her eyes and tense shoulders gave her away.

"Stop being such a drama queen. What difference does it make what I do outside the band?" she asked what Tanner assumed was a rhetorical question.

Jayce didn't take it that way.

"If you're screwing someone in the band, there is no outside. No separation. Isn't that why you have your precious rule? It's what you told me when I joined," he snarled.

She sighed. When she spoke, she sounded tired. "We didn't plan for it to happen. And remember, he isn't a true member of ThreePence. He's with us until Scarlett returns."

She winced. Tanner wondered if it hurt her to think about him leaving. It made his chest tighten as if a fist was squeezing his heart.

Jayce acted like she hadn't said a word, saving his fury for Tanner. *Double shit.* "You know the only reason she's with you is you're convenient, right? Once you go back to your boring, insignificant life counting numbers, she'll forget you ever existed."

Tanner's pulse pounded in his ears. He wanted to jump over the table and strangle Jayce. Instead, Tanner growled, "Fuck you."

Jayce, for his part, was like a can of pop that'd been left in the hot sun all day. Slowly building pressure, ready to explode in a mess of hate and jealousy. His lips contorted into a cruel grimace as he faced

Lincoln. "Maybe you'll get a taste next. Or the whore might come crawling back to me."

Tanner saw red and sprang from his chair. It knocked against the wall as Maggie shouted, "Hey!"

Before he reached Jayce, Lincoln pushed them apart with his strong drummer's arms. "Enough!" he yelled. "Let's take a break. Cool off. We'll come back to this shit later."

Tanner inhaled deeply through his nose. After getting himself slightly under control, he nodded at Lincoln, then Jayce.

Jayce snarled. "Fuck this! There's nothing to discuss. I'm not sharing a room with either of them." He stormed from the kitchen, snagging his coat before crashing out the front door.

"At least he didn't quit. Or threaten to evict," Zia muttered.

Lincoln let his arms drop to his side and focused on Tanner. "Seriously? You two are together?"

"I told you," Zia said to Lincoln. "Has this been a thing for a while?"

Maggie scratched her nose. "I don't know. Sometime in the fall."

"That long? And you didn't tell me? Why?" Zia sounded hurt.

"I'm sorry." Maggie sat, and Zia did the same. "As my manager, I knew you'd be pissed. You'd already warned me in the spring."

Surprise bloomed in Tanner's chest. *Had she?*

Maggie continued talking to Zia. "Anyway, we wanted to keep it private so it wouldn't mess with the band."

Everyone understood she meant Jayce.

"Speak for yourself," Tanner grumbled, returning to his seat. "I didn't care if the asshole knew."

"Fine." Maggie sighed. "*I* wanted to keep it quiet. Tanner wasn't happy about it. But I was right. Our tour starts in less than a month. What are we going to do if he doesn't come back?"

"He'll be back." Lincoln didn't have any doubt in his voice.

"What makes you so sure?" Maggie asked.

"Because, where else is he going to go?" Zia rubbed her temples, smiling weakly at the group. "I'm really glad you guys don't need me on this tour."

Chapter Sixteen

Maggie leaned back into the worn leather couch, propping her feet on the scarred metal table. She tried to dampen the excitement zinging through her. It was impossible. Before the show, J.Hoffa asked ThreePence if they wanted to play a song or two with them during their encore.

Maggie was beyond thrilled. The Columbus crowd was enormous. The added publicity at their first major stop outside of Michigan would be killer.

They had an hour and a half before joining J.Hoffa on stage. She closed her eyes trying to appreciate the downtime. There were friends and fans backstage, but for now, everyone was leaving her alone.

Good.

A song tugged at the corners of her mind. She needed a little uninterrupted time to play with her muse. To let her mind drift to the dreamlike place where lyrics and music came together.

A woman's high-pitched giggle slammed into Maggie, bringing her back to reality. Cursing, she opened her eyes, her focus falling on Tanner.

He sat on a barstool, feet resting on the lower rungs, relaxed, chatting with two women. One of them was well into his personal space, tittering and giving out all the 'fuck-me' vibes.

Ah, the obnoxious giggler. Of course.

The woman leaned forward, offering Tanner a spectacular view of boobs nearly tumbling from her halter top. Giggler's friend, who most definitely had some work done to look like Barbie's twin, bent forward, placing her hand on his upper thigh. Her thumb was close enough to brush his dick. The women were moving in like two vultures.

A possessive fury beat inside Maggie's head, keeping time with her heart.

Not cool.

His gaze swung from the women to Maggie. He smiled sheepishly before shifting his legs. The two Barbies gave matching pouty frowns, then moved in closer.

Maggie's pulsating anger shifted from her heart, racing through her veins, making her fingers itch to claw flesh. She wasn't sure if her jealous rage was directed at Tanner, or Barbie and Skipper.

Forgotten, old insecurities popped up like weeds. They whispered she wasn't enough to keep a man from straying. Reminding her how she gave her heart and virginity to a man who treated both like cheap, dime-store trinkets.

The men who followed weren't much better. She found it easier to freeze her heart. To use them as they used her.

It had been so long since she cared about someone she was sleeping with, she'd forgotten the misery disguised under a simple word: jealousy.

"Are you regretting it? Forcing him to sing?"

Maggie jerked, startled. She focused on Jayce. He was hunched over and resting his arms on the back of the couch, way too pleased with himself.

She scooted back, putting some space between her and his smug expression. He shifted his attention on Tanner and the two women.

Maggie folded her arms across her chest. "I don't know what you're talking about."

Shut up. Don't give him fuel.

Besides playing bass, it seemed Jayce's sole purpose was to stir shit between her and Tanner. She just offered him a match and gasoline for his fire.

Jayce tipped his chin. "Putting the accountant front and center made him more noticeable." His tongue darted out, playing with his lip ring. "Though, what a woman would want with such a boring straight-laced guy is beyond me."

Maggie's mind wandered back to earlier in the morning, to the things Tanner had done to her body. The man was *not* straight-laced.

"Maybe today will be different. The way those two loyal fans are hanging on him, I'm willing to bet they'll teach him the art and splendor of a threesome. I bet even a dull shit like him wouldn't refuse. What do you think?"

Jayce was trying to piss her off and was succeeding. Not that she was going to admit it.

Standing, Maggie gave a dismissive wave. "Not all men are pigs. Some guys aren't man-babies, unlike you. Some manage to control their dicks."

"Doesn't seem like he's very interested in controlling his," Jayce taunted.

His mocking words following her as she made her way to Tanner.

Don't let them penetrate. He's a shit-stirrer, nothing more.

Though, it'd help if Tanner wasn't so freaking cozy with his two Barbies.

Stopping next to him, Maggie plastered on a smile she hoped hid her jealousy.

His arm went around her waist. He kissed her shoulder, moving to her neck, making it clear to the two women he was with her.

Her resentment popped like a fragile bubble. She still shot the two women a warning glare.

Barbie took in Tanner's familiar hold on Maggie. "So, the rumors are true? You two are together?"

She didn't sound happy.

"Yeah," Maggie replied flatly.

These two were ThreePence fans. She needed to put away the claws, but she couldn't seem to retract them.

Barbie's friend seemed to be sizing them up, appearing more speculative than upset. She smiled at Maggie, thrusting her double D's forward. "You guys interested in a three-way?"

Maggie's gaze flew to Tanner, and she stifled a laugh. His cheeks were crimson and didn't seem to know where to look. The poor guy was probably going to start stuttering and shuffling his feet like some bashful schoolboy.

She decided to rescue him. "Sorry, I don't share."

Skipper shrugged a delicate shoulder. "I figured it couldn't hurt to ask. Hell, being the meat in a sandwich with you two would be hot." She winked, taking Barbie's hand they moved toward Lincoln.

"You okay?" Maggie tried and failed to hold in her laughter. Tanner's stunned expression was priceless.

He ran a hand down his face, shaking his head. "Life on the road is way different than academic life. Jesus, I thought going to the shows with my mom's old boyfriends was bad. At least I was never on the receiving end of this crazy shit."

"You know, for most men, this 'crazy shit' would be a dream-come-true. Hot women throwing themselves at you." She tilted her head back, studying Tanner. "Were you tempted? Even a little?"

He scratched his chin. "Okay, I admit, watching you with another woman would be scorching hot."

"But you don't want to be involved?"

He smirked. "Well, I like to be a helpful guy."

She smacked him on the chest. *Hard.*

“Ouch.” He stumbled back a step, smiling and rubbing his chest where she’d hit him. “I was kidding. You’re all the woman I need.” Hugging her in a tight embrace, he pinned her arms at her side. “Seriously, a midnight fantasy is one thing. In reality, I’m like you. I don’t share. Man or woman, doesn’t matter.”

She rubbed his chest with her palm. “Okay. You can let go. I promise not to hit you again.”

“Thank God. You have a mean right hook.” He shifted, taking her hand. “Come on, Muhammad Ali, I heard there’s a haunted bunker under the stage, want to explore?”

Maggie nodded, naughty thoughts of christening haunted rooms pole-danced in her mind.

Chapter Seventeen

Tanner stumbled to the hotel bed, falling face down. "Exhausted," he mumbled into the pillow. Everything was tired, even his toes.

"So you don't want to get your nerd fix and check out the National Archives?" Maggie teased.

Rolling to his side, he watched her remove large silver hoop earrings. After setting them on the table, she perched on its edge, bending to slide off black, sexy heeled boots. He was able to see straight down her loose-fitting burgundy shirt. The woman's breasts were perfect; not too big or too small.

His fatigue began to fade. "It's after two in the morning. I'm betting it's closed," he said to her boobs.

Sitting up, he shifted his feet onto the ground. When she straightened, he gripped her waist, bringing her to him. Resting his face against her stomach, he inhaled her scent of leather and jasmine. "Who are you calling nerdy?"

"You." She giggled. "D.C. must be heaven for a geek like you."

"You like it here, too. You seemed to enjoy the Tidal Basin."

"Whatever, sure. The blossoms were gorgeous." She ran her fingers through his short hair, scratching his scalp. He hummed in appreciation, loving the bite of her nails.

Lifting her shirt, he ran his tongue along the waist of her tight black jeans. "Yeah. Gorgeous."

A shiver of desire warmed her flesh. She let go of his hair to peel off her shirt. Her sheer bra and the raw need radiating off her made his knees weak.

Hell, he would've dropped to them if he wasn't already sitting.

Maggie was the perfect mixture of sugar and spice. She was infuriating, selfish, and demanding. Also, generous and devoted.

He could love her.

But shouldn't.

There was truth in what Jayce had said and Levi hinted at those weeks back. When Tanner left ThreePence, he was also leaving Maggie.

Not because she didn't have feelings for him. It was more her focus on the band didn't leave space for much else. She didn't have time for outside distractions. Her true love was music.

So instead of declaring his love, Tanner shoved his growing feelings into a steel box, storing them in a shadowy corner of his heart. He ran his palms down her thighs then back up, to rest them on her curvy waist.

Looking into her eyes, he said, "You're beautiful."

I could love you if you'd let me.

Tenderness, maybe something more, flashed across her face. A sinful smile quickly replaced it. She bent, kissing him roughly while also pushing him flat on the bed. Maggie fell on top of him and wasted no time, working the buttons of his jeans.

She was all demands and frantic hands. Their first time was explosive. The heat never dimmed. Hiding their relationship for months, so many stolen moments, led to fast and feral sex.

That part was behind them, the sneaking, not the furious lovemaking. Their need for the other always seemed too great to pause and take things slow.

Tonight, he was determined to make love to Maggie, not just have sex. He wouldn't tell her he loved her, wouldn't even think it, but dammit, he'd cherish her body.

Taking her hands, he clasped them with his as he rolled over, pinning her under him.

"Take off your clothes," she panted.

He smiled, loving that she wasn't shy and demanded what she wanted. Rolling away, he stood, removing his shirt. His gaze never left hers while he popped one button at a time on his jeans.

She hungrily ate up his movements. Running his thumbs along the waist of his pants, he stopped, waiting to see what she'd do.

"Do you need some help, Tanner Reid?" she practically growled.

Tanner shook his head, pushing his jeans and boxer briefs down, kicking them aside. Her gaze fell to his erection, and she licked her lips.

He almost caved. Taking a deep breath, he tamped down his desire, then commanded, "Move to the center of the bed."

She listened.

He crawled up the comforter, methodically removing her clothes and kissing recently covered areas. Once naked, he lingered, taking in the rapid rise and fall of her breathing. Her desire amped his.

He caressed her breasts, reveling in the rapid beating of her heart. She arched into his touch, while also wrapping a hand around his erection.

The pleasure of her firm strokes flowed over him. Closing his eyes, his head fell against her chest

When she whispered for him to get a condom, he searched his willpower. Found a trace and scooted back.

Maggie huffed, scowling at him. “What are you waiting for?”

He bit back a smile. “Not yet.” He leaned in, brushing his lips lightly across hers.

He trailed kisses to her stomach. He stopped at her inner thigh, hovering less than an inch from her flesh, basking in her arousal.

“Tanner,” she whimpered. “You’re killing me.”

No more urging required. He claimed her with his mouth. Her legs opened for him, moving them onto his shoulders. Within no time, she was panting and calling out his name, his favorite melody. Finding her favorite spot, he sucked while also gliding two fingers inside. The combination sent her over the edge.

Her legs tightened viselike around him as she shouted through her release. Vaguely, he hoped the hotel had thick walls. Otherwise, their neighbors were probably getting sick of them. Or turned on.

Right now, he didn’t care. All his focus was on her taste and the sounds of her orgasm.

When her shouts became whimpers, he kissed her soft skin, taking a leisurely and delicious path up her body. He paused, reaching for the condoms in the drawer at the bedside table. Maggie stopped him.

He raised his brows in question. Besides their first time, they’d always used protection.

“Can we skip it?” Her words came out in a rush. “I’ve been on the pill for years. My doctor ran the usual tests a month before we left on tour. All was good. And besides our first time together, I’ve always used a condom.”

“Me, too.” He’d been tested a while back, during his yearly physical and hadn’t been with anyone since then besides Maggie.

What he wanted to ask was, why now? Why tonight? Did she share his need, the desire to be closer?

To not have sex. To make love.

In the end, he didn’t ask. He’d learned at a young age not to ask a question if you didn’t want to know the answer.

He kissed her. Hovering, he entered her slowly, watching. Engulfed in her heat, reality went blurry around the edges.

His gaze moved to her face and saw adoration. He desperately wanted to believe they were her true emotions, not a reflection of his wishes.

Once buried inside her, she wrapped her legs around his waist and sighed. It sounded like satisfaction and a demand for more.

Again, he couldn't deny her. His thrusts were slow, like he wanted to prolong their pleasure all night, but Maggie urged him on with her hips. She moved in a hungry rhythm, making his release build.

When she started to go over the edge, she closed her eyes.

"No," he said gruffly. "I want you looking at me when you come apart."

She did as he demanded. Seeing longing, and possibly love, stopped his heart. When it began to beat again, she owned a large part of it.

Chapter Eighteen

Maggie scanned the small room given to the club's performers. The Baltimore show had sold out, and the afterparty was packed. The walls plastered with concert posters and people, leaning on them talking, or making out. None were Tanner. In a crowd filled with crazy hairstyles and dye jobs, it should be easy to spot his neat russet hair.

Where the hell is he?

She was pumped. Sitting around backstage drinking and chatting held no appeal. She wanted to celebrate. Either by hitting one of those jazz shows in the Northern Liberties, or going back to their hotel.

She needed Tanner for both options.

"Hey! Anyone seen Tanner?" she asked to no one in particular.

"He's the hot guitarist you sing with, right?" asked a woman in a red tube top and matching miniskirt.

Maggie nodded, pushing down a cutting retort. His growing admiration from ThreePence's lady fans was difficult. "Yup. That's him."

"He left with some girl. Maybe ten minutes ago." Ms. Tube Top wrapped a lock of her hair around her finger and pouted. "Lucky bitch."

Not if I find her.

Maggie stomped out. Anger and betrayal were making it next to impossible to breathe. Had Jayce been right? All guys were led by their dicks.

At least she now knew what to do with her excess energy from the show.

I'll use it to kick Tanner's ass.

The first door she came across, Maggie yanked it open. An empty janitor's office. The sight deepened her fury. It reminded her of the first time she'd been with Tanner.

She slammed the door shut, and a group of roadies stopped talking to watch her. Ignoring them, she turned the corner and found herself in an empty corridor. Seconds later, Tanner's deep laughter floated out from the nearest open door.

Stepping inside, she distractedly noticed tables and large vanity mirrors on the far side of the room, along with the many empty clothes racks. However, what held her attention was the black, leather sectional. Sitting dead center, with their backs to her was Tanner and some woman with long blonde hair. They were bent over something, their heads almost touching.

"What the hell's going on?" Maggie barked.

Her anger bounced around the small space, smacking against him. He jerked back, and something clattered to the floor.

Tanner jumped to his feet, looking guilty but sounding pissed. "Jesus, Maggie, are you trying to give us a heart attack?"

The fucking nerve of him.

She took in the woman on the couch. She was stunning. Wide, innocent blue eyes, cupid's bow lips, and flowing blonde hair. Tanner's perfect match.

Good. She can have his cheating ass.

He swallowed. "This is—"

In no mood for introductions and excuses, Maggie cut him off. "Would you please fuck off?" she told the blonde.

The woman gasped, her gaze swinging to Tanner as if waiting for his direction. *Wow, submissive too.*

His head lowered briefly, then he faced the woman. "I'm sorry, Ester. I guess this isn't a good time. We'll talk soon, okay?" Anger tinged his words.

Maggie's simmering indignation became a boiling fury.

I caught him with another woman, and he has the gall to be angry? Asshole. Fucking asshole.

The blonde stood, brought up her arms like she was planning on hugging Tanner, then cut a glance at Maggie. She let her hand fall back to her sides. Guess there were some brains in her cute little head.

Instead, she muttered a goodbye, darting for the exit. She quietly closed the door behind her.

Tanner stomped toward her. "What the hell, Maggie?"

"Excuse me?" she stuttered, taken aback by his anger.

She'd caught him with another woman, practically kissing. He had no right to self-righteous wrath. He could at least have the decency to sound contrite.

Shit. I'm such a fool. I thought he was different.

He looked at the ceiling, muttering about patience. Her palm itched to slap him.

He bent, coming back with his phone. *So that's what he dropped.*

He slid it into his back pocket. "Yes. What's your excuse for stomping in here and acting like a damn two-year-old? Why were you rude to Ester?"

"Oh, I'm sorry," Maggie spat, her chest heaving with rage. "Did I come in too soon? You were only able to exchange numbers instead of bodily fluids."

Every muscle in his body tensed. Two beats later, he exploded like a volcano. "Fuck, Maggie. I was showing her pictures from the tour. She's a friend. I used to tutor her."

The beginning tendrils of doubt snaked around her, yet she was too wound up for it to extinguish fully. "If she's just a friend, why run off to a private room so far from the party? From everyone." *From me.*

He came around the couch, his angry strides eating the space between them. He gripped her waist, fingers digging in, not hurting just getting her attention. "Why don't you trust me? Have I ever given you a reason not to?"

She stared back at him, refusing to answer because shame wrapped around her throat. What he said was true. She was being unfair.

Defensiveness gripped her. "Then why'd you sneak off?"

His mouth flattened into a thin line, pushing in his full lips. He let go. "I didn't sneak off. It was loud. I was tired of shout-talking."

Humiliation pricked her flesh, began a slow burn in her gut.

Oh, God. Did I read the whole situation wrong?

Her mouth opened as she searched for justification. One that didn't sound like shit smeared over excuses. She had none and closed her mouth, watching him.

His gaze ran over her. Her black dress was lowcut, and her angry, choppy breaths put on quite a display. He was definitely noticing, but made no move to come closer.

His jaw clenched, and his stance oozed fury and desire.

Her emotions licked against his, mingled and formed into lust.

She grasped his face, brought it to hers. Her lips against his weren't gentle.

Neither was his reaction.

He was rough, angry, and oh-so-hot.

He ravished her mouth, walking her backward, not stopping until her ass bumped against something. The vanity table. The mirror crashed dangerously against the wall but didn't shatter.

What did was their restraint.

Tanner spun her around. Their reflections met in the mirror. Lust, anger, and hurt battled behind his lovely hazel eyes.

Maggie didn't know what she wanted more, his body or his

forgiveness.

He waited, as if wanting her permission to continue.

She nodded.

His hand skated along her back, unzipping the closure running from the top to the bottom of her dress. He bent when the zipper ran past her ass to her calve.

On the way back up he ran a palm up her inner thigh, stopping to grip her ass briefly before moving to her shoulders. Once standing upright, he pushed the material from her shoulders, letting it fall to the ground.

Cool air caressed her naked flesh. The dress had a built-in bra and was tight enough she'd again, skipped panties. She stood naked before him, in only her red heels.

He caressed her ass, then stopped. Letting his hand rest there, looking into her eyes. He cocked a brow, his fingers twitching as if he wanted to slap her ass.

She wiggled her bottom. Daring him to do it.

His eyes narrowed. A ghost smile danced on his lips. Then he did it. *Hard.*

The *whack* echoed against the walls. Followed by her needy moan.

"Jesus, Maggie," he growled, his palm rubbing the overheated flesh he smacked seconds ago. She wanted more. The hunger stamped on his face mirrored hers. "What am I going to do with you?"

"Right now, you're going to fuck me."

He shifted back, and she whimpered from his absence. She started to turn, about to demand more, but he stopped her with a big hand on her back.

She watched his reflection in the mirror. He yanked open his jeans, pushing them past his thighs. Gripping her waist, he thrust into her. The sudden fill of him was a shock and what she desperately needed.

"Yes," she moaned. Her head dipped past her shoulders, and she gripped the edge of the counter widening her stance, slamming back into him, her orgasm already on the razor edge.

His palm crashed against the mirror. Her head whipped up, snagging his gaze. It brimmed with lust, with anger still sparking at the edges. "Should I put on a condom? Since you're convinced I'm screwing around."

Guilt flooded her, washing away most of her lust.

"No," she whispered. "Step back."

He did, and the loss of their connection caused tears to prickle along her bottom lashes. She faced him, and craving his warmth, slid her arms around his waist.

In heels, she was able to rest her chin on his shoulder. "I'm sorry," she whispered into his ear. "You're right. I shouldn't have thrown my hang-ups at you."

He sighed. It sounded heavy, regretful. "No, I'm sorry. I shouldn't have started this when I was pissed. I don't know what the hell got into me."

Maggie laughed against his warm neck. "Angry sex with you is great." She rubbed against his erection.

He sucked in a breath, scooting her onto the vanity table. She removed his shirt then wrapped her arms around his neck and her legs around his waist, bringing him closer and back into her.

They were joined but didn't move. She searched his face for forgiveness. Thought she might have found it. She brought his head to hers, their foreheads resting together. "I'm sorry. I overreacted."

He opened his mouth to say something. She quieted him with a gentle kiss. "Let me finish. Half is Jayce. He's filled my head with shit about you since the tour began." Tanner scowled at the mention of their bassist. "The bigger factor is my feeling for you. I've never cared for someone like I do you. Tanner, I might be falling in love with you. Scares the hell out of me and apparently turns me into a jealous harpy," she finished lamely.

God, saying the words made her heart skip a beat and tumble to her stomach.

Tanner's eyes widened, then he broke into an angelic smile. "I fell for you months ago, Maggie May." He swiped his lips back and forth across hers. "I haven't told you because I was afraid it'd freak you out."

Warmth and happiness spread through her, even as reality refused to be ignored. "What will we do when Scarlett comes back?" Maggie asked.

He kissed her neck. "Let's not think about the future, right now," he whispered between nips and licks.

He grasped her hips, began to move in her. When he did that, disregarding everything but his touch was easy. She buried her fingers in his hair, following his intoxicating rhythm.

Words and worries fell away, pleasure and release taking its place.

Chapter Nineteen

"Are you busy?" Lincoln asked.

Maggie set aside her book and dropped her feet that she'd stretched across to the diner's bench seat. He slid in, stooped and exhausted.

"What are you doing up?" Her phone was resting on the table, and she checked the time. "It's barely after nine. Why aren't you sleeping?"

He practically whimpered, letting his head fall back against the booth. "Fucking Jayce. He came stumbling in about an hour ago. I couldn't fall back asleep. I texted you, and when you didn't answer, I tried Tanner. He told me you were here."

"Sorry. My ringer must be off. Yeah, he's doing his tutoring stuff. Every time I interrupted he'd sigh, sounding pissy. I decided to give him some space. I came here for coffee and to read." She held up her book.

"Nice cover."

Maggie flipped it around, taking in the nearly naked man plastered under the title. She smirked. "Yes, yes, it is."

She marked her page and nodded when the waiter stopped at their table asking if Maggie wanted a refill. He then asked Lincoln if he wanted anything. He pointed to the carafe like words were too much without coffee.

After the waiter filled their coffees and asked for their orders, Lincoln swallowed a healthy slurp from his steaming mug. It seemed to be what he needed because he sighed in contentment, then spoke in complete sentences. He started with asking, "Has Tanner been stressed? The traveling and late nights have to be rough."

"Um. We're all living that life right now."

"He's also tutoring and studying like a madman. I'm sure failing the CPA test was a bummer."

Maggie got it. Tanner took it right before leaving for the tour and failed. He was stressed and disappointed. However, right now, she was in a selfish mood and could only manage a half-hearted shrug. "We're visiting all these fun cities, and he spends half the time holed-up in whatever hotel we're at, studying or taking video chats for tutoring students."

"It's not like he didn't warn you. Plus, I'm sure when he joined us, he didn't plan on touring."

Her drummer's sound reasoning was ruining Maggie's pity-party. "Lincoln."

"What?"

"Take your logic and shove it."

He chuckled, sipping his coffee. "Tanner hasn't asked you to sit around while he does school stuff. You and I have gone out plenty. Seen some cool places. Am I such bad company?"

Damn Lincoln, and his reasonableness.

Maggie patted his hand. "No. Not at all. I just want to pout. Listen, if you can't sleep in your room, head over to mine. Believe me, listening to Tanner's online sessions with his students will put you right to sleep."

"Thanks for the offer. I'll pass. For now." After another loud slurp he set his mug aside. His smile dimmed. "We need to talk."

"About?"

"Jayce."

She'd figured, but had held on to a small hope it'd be something else, something more pleasant. Like, say, a root canal. "What about him?"

"Are you shifting from pity to denial, Maggie? Don't act like you don't see it. Things are getting out of control with him. Jayce is partying every night, coming back high as a kite and usually bringing back sketchy people. I'm worried about him and the band." Lincoln ran a hand through his chin-length hair, knotting it around a fist. "I've tried talking with him. He either gets pissed or calls me Dad."

The waiter returned with their breakfast. Maggie leaned back, rubbing her belly. Worry made the three cups of coffee sloshing around in her churn uncomfortably.

"What do you want me to do? Even before Tanner, Jayce barely listened to me. Now," she leaned back, crossing her arms over her chest, "he can barely tolerate my presence."

"Yeah, you too hooking up sure didn't help," Lincoln said distractedly, inspecting the heaping plate of eggs and toast the waiter was setting before him.

Gee, thanks for the added helping of guilt to go with my coffee.

Her aggravation must've shown because Lincoln raised his palms in surrender. "I'm not blaming you. I'm happy for you. Tanner's a good guy. The opposites attract thing is cute."

"Cute?"

He broke into a wide grin, and it seemed to chase away his worry. “Yup. It’s like watching Tom and Jerry cuddle.”

Maggie snorted, throwing a creamer packet at him. “Which one is Tom and which is Jerry?”

Catching the packet, Lincoln laughed. Opening creamer, he dumped it into his coffee. “I haven’t figured that part out yet.” He paused, the humor seeping from him.

Crap. Back to Jayce.

“It’s time, Maggie. We need to talk to him. If he doesn’t slow down, we have to consider replacing him. We could start looking when we get back to Michigan.”

Her heart fluttered in low-grade panic. What if they couldn’t find a decent replacement? Sure, the more he partied, the worse he performed, and his asshole side was showing. However, he wasn’t some stranger to be tossed aside at the first signs of trouble.

She voiced these concerns. “Seems a bit extreme. We got lucky with Tanner. What makes you think we’ll find a replacement as good, or better, than Jayce?”

“Come on, Maggie, he’s no Geddy Lee. And I’m not being extreme. I’ve been rooming with the dude. I know you don’t want anything to disrupt ThreePence’s flow, but let me tell you, keeping Jayce might make things harder for us. He’s getting pretty bad.” Lincoln drummed his fingers on the table for a beat, then said, “Hell, if worse comes to worst, we could have Tanner switch. Have him play bass guitar once Scarlett comes back.”

Thrown by Lincoln’s comment, she didn’t bring up the fact that once Scarlett returned, Tanner’s time with the band would be over. He’d probably be high-tailing back to his normal life. Instead, she asked, “He can play bass?”

Lincoln scoffed. “You’re sleeping with the guy, but have no idea he can play multiple instruments?”

“Yes. I knew he could play more than a guitar. His learned the piano first.” Maggie huffed.

“He can also play the trumpet and the drums. Not at the level where I have to worry, but impressive, nonetheless.”

Huh. He’s a man filled with surprises.

Maggie waved aside the interesting and new information about Tanner being a multi-instrumentalist. “It doesn’t matter. Tanner isn’t an option. He doesn’t want to stay on any longer than necessary. I’m sure the minute Scarlett’s back, Tanner will be gone, like his ass is on fire. He’s not going to hang around because of Jayce’s shit. He’s our problem. Not Tanner’s.”

"You sure, Mags? He's rather enamored with you."

"Not enough to give up his *Pleasant Valley Sunday* dream life in suburbia."

Tanner might love her. However, he'd never said he wanted to stay with ThreePence. Was it the life of a musician he hated or was it because he didn't want to take Scarlett's job? Did she even want it back? Right now, it didn't seem like it. Although, that could change when motherhood wasn't so new.

Maggie rubbed her temples; a headache was starting behind her eyes. Too many uncertainties. She shoved them aside to focus on the current topic. "Why are you coming to me about Jayce now?"

She held up a hand when Lincoln started to repeat his earlier spiel. "I get you're not happy with Jayce. Why not wait until we're with everyone else? Scarlett, Zia, and Tanner."

"Because Zia's not here. You formed this band, and I've been with you almost since the beginning. We, including Jayce, are the core of the band. Not Scarlett or Tanner. Right now, both are temporary. You and I aren't. It's a decision we need to make. After, we'll talk to Zia."

Maggie's shoulders dropped. Lincoln was right. Talk about an unhappy realization.

The waiter stopped at their table, refilling their mugs and leaving the bill. Maggie lifted her cup to her lips, taking a large sip, loving the strong and slightly bitter taste. "Okay, fine I'll think about it. Let's try talking to him, see how the rest of the tour goes."

"Fine." Lincoln shrugged, pointing at her. "But I swear, if he keeps partying this much and bringing strange people back, I'll be on your couch, putting a damper on your love nest."

Maggie gave her sauciest smile. "Go ahead. We'll keep the lights off, get it on under the covers. For you, we'll try to keep it quiet. Though Tanner's a screamer."

Lincoln's pained expression made her laugh a little too loud, catching the attention of a few people at nearby tables. She bit her lip, trying to keep it together.

"Ahh, Mags, why?" Lincoln shuddered dramatically. "Forget it. Maybe I'll find someone to take me in. A woman at every port and all that. I'll be one of those guys."

"I'm thinking your plan might upset Jeanne. Your girlfriend might have something to say with this sailor like behavior."

"We broke up."

Maggie's smile slipped. Jeanne was a sweet woman—fun, kind and seemed to adore Lincoln. "I'm sorry. Why didn't you tell me?"

He waved off the sympathy. "It's fine. She wasn't the love of my life or anything. She didn't like my busy schedule back when we were mostly playing in Michigan. We figured it'd only get worse. Why avoid the inevitable."

"Still. Why didn't you tell me?"

"Like I said. It's not a big deal. Or a surprise."

An awkward pause fell between them. They were close friends. Maggie could read Lincoln easily. He wasn't thinking about his ex; he was wondering if Maggie understood this and what she'd do when Tanner left. How she'd handle it.

She didn't have a clue and didn't want to dwell on it.

Clearing her throat, she stood, grabbing the bill. "Tanner should be done tutoring. I'm going to convince him to do some sightseeing. Want to come?"

Lincoln snatched the receipt from her. "Let me pay. If you don't mind, yes, I'd liked to come with you guys."

"I don't mind. Neither will Tanner. In fact, you can help me convince him to skip the Museum of Art. I want to go to the Eastern State Penitentiary."

"Umm. I've wanted to visit the Liberty Bell. Isn't it by the museum…?"

"Figures," Maggie huffed. "Fine. Don't take my side."

He nudged her shoulder, chuckling. "Am I still invited?"

"Yes." She narrowed her eyes, trying to keep her smile tucked away. "I guess."

"Cool." He wrapped an arm around her shoulder as they left the restaurant. At the exit, he said, "You will think about it? Later? What we should do with Jayce?"

Wow. This is unlike Lincoln, not letting it go. Jayce must be an awful roommate. Or his partying is worse than even I realized.

The unpleasant realization made her heart hurt. Jayce was burning through his talent and right when success for his music might be within his grasp. For some reason, that made it worse.

Maggie sighed, deep and heavy. It matched her worries. "Yes, I will. Just not today, okay? Let's finish this show. We'll talk to him in New Jersey. If he doesn't want to rein it in a bit, we'll start looking when we get home."

Chapter Twenty

Tanner stepped through the wide entrance of the hotel's restaurant, scanning the area for Maggie's purple streaked hair. Finishing early with his tutoring, he hoped to have dinner with her and Lincoln.

The dining room was dim, three shades away from darkness. Moving farther inside Tanner saw wrought iron tables strewn with dark purple runners, red lights hanging low at each table. Reminded him of pictures he'd seen of the Moulin Rouge. Not the easiest decor to find people in, even those as distinctive as ThreePence.

Somewhere to his left, Jayce's angry voice cut through the murmured conversations. "You kidding me?"

Diners turned in the direction of his anger, and Tanner spotted them. Each wore a pissed off, defensive stance. They sat at a table next to the floor to ceiling windows that ran along some street he couldn't name somewhere in New Jersey.

Tanner debated leaving, going back, and ordering room service. Except Maggie had spotted him, and she was waving him over.

Damnit.

Cursing inwardly, he walked toward them, discovering the only empty seat was the one right next to Jayce. Fantastic.

"Did you finish early?" Maggie asked, her smile a little worn at the edges.

Before he could answer, Jayce broke in with his usual spite, his furious gaze landing on Tanner. "I bet this lecture was your idea. You're just too much of a pussy to be here for its delivery."

Anger mixed with his confusion and exhaustion, made him speak louder than intended. "What the hell are you talking about?"

"Tanner, take it down a notch," Maggie pleaded.

People at the closest tables were staring with open curiosity. He visibly calmed himself before sitting. In a quieter voice, he asked, "What's going on?"

To his surprise, Jayce answered, "I've been told I need to cool my partying. Lay off the sins. Women, drugs, and booze." He was peeling the label off his beer and stopped to sneer at Tanner. "They want me to be boring. Like you."

Tanner leaned forward, setting his hand on top of Maggie's. He stared back at the other man. The flare in Jayce's eyes let Tanner know he'd made his point.

Childish, yes, but damn satisfying.

Maggie gave Tanner a warning look before facing Jayce. "This has nothing to do with Tanner. This was something Lincoln and I discussed. We're worried."

"Whatever." Jayce slouched, flicking a crumb from the table. "I'm having a little fun. Nothing for you to worry about. Have I missed any shows or practice?"

"Dude, I've been sharing a room with you for weeks now. Almost every night you've been drunk or high." Lincoln leaned forward, elbows on the table. "What the hell are you using? I know it's more than weed."

"I got it under control." Jayce crossed his arms over his chest.

Tanner was again reminded of his friend, Will. Back in the days when drugs and denial had him by the throat.

"I am worried," Lincoln continued. "Yes, you're showing up. But you're usually late and not playing your best. You're dragging us down."

Jayce bared his teeth, looking feral. "What exactly are you saying?"

"You can't keep going on like this," Maggie said. "You need to stop. Or, hell, at least slow the hell down. We don't want to replace you, but your performance *is* slipping. We can't have you playing half-assed when we're starting to get some real attention. Don't force our hand."

Jayce's chin dropped, his gaze shifting to Lincoln as if asking if he agreed. He nodded.

Tanner felt for Jayce. He didn't like the guy, but what else did he have besides the band? ThreePence seemed to be his whole identity.

Although Tanner had to agree with Lincoln and Maggie, Jayce was on a head-on collision with destruction. Hopefully, this would be his wake-up call.

Jayce's glare bored into Tanner. His sympathy vanished. The blame would fall on him.

"Now you have the accountant. You don't need me," Jayce spat.

Yup. There's the blame.

"Don't be an ass." Maggie sighed. "He doesn't even play the bass. Nor is he permanent."

He could, in fact, play the bass. Not that it mattered. She was right; he wasn't permanent.

Why did this fact bother him more each day?

She slid from Tanner's grasp, gripping Jayce's forearm. "Can't you cut out the drugs, cool it some with the drinking?"

Jayce covered it with his hand. "Is that what's bothering you? Or is it because I'm having fun without you?" He leaned forward, tracing his thumb along her wrist. The gesture seems almost tender, but his tone was poison. "You're welcome to drop the stiff. Come back to me."

Tanner managed to stay seated, though he wanted to break each of Jayce's fingers. Slowly. However, this was Maggie's fight for her band. She didn't need him to muddy it with his possessiveness.

She straightened. When she spoke, there was steel in her voice. "Listen, Jayce, as a friend, I'm worried about you. As a band member, I'm telling you I won't let you ruin us. Get your shit together."

"I show up. I play. What the fuck do you want from me?" His anger cut to Tanner. "Half the time he's late for one or both. Though, I guess when you're fucking the founder of the band, then it's okay."

Enough of this shit.

"When I'm late it's due to classes or my other job. Not because I'm trying to consume every drug within reach. Or sticking my dick in any nameless woman. Plus, when I show, I don't fuck up my chords."

Jayce sprung to his feet. His eyes were as wild as the tattoos covering his arms. He leaned in, inches from Tanner's face. "Fuck you, you smarmy prick." Jayce's stale breath reeked of sage and vinegar.

The scent propelled Tanner into the past. To the time he and Jacob, once again went searching for his brother, Will. They'd found him that time at another decaying drug house. Jayce smelled like that house.

Tanner stood. "I'm done. I'm not listening to your shit."

Jayce shoved Tanner. "You're done when I say so."

Months of pent-up aggravation and biting his tongue at the other man's rude comments made Tanner's hands curl into fists.

Lincoln and Maggie were around the table, between them in seconds.

"Enough," she whispered, placing a palm on their chests, pushing them apart. "Not only do I *not* want to get kicked out of our hotel, I don't need you two to fuck up your hands. If I lose half my band because you two get into a pissing match, you won't have to worry who wins the fight because I will personally kill you both."

Tanner looked down at her grip on his shirt, then around in the restaurant. People were staring open-mouthed, some even snapping pictures with their phones.

"This isn't the kind of publicity we need," she hissed.

"Yes, we can't forget the band comes before everything," Jayce sneered. "Remember that, Accountant," he threw out before stomping from the restaurant.

"Well, that could have gone better," Lincoln muttered, sitting back down.

"Yes, it could have," Maggie spat. "I'm going to my room."

"Don't you want to eat first?" he asked.

"No. I've lost my appetite."

Guilt tugged at Tanner's gut. He'd made a difficult conversation a hundred times worse. "I'll go with you."

"No. Stay. Eat something. Keep Lincoln company. I don't want any." Without a backward glance, Maggie left.

Tanner fell back into his chair, guilt shifting to annoyance. He wasn't sure if it was aimed at her, or himself.

He caught the waiter's attention. When he stopped at their table Tanner, ordered a Black Russian.

"You having a liquid dinner?" Lincoln asked, after ordering a steak and a beer.

Tanner waved away the sardonic question, asking his own, "Why's she pissed at me?"

"I think it's more she's worried. Jayce is screwing up big time. We've been together for years. Worked our asses off. It kills us to see the way he's pissing away his talent and hard work." The waiter dropped off their drinks, and Lincoln continued, "Plus, I'm sure she's worried about the aftermath this fight will cause. Jayce owns the house we live in. We borrowed a hefty sum of money from his parents to buy better instruments, along with the down payment for the house. Thank Christ we recently paid off the instruments. Next is the house. We need to get it out of his family's name."

Tanner was silent, sipping his drink, taking in Lincoln's words, shocked at how much leverage Jayce held over Maggie and the band. Tanner couldn't decide if Maggie was ridiculous for putting everything, everyone behind the music, or if she was justified. If someone had a dream, a passion, shouldn't they give their all to make it come true?

At the same time, it made him wonder if there was some truth in Jayce's spite. Was Tanner nothing more than a convenience to Maggie? Someone to toss aside when Scarlett is ready to come back?

He slammed back his drink. His gut churned with alcohol and doubts.

He motioned the waiter to bring another one, hoping the former would block the latter.

Lincoln grimaced. “You might want to take it easy. It probably won’t help matters. You returning to Maggie shit-faced.”

“Yeah, yeah. We must worry about Maggie. And she must worry about the band. Above all else, everyone else.” Tanner stared at the droplets of amber liquid in his glass.

They sat in silence for so long he wondered if Lincoln had left. He hadn’t and was studying Tanner with a worried frown.

I need to get my shit together.

Running a hand through his hair and down his neck, Tanner sighed. “Sorry. I’m an asshole. You’re right. I’ll eat. Let’s talk about something else.” He searched his slightly foggy mind for a new topic. “Which cities have you liked visiting the most during the tour?”

“Let me say one thing. Then I’ll drop it, okay?”

Tanner exhaled. “Do I have a choice?”

Lincoln smiled around his beer. “No.”

“Go ahead.”

“The band has always been Maggie’s first priority, but it doesn’t mean she doesn’t care about you. I’ve never seen her this happy with anyone. Hell, when you enter the room, she gets the same smile my nephew has when he spots his favorite teddy bear.”

“And like your nephew, as time goes by he’ll tire of it, tossing it aside,” Tanner grumbled.

“I’m no fortune-teller. I have no idea if you two will last. All I know is, if a woman looked at me like Maggie does with you, I’d be one happy man. No matter if it lasted a week or until the day I die.” Lincoln swallowed the last of his beer. “No doubt, you two make an odd couple, yet somehow it works.”

The drummer’s words stay between them. Tanner mulled them over, and when the waiter stopped at their table, he ordered two club sandwiches to go, refusing the suggestion of another drink. A warm drunk was already enveloping him.

“You’re right,” he said. “I’m overthinking. I should let things ride out. I’ve never been good at that. Plus, my life doing a one-eighty hasn’t helped. Last year around this time, I was dating a quiet bookworm from the accounting office I was interning at. My biggest stress was getting a letter of recommendation from my boss. Now I have Maggie, a force all her own, while also traveling with a band and trying not to lose my tutoring students. Oh, to top it off, I’m studying for the CPA exam I’ve already failed once.” He rolled his empty glass between his palms. “The way I bombed it shows I’m not managing very well.”

"Are you having fun?"

"Yeah. Most of the time. When I'm with Maggie, or on stage, it's sublime." Tanner played with his fork before dropping it. "Not so much when Jayce is busting my balls, or I'm stressing because I missed another window for the CPA test or lost another tutoring job."

"Have you considered putting the accounting stuff on hold? There are lots of undecided stuff. Scarlett might not come back. Jayce might implode. With you writing the songs, I know you could take on the bass. We'd make an excellent rhythm section."

He hated letting down others, and ThreePence would be screwed if Jayce went AWOL. Tanner was in the position to help, but what about his tutoring students? They needed him too. Also, was he supposed to toss aside his wants and needs? He'd worked his ass off for so many years. There was no way he was giving up at the final stretch.

Shit. Too many people depending on him. Everyone's expectations and needs were too much. It made him want to order another drink. "Those are a shit-ton of maybes, Lincoln."

"For most artists, the day job is the backup plan. In case their dream careers don't pan out. You, on the other hand, get one in spite of a promising future as a musician." Lincoln chuckled, then turned serious. "You know, you'll always have a place in ThreePence. No matter what happens with Jayce or Scarlett."

Tanner wasn't sure how to answer.

All his life he wanted stability. A house, a steady job, a comfortable life. Everything his father couldn't bother to stay around to offer.

Also, Tanner wanted kids, and he didn't want them to have his childhood. An absentee father, always traveling with his band until maybe one day he won't bother to come home.

The waiter dropped off his to-go containers, allowing Tanner to bury those unanswerable questions. "I better get this food to Maggie. She hasn't eaten since breakfast."

Lincoln pushed back his empty plate, then gave the waiter cash to cover his bill. "I'll ride up with you."

"Good. After downing two Black Russians that were mostly vodka, I'm afraid to stand," Tanner confessed.

Lincoln's lips twitched. "This I have to see. You, drunk and stumbling."

"I'm not drunk."

"Famous last words…"

Chapter Twenty-One

Once up and moving, Tanner found he wasn't as sloshed as he feared, merely warm and tipsy. Feeling damn good. The alcohol made Jayce's anger and Maggie's anxiety distant and indistinct.

Lincoln parted ways with Tanner in the hallway of their floor. After using his keycard, he pushed the door handle, calling to Maggie.

He was met with silence.

A dim headboard lamp shined above the bed, illuminating the tan blankets, pulled back and unoccupied. He glanced toward the bathroom. The door stood open and dark.

He caught movement from the small balcony. Maggie was bent, leaning on the glass balustrade. A breeze wafted around her lose, knee-length wool skirt. He hoped the tall leather boots were enough to keep her warm.

Tanner set the food containers on a small faux wood desk, sliding open the heavy glass door. A chilly, pleasant breeze stroked his face.

The balcony was small, with high walls separating them from their neighbors. He angled around a set of armless wicker chairs, watching Maggie.

Her body was silhouetted against the lights from the hotel's closed and deserted pool. Farther off, the city lights of Newark twinkled.

Tanner stood behind Maggie, she leaned back, and he wrapped his arms around her waist, burying his face in her hair.

"Aren't you cold?" He breathed in her jasmine scent, loving how it mixed with the chilly, spring nights.

"Between these leather boots, skirt, and sweater I was melting at the restaurant. This is heaven."

"I'm sure butting heads with Jayce didn't help. Sorry I made it worse."

She rested her head against his shoulder. "You didn't. I should apologize. Jayce was out of line. I should've shut him down. I was too upset to think straight. ThreePence is finally making a name, at the same time we're falling apart. First Scarlett. Now Jayce."

"Everything will be fine." Empty words, but he needed to say something. Her despair was his own.

"I've seen enough failures, teetered on a few to know that isn't true."

It didn't surprise him Maggie didn't accept his empty platitudes. Still, he persisted. "It will. You want this too badly to ever settle for failure."

She laughed quietly. "How much alcohol did you drink? By chance, was it spiked with a happy drug?"

He chuckled. "No. I'm just not willing to count disasters before they've happened. Sure, Scarlett left, but it's temporary. Plus, you have me."

"For now."

"Yes, for now. I'll stay until she comes back."

He'd already stayed on three months longer than planned. He shouldn't make further promises, however the desolation in Maggie's voice was a knife to his gut.

If he was honest, the prospect of leaving bothered him. A lot.

What he couldn't figure was the reason behind it. Was it because he liked playing in the band or was it he feared losing Maggie? If he stayed, would he grow to resent her?

"Anyway," he continued. "I'm not going to leave. Neither will Jayce. He doesn't strike me as a man with a backup plan."

Maggie sighed. "Maybe you're right."

"I am," He kissed her exposed neck.

She shuddered against him.

"Cold? We can go inside. I brought food."

"No. Not yet. Continue what you were doing."

"Bossy woman," he murmured, smiling, following her command. He skimmed his fingertip over her soft sweater, finding and caressing her breasts.

She moaned, her warm exhale puffed on the cool night air. He gripped her chin, capturing her lips.

His blood rushed south so fast Tanner was surprised he didn't pass out.

"Maggie," he growled, finding the hem of her skirt, lifting it. He slipped one hand under, skimming it up her thigh and choked when met by nothing but bare skin. No panties. "You are trying to kill me, aren't you?"

"You'd think by now it wouldn't be such a surprise." She laughed huskily.

He caressed her hip before moving between her legs. She rocked to his rhythmic touch.

"More," she demanded into the night air.

In complete agreement and silently thankful for the empty courtyard, he fumbled with the fly of his jeans. Pushing them down, he freed himself, joining her, fully and deeply.

He grunted her name, his fingers digging into her waist, his control dissolving. He wanted to slam into her until they both saw stars.

Maggie widened her stance, gripping the railing before tossing a saucy smile over her shoulder. "If I'm able to walk after this, we'll stroll the cherry blossoms all day tomorrow."

"Woman. You are trouble." *And I love it.*

He let his control off its leash. She embraced it, matching him thrust for thrust. Her urgent pleas and the erotic echoes were the only sound on the late-night air. It nearly sent him plummeting over the razor edge of pleasure.

Wanting her to go first, he slid a hand between her legs, seeking her sweet spot. Finding it, her breaths became erratic, her movements stiff.

She was there. Begging for release, when the lights from the balcony next to them switched on.

They froze as voices floated from the next room, both male and female. Lots of them.

Shit.

"Come here," Tanner whispered in her ear.

They separated, and Maggie faced him. He shuffled backward with her pressed against his front. The backs of his legs hit the wicker chair, and he fell into it, taking her with him. The metal back crashed into the thick glass, not breaking it but the reverberating bang was loud.

The gathering next to them went silent.

Maggie's eyes widened, losing none of their heat. When the group began talking again, she readjusted herself, straddling the chair, then lowering herself in a measured, unhurried pace, sheathing him. He'd never been so happy for armless chairs and balcony walls.

She took control.

Maggie gripped his neck, crushing her mouth against his, devouring him with her needy kisses and demanding tongue. Her reckless desires tempted him to follow. She tightened around him, racing toward her release. It fueled his own.

Her legs trembled as her gasps became pleas for release. Tanner tried muffling them by kissing her deeper.

A subtle shift brought him impossibly deeper, taking him from almost-there, to there. Worrying about how much noise they were making fell away as she pulsated around him and his climax wracked through his body.

After the thudding in his ears and body quieted, he heard clapping and whistling.

"What the hell…"

Maggie leaned her forehead against his, a wicked smile tugged at her kiss-plumped lips. "Our neighbors," she whispered.

"Shit. You were quite noisy," he teased.

She leaned back, quirking a brow. "Me? Did you hear yourself?"

Tanner's cheeks and neck warmed. "What? Did I shout your name or something?"

"No. Not this time." Her smile widened. "Just a few sexy grunts. A rather loud, satisfied groan."

He let his head fall back. "Come on," he said over their neighbors' catcalls. "Let's go inside."

Chapter Twenty-Two

Maggie dragged her feet down the carpeted hallway of yet another hotel. This one was outside of New York, though it could've been in Cleveland, Detroit, or Mars. They all looked the same.

Her mood hung as heavy as the messenger bag digging into her shoulder. She hoped fresh air and time alone would shake her morose mood.

Hadn't worked.

She'd left Tanner to his computer in the early afternoon. He, once again, needed to catch up and answer emails from students. So, she packed her bag, heading to a quaint park within walking distance from the hotel, doing the things that usually helped to find her center. She messed around with the lyrics from some new songs, read a couple chapters from a favorite romance author, and snapped a few pictures with her D3400 Nikon.

She discovered her center was off kilter. It was on a drunken bender, couldn't even stand, let alone find the bull's eye.

Nothing was working, so she returned to her hotel, still trying to shake her mood. The reasons were clear. The solution was not.

The tour was going spectacularly well. They were at their final stop. Opening for J.Hoffa was fantastic. They were good people, and their star power helped ThreePence immensely. A couple record companies had contacted them, and most venues asked them back. As the main show!

Plus, they were in freaking New York City. The Big Apple. A city brimming with fun, sin, and sights.

Yet, it didn't chase away the misery plaguing her, biting at the heels of her happiness.

It was a house of cards.

Tanner didn't want to stay. And while Scarlett was a fantastic guitarist, the crowds loved the duets. They loved Tanner. Also, many popular new songs were written with him. Could she go back to composing them alone?

Then there was the growing problem with Jayce. The talk hadn't done a bit of good. Instead of slowing his partying, he'd taken it to a whole new level. It hurt watching him destroy his body and career.

He was arriving late for performances, making stupid mistakes. Luckily, the slipups were small, easy to hide. Nonetheless, it ate at her. And damn it, she didn't come this far for others to fuck up her dream.

She finally broke down, and talked to Zia. Asked her to put out feelers for a new bassist. She didn't seem very surprised. Drug abuse ran rampant in this profession, and Jayce was teetering on the cliff, falling from abuser to full-blown addict.

Zia quieted Maggie's fears, telling her the record label wouldn't care if Jayce left, if he was replaced before they started recording. Still, it probably didn't look good to have ThreePence going through band members like toilet paper.

The elevator dinged, opening. After stepping inside, she pressed the button to her floor. The door shut, and she put on her happy face.

She didn't want to nag Tanner with her worries. He'd made his position clear when he signed on; he was temporary.

Pushing her problems onto him was unfair, even if her less magnanimous side wanted to use his love to guilt him into staying.

The elevator stopped. She made her way to their door, digging in her bag for the key card. After searching every damn pocket, she gave up and knocked. Seconds later, Tanner swung open the door, cellphone to ear, a huge grin illuminating his handsome face.

She couldn't help smiling back. His happiness brightened everything around him, like a sunny afternoon. Maggie soaked in his rays, letting it melt some of her gloom.

"Yeah, it's Maggie...okay, we'll talk soon. Again, congrats," Tanner told whoever was on the phone. He hung up, tossing his cell onto the closest counter, before hugging her. "I missed you."

His open affection was a balm, and she let it soothe her, kissing his cheek. "Same. Who were you congratulating?"

"Jacob."

"Oh yeah. What's new with him?"

"He and Greta are getting married. They set the day for June of next year." Tanner picked her up, nuzzling her neck.

"Wow," Maggie giggled. "You sure are happy for your friend."

"Oh, I am, although that's not why I'm ready to celebrate with you and your lovely body."

"Are you going to tell me, or are we going to skip straight to the merry-making part?" She wrapped a leg around him. "Works for me."

He moved to the bed. "Me too."

Curiosity mixed with the first tingles of desire, she met his eyes. “What made you so happy?”

Tanner sat on the comforter, keeping her on his lap. “Right before Jacob called, an accounting firm I interviewed with a few weeks ago contacted me. They want me to come in for an interview when I get back. And I signed up for the next scheduled CPA test. I’m confident I’ll pass it this time.”

And the gloom is back. Tenfold.

“To hire you? Um, we need you.”

I need you.

She was sure desperation oozed from her, but she couldn’t hide it.

“Don’t worry. Even if they wanted to hire me, they have to see if I pass the exam. The test isn’t until the end of next month. By then I’m sure Scarlett will be ready to come back. Noella will be six months old.”

An invisible fist squeezed her heart, but she plastered back on the plastic smile. “Fantastic. Great.”

He chuckled. “Uh, huh. Then why you’re shaking your head from side to side?”

Oops. She stopped. “Sorry. I’m happy for you, just worried about ThreePence. So many changes have me freaking out.”

Tanner pulled her in closer, she tucked into him, resting her head on his shoulder. “Nothing’s going to happen,” he said into her hair. “Nothing will change. We’ve survived the pressure-cooker of traveling and living with each other these last months. We haven’t even tried to kill each other. We can handle these challenges as well.”

She wasn’t sure his reasoning worked. Having him around all the time didn’t worry her. She loved having him near. No, what troubled her was when their conflicting schedules and her constant traveling made it difficult to see each other. It wouldn’t matter if she loved him, once he became a CPA, they’d grow apart.

The fist around her heart squeezed tighter, making it hard to breathe.

Her silence must’ve bothered him because he shifted back, taking her face between his palms. “Well, I still love you.”

She smiled. “I love you, too.”

He kissed her deeply, running his palms from her face to her neck. One gripped her neck, the other slid into her hair.

Maggie drew back, kissing him softly on the lips. “I love you,” she repeated, tracing a thumb across his full bottom lip. Looking at him, she lied, “I know you want to get back to your normal life. I’m sure we’ll figure it out. We’ll be okay.”

"I do want my old life back. I also don't want this new one to end," he admitted.

Hope flooded her. Maybe he'd stay. Even if Scarlett wanted to come back, which Maggie sincerely doubted, Tanner could take on a more significant role singing and songwriting. They could add a second guitar to the mix. Something, anything so he didn't have to leave. Optimism and happiness zinged around her brain making her a tad dizzy.

"Whoa, slow it down, Mags. I can practically see the plans you're making for me," he said, breaking into her swirling thoughts. "I want it all. You, the music, and my accounting career. Yet they aren't compatible. Late nights and frequent traveling aren't compatible with the nine to five."

Hope is a fickle, cruel bitch.

She shrugged, pretending the choice didn't mean everything to her, or that her happy high was crashing. "Let's see what happens after you take the exam."

Or I'll get really lucky, and he'll fail the exam.

Shitty, selfish hopes.

"Yeah, let's." He began working at the asymmetric buttons of her sweater, fumbling with the different sizes. "What the hell are you wearing? This thing is more difficult to take off than your red bra."

"You mean the one I *had*, as in past tense?" He'd ripped it after growing impatient with its complicated clips.

He grinned. "Yeah, that one."

The man wasn't even sorry.

She slapped at him. "I'll do it. I like this one. I don't want your bear paws to ruin it."

He chuckled, skating a hand inside the growing gap in her sweater, palming her breast through her thin bra.

"Anyway," he continued, "I won't leave you in a lurch. I'll stay on until Scarlett comes back. And I won't leave you. Ever." He pushed off the sweater. Still talking, he kissed a trail on her bare shoulder, making her flesh pebble in anticipation. "Unless you want me to. Sometimes it worries me. I wonder if you're the real reason I don't want to leave ThreePence. Not because I'll miss the music, but you. I don't want to lose you."

"You won't." She cradled his head, fearing if he saw her face, he'd see her doubt.

Deep-down, she doubted they'd survive after he left.

His kisses moved to her neck, then cheeks. She shifted to meet his lips, wanting to lose her chaotic, troubling worries to his masterful touch.

Chapter Twenty-Three

Maggie studied Lady Liberty's tablet, before looking past it, to the people *way* below. They seemed like scurrying ants. She returned to the Roman numerals that read July 4, 1776. She knew this because Tanner had told her.

Over the weeks of the East Coast tour, she'd learned he was a history nut. Her sexy nerd.

Glancing to her left, she studied his profile. At the moment he was pointing through the large vertical slits in the crown, talking to Lincoln and Zia about some massive hurricane that had plowed through New York in 1821.

She didn't pay much attention to his words. Instead, she focused on the warmth of his hand on her lower back, trying to forget they were expected to leave sooner or later. Picturing the tight, winding staircase made her insides quiver.

Tanner cut another side glance at her. He was probably still bemused with her crazy, stupid fear. The odd thing was heights didn't scare her. No, what had panic clawing at her was the tight, confined spaces. To top it off, there were too many damn people. It set her nerves on edge. Tanner tried to distract her with jokes and stories. That had mostly worked. By the time they reached the top, she was frazzled but in one piece.

She leaned into Tanner, tucking herself under his arm. He accepted her, shifting to wrap her in tighter. The man's quiet, gentle ways filled her sharp edges, made her softer.

The sensation was strange, yet Maggie craved it. Craved him, more and more.

Zia laughed, catching Maggie's attention, mouthing, "Okay?"

She nodded, chewing on the corner of her lower lip. Anxiety gnawed at her stomach lining. However, having her best friend here, along with Tanner's comfort, made the eventual trip back down almost bearable.

Zia joined them for their last performances in New York. The tour ended two days ago, and after everyone slept for almost twenty-four hours straight, they decided to explore the city.

They spent most of the morning in Central Park, wandering its many tree-covered paths. Maggie loved the green space, dotted with ponds and old bridges. How she was surrounded in green nature, yet the skyline was crowded with buildings straining for the clouds.

Now, they were spending their afternoon in the steel hell, better known as the inside of the Statue of Liberty. Okay, the view was spectacular, but the hike to the bottom would be vile. If only they'd let her climb out the crown and parachute to the bottom.

"You ready?" Tanner asked, concern etched in the furrows of his forehead.

Maggie blew out a shaky breath, twisting around into his solid chest. "I'm such a wimp."

He kissed her head, speaking into her hair. "We all have our things. Even the invincible Maggie."

"What's yours?"

"I hate bugs," Zia volunteered, shuddering. "No. I loathe bugs. The bigger, the more terrifying."

Maggie snickered. "Ah, yes. I remember the cockroach incident."

Zia rubbed her hands up and down her arms as if brushing away invisible bugs. "It was in my computer bag."

"It was dead."

"Whatever. You know the saying, if there's one, there's a million."

"Birds creep me out," Lincoln offered, his voice drifting from somewhere behind Tanner.

Not letting go of Maggie, he faced her. "Really? Birds? Tiny creatures tweeting pretty noises."

"Dude. Don't judge. Have you seen Hitchcock's movie *The Birds*? Plus, when I was a kid every spring, fucking robins would throw themselves at our kitchen windows." Lincoln scanned the openings in the crown like he expected birds to start flinging themselves at the glass. "Freaky shit."

Tanner nodded. "Yeah, a house I lived in had a sliding glass door next to a big oak tree. Damn robins loved to fly into it. My mom would tape owl decals on it to stop the kamikaze birds. Though, I found it more annoying than terrifying."

"Okay, tough guy, what are you afraid of?" Lincoln narrowed his eyes and smirked. "Besides the open road. Terrifies you so much you start puking all over the place."

Tanner snorted. "That's motion sickness, asshole, not terror. And it only happened once."

"Twice," Maggie and Lincoln said in unison.

Tanner's neck reddened, and she kissed his throat before stepping back.

"Not like I threw up in the van," he muttered. "I made it to the side of the road."

"We thank you for that," she said with complete sincerity. "Now tell us, what's your phobia?"

She recalled his nervousness the first time he'd gone on stage. Stage fright couldn't be his fear. It had only happened once. Did he have one?

He cleared his throat. "Um, crowds."

Crowds?

Confusion clouded her anxiety, making it nearly disappear. "Then how do you go on stage with us? And," she glanced at the crowded, tight space they were in, "you seem fine now."

"They're not pressing on me. Crowding me, bumping me…" A slight shudder ran over him.

"Why didn't the climb here bother you? It's a tight fit."

"True." He swept back a strand of her hair, hooking it behind her ear. "This time, I was too worried about you to let the crowds get to me."

"What about when on you're on stage?" Zia asked the question on Maggie's lips.

"It's fine. I wouldn't say I'm relaxed, but I'm not ready to crawl out of my skin. It's when I'm in the crowds. People pushing on me. I don't like it. My mom and I used to go to my dad's shows when I was a kid. Most of the time everything was fine. But there were times I'd get caught in a crowd with too many rowdy drunks and get knocked around or elbowed. Once my dad took off, I didn't go back to gigs until I was a teen. Then I mostly stayed backstage, only coming out during set up and break down. Or when they needed me to play some instrument on stage for them. During those times, I was kept in the back. They didn't want the bar's owner to notice the underage kid." He shrugged. "Anyway, sometimes that old hopeless panic wells up."

The group fell silent. Probably, like her, digesting his sad story. She adored Carleen, but right then, some of her idolization fell away.

Tanner kissed her cheek. "It didn't happen often. My mom made me sit at the table. Or she'd give me a fist full of quarters to play the pinball machines, keeping me well away from the crowds." He smiled, some even made it to his eyes. "Just don't expect me to stage dive anytime soon."

Lincoln snapped his fingers, breaking apart the heaviness that had settled on them. "Damn, I was going to suggest it for our next show."

Tanner tilted his head. "You have a birthday soon, right? What kinda bird do you want?"

Lincoln flipped off Tanner.

He laughed. "Oh. I see not all birds bother you." He turned to Maggie, and softening his tone, he asked, "Ready to go? If you want to make it to Ground Zero before dinner, we'd better get moving."

Their group shuffled toward the exit. Maggie's legs wanted to lock.

Tanner came around to face her. "How do you want to do this? You want me in the front or behind you?" He broke into a wide grin. "Or should we scoot down on our butts."

Her mouth twitched. "No. Jerk. You go first. Then if I faint, I'll crash into you. You'll cushion my fall."

"I'll catch you, my damsel." He smirked.

"You are having way too much fun at my expense. See if I comfort you next time you're heaving your guts on the side of the road."

He clutched his heart. "Aw, you wound me." He spun her gently, wrapping his arms around her in a comforting cocoon of warmth, scent, and safety. "I'll be right here with you. We'll go slow or fast. Whatever you need."

"Let's try for a normal pace." Unlike her heart, which was racing and pounding in her ears. "Tell me something that'll make me forget the hike to the bottom."

Tanner started down the stairs. "Any suggestions?"

"Hmm. I've always found your body a lovely, sinful distraction. Want to have a kinky New York experience? Sex in a cab or maybe at Central Park?"

Tanner swiveled around, but Lincoln spoke first. His words and laughter echoed from somewhere below the twisty stairs.

"Hey, Mags, we've already visited Central Park. Apparently, you have a different sort of experience in mind. The trip we planned for Times Square tonight, you two are taking your own cab."

"Ah shit," she mumbled. "Was I shouting? Talking loud?"

"Nah." Tanner chuckled. "I'm sure no one past Ellis Island could hear you."

She refused to look around. Instead, she scooted closer to Tanner. "I talk loud when I'm nervous."

"That so?" He turned, sparks of humor danced in his hazel eyes.

"Oh, shut up. New subject." She floundered around for

something, gripping his shoulders tight enough to leave marks. "I want to try calling Jayce again."

Tanner's muscles tensed, yet his tone was mild as he said, "You've tried since he bailed after the final show. You've left, how many messages?"

She shrugged. "What if something happened to him? What if he needs our help?"

He opened his mouth to speak. She suspected he was going to say something along the lines of, "Who cares."

She held up a hand to stop him. "I get he's been a pain-in-the-ass lately—"

"Just lately?"

"Anyway," she continued, "I'd feel better knowing if he's merely being a fuck-face and blowing us off, or if he's in real trouble."

"Fine. Then keep trying." After a pause, Tanner added, "If it makes you feel better, we could try phoning the hospitals in the area. You work one area code, while I do another."

A soft warmth swam beside her anxiety. He was willing to search for a man he disliked. It meant the stars to her. More meaningful than roses and jewelry. A kind heart was worth more than diamonds.

"Thanks, Tanner." Her mind drifted, wondering how many ERs would be in such a massive city.

"You okay?"

"Yeah. Why?"

He eyed her from over his shoulder. "You got quiet. I wanted to make sure you weren't about to pass out on me."

Her gaze flickered to the people in front of her. Then to the copper walls.

Are they shifting closer? Crap.

She tried to find the exits

Shit. Where are they?

"Thanks for reminding me where I was." Her voice sounded weak, pathetic. Like her.

"Shit. Sorry." He reached back, squeezing her hand.

"Quick, give me something else to occupy my mind, before my brain seizes."

Panic whispered and bit when he shifted away, moving from her grasp. "Tanner," she squeaked.

"I have you." He swiveled around, taking the steps backward. One hand gripped the rail while the other held her. With his height and her one rung above, they were eye-level. She found it comforted her. His warm breath caressed her face, helping to slow her racing pulse.

"Since I'm better at keeping my voice quiet, I could tell you some ideas for the evening."

"Oh yeah?" Her anxiety faded into a climbing heat. "Such as?"

"A cab ride from Time Square back to our hotel is at least fifteen minutes. You could wear the flowy dress you packed, skip the panties…"

For the rest of three-hundred and something steps, Tanner whispered exactly what he'd do to her. By the time they stepped from the exit, her thighs and glutes were sore, though her ache for him ran way deeper.

Chapter Twenty-Four

Maggie's favorite singer began crooning from the nightstand. It didn't make her journey to wakefulness enjoyable. Cursing, she answered her phone, cutting off the song.

"What?" she grumbled.

"Have you read *D Notes* yet?" Zia asked, forgoing any pleasantries.

Maggie pulled back her cell, checking the time. "Why are you calling me at the butt-crack of dawn asking about a local music magazine? No, I haven't read it. I'm in bed. Sleeping. Or at least, I was."

"Get your ass up and to your mailbox. You need to read it. Looks like Jayce didn't head for Canada. Or crawl under a crack rock. Get it, read it, call me back." Zia hung up without even saying goodbye. She really was upset.

"What's going on?" Tanner muttered, wrapping a warm arm around Maggie's naked waist, his groggy voice thick with sleep.

"Hell if I know. Zia ordered I read *D Notes*. She mentioned Jayce." Maggie made to get off the bed.

He tightened his hold. "Can't it wait until the sun is a little higher in the sky?"

"Tempting. However, Zia was damn near frantic. I need to know why" She rolled away and stood. "Go back to sleep."

Zia's slightly hysterical tone put Maggie on edge. There was no way she was going back to sleep. Plus, mentioning Jayce made her curious. More than a month had passed since the tour, and no one heard a peep from him.

He never came by to demand they leave, or even pack up his stuff. Still, to be on the safe side, they took the money they made on the Cabin Fever tour and used it to pay off the rest of the loan to Jayce's parents. The house and instruments were ThreePence's free and clear.

All those months worrying and anxiety for nothing.

Though it still ate at her, how things ended with him. Yet, she doubted there was ever an easy solution when it came to Jayce.

Slipping on a tank top and lounge pants, she studied Tanner's sleeping form. On the plus side, without Jayce's hostile glances and comments, Tanner spent more nights with her. He still had his townhouse with Colton, but hardly ever stayed there.

Tanner peeked open one eye, caught her ogling. He trailed a palm up her thigh. "Change your mind?"

"No, no." She sighed. "If I crawl back under those covers, I'll never make it to the mailbox."

"Why's this a problem?" he murmured, his palm skimming higher.

She stepped away before her resolve crumbled. "Because if Zia doesn't hear back from me soon, she'll be here within a half-hour, pounding on the door, interrupting us anyway." She ran a hand through her tangled hair. "Don't you have to get ready for another interview?"

He groaned. "Yeah. Okay, you get the mail. I'll make coffee. Though after you talk with Zia, we're going to multitask."

Maggie raised one eyebrow. This sounded interesting. "Multitask? How?"

Tanner rolled onto his back. "We're taking a shower. Together. I'll make sure you're clean and satisfied."

"Then you'd better get the coffee started." She moved to the door.

"Coffee, followed by shower fun. You're my dream woman," he yelled cheerfully after her. "You know me. I'm all for good, clean fun."

She smiled, opening the front door.

~ * ~

Hearing Maggie's soft footsteps, Tanner grabbed the mugs, about to suggest they take them to the patio. The thought died on his lips.

Fury was radiating off her in waves. She was reading the magazine.

"You okay?" he asked.

Her head shot up. "That fucking asshole."

"Who?" He set the mugs on the counter, coming around to read the article.

All he could decipher was the title: *Is Detroit's Rising Star Already Burning Out?* He couldn't read anything else because she was shaking the paper, making it impossible to read.

He gently slid it from her tight grasp. She slumped against the counter. Reading it, he understood her reaction. His own annoyance rose.

Stupid fucker. Jayce doesn't know when to quit.

He'd made ThreePence sound like an imploding disaster with

him in the middle, the poor, innocent victim. He overdramatized fights within the band. Seemed to have forgotten he was usually the cause of them. The article painted Jayce the saint, Tanner the callous asshole, and Maggie as some female Don Juan. Ending with the speculation that Tanner might quit because she was setting her sights on Lincoln.

The whole thing was ridiculous. Tanner threw the magazine onto the counter in disgust.

"Should've known he wouldn't slink away. No one tells Jayce what to do," Maggie grumbled. "He had to take his pound of flesh."

Tanner leaned a hip against the counter, studying her. "Don't worry. No one will pay attention to this. Craziness and music go hand and hand." He motioned with his chin to the magazine, shrugging. "Your fans will think you're a player. Who cares? The women will want to be you. Men will want to be with you."

She swept the magazine off the counter. "Doesn't it bother you?"

He wrapped her in his arms. "Only if it were true."

Lincoln stumbled into the kitchen, half asleep, his blond mop in a tangled mess. "What's true?"

"According to *D Notes,* I'm a manizer, and you're the next notch in my bedpost."

His drowsy gaze shifted to the discarded magazine back to Maggie. He wrinkled his nose. "Ew. It'd be like messing around with my sister." He snagged a mug, smirking. "However, I'm not opposed to messing around with *your* sister…"

She laughed, picking up the magazine then hitting Lincoln with it. "Believe me, she's not worth the hassle."

He shrugged. "You're wrong. Until then…" He turned to Tanner. "How about you introduce me to the redhead you were tutoring the other day."

Tanner wasn't surprised. He'd noticed Lincoln hanging around whenever Stacey was at the house for her tutoring lesson. "Next time she comes over, I'll let you know. You can answer the door and work your magic."

Maggie's cell blasted from the bedroom. "It's probably Zia. No doubt she's freaking out because of tonight's meeting with Motown Recording Studio. I hope this stupid article doesn't make them reconsider taking us on with those two songs."

"Way to keep it positive," Lincoln said to her retreating back.

"Fine, fine," she said while walking away. "She's calling to tell me Motown wants to record a full album, along with paying all our promotion and recording costs."

“That’d make my morning,” he said before taking a sip of his coffee.

Tanner raised his brows. “Just your morning?” He checked the oven’s clock. “Crap. I better get ready. I have a job interview in a couple hours.”

“You need a couple hours to get ready, Princess?”

Tanner shoved Lincoln’s shoulder, laughing. “You’re the one with long, golden locks.” He ran a hand over his messy, short hair. “The office is close to an hour away, and with I-75 torn up, I need the extra time.”

“Ah well, good luck.”

“Thanks. You mean it?”

Lincoln smirked. “Hell no. We’re having a problem holding on to guitarists. And your singing voice isn’t too bad.”

“What about my winning personality?”

“What personality?”

Tanner snatched the hanging dishrag, throwing it at Lincoln’s head before starting down the hall. “I’m outta here. I need to get in the shower. It’ll hide the tears I’m holding in from your cruel words.”

“Aw man, I’m sorry,” Lincoln called, laughter making his voice shake. “You’re my BFF. Really.”

Maggie popped out from her bedroom as he passed, cellphone pressed to her ear. “Will you be able to come to the meeting?”

Tanner stopped, considering. His interview was at least an hour away, but meeting with the record label wasn’t until late afternoon. He nodded. “Yeah. I should be able to make it.”

She kissed him. “Thanks.”

He waggled his brows. “Want to thank me, let’s stick to our original plan. Meet me in the shower.”

“Let me finish with Zia, and I will.”

Perfect. Suddenly he was certain an extra hour of driving time wasn’t necessary.

Chapter Twenty-Five

"Tanner, where are you?" Maggie tossed her keys onto the counter and hurried through the kitchen, stopping short in the living room.

He was sprawled on the couch with a half-empty beer between his legs, staring blankly at the TV. His gaze flickered to her, then back to the screen.

"I'm here," he muttered.

He didn't sound drunk, yet something wasn't right. He'd blown off the meeting, plus his body language screamed "fuck off."

"Where were you? Why didn't you show up? Or answer your phone? I've been calling and texting you for hours." She waved a hand in front of his face, steadily growing annoyed."

He shrugged, his gaze fixed ahead. "As you can see, I'm fine."

Her patience snapped. "What the fuck, Tanner! No show. No call. Our meeting ended hours ago. I worried something happened to you. And all you can say is, 'I'm fine'?"

He blew out his cheeks, finally turning to her. He looked beaten. "Yes, I know, can you believe it, I wasn't responsible. I didn't do what everyone else wanted and needed."

Seeing the pain under his surliness, she ignored his sarcasm and sat next to him. "Tell me what happened."

"I didn't get the job."

She figured but suspected there was more. "And…"

"Ms. Caroline of Noxon Accounting believes someone like me to be a bad fit for the team."

"Someone like you…" Maggie didn't know anyone more responsible than Tanner. Hell, he'd give her mother and father a run for that award.

"Someone came across the article in *D Note.* HR decided hiring me would be a risk. I might give the company unwanted negative press," he finished bitterly.

"A risk," she parroted, shocked. *Seriously*? He wasn't applying for a job at a preschool or church. "How? It's not like the article made you out to be out-of-control or unreliable."

"No. I'm a skirt chaser with no morals."

She gave a mirthless laugh. “Um, are we talking about the same article? That was me. You’re just my innocent victim.” She kissed his cheek, relieved when a small smile played at his lips.

Tanner shut off the TV, then stood. They were less than a foot away. Her heart echoed with the distance between them.

“I’m sorry I missed the meeting.” He exhaled, his shoulders slumping. “I didn’t want my mood to bring anyone down. Still. I should’ve gone. This is my life now. At least you’ll get what you’ve wanted.”

“Which is…” She wasn’t sure what to make of his rant. He was aggravated, had reason to be, but how did it circle around to her?

“Thanks to the damn article, no one’s going to hire me. You’ll have me for however long it takes Scarlett to return.”

Maggie buried her irritation. He was hurting, lashing out. Plus, his point was valid. They both knew she wanted him to stay. What he didn’t understand was she didn’t want it at the cost of his happiness.

He’d managed to crawl into her heart and now mattered as much as the music.

She reached for him, trying to bring him back to the couch. He resisted for a split-second before taking the seat beside her.

He slid his fingers through hers, grasping her tight. They sat in the dark silence. There was nothing else for her to say. She waited for him to speak.

“In truth, I want both.” He exhaled. It sounded so heavy, full of frustration. “A nice stable life, and one where I continue writing songs with you. I want to play the shows and have a steady, predictable job. Guess I should be happy the choice was taken from me.”

Her selfish parts wanted to encourage this line of thinking. Give up on his career, to focus on ThreePence one hundred percent.

Her conscience overruled her greedy heart. “Nothing is written in stone. It was one interview. By the time you take the CPA test and start actively looking for a job, the article will be buried and forgotten.”

The couch dipped as he leaned forward, grabbing a beer from the coffee table. He drained it. She rubbed his back, then massaged the base of his neck.

“Plus, come on, most accounting firms aren’t going to read or even care what *D Notes* wrote. Trust me this article will be forgotten in a week or so. When some other Detroiter does something newsworthy, you’ll drift back into obscurity.”

He studied her, a line appearing between his brows. His scrutiny made her uncomfortable, and she shifted. “What?”

“Does leaving the band mean I’m leaving you?”

The sudden topic shift threw her. Maggie tilted her head in question. “Where is this coming from?”

“Earlier, you said it’ll upset you when I left the band. When I leave you. Why do the two go hand in hand?”

Hell if she knew, but they did.

“I didn’t mean I’d break it off because you’ve left ThreePence, it’s more I’m a realist. My constant traveling and late shows won’t mesh with your nine to five job. It won’t be easy.”

“Doesn’t mean it’s impossible,” Tanner argued.

Resting her forehead against his, she whispered, “No, not impossible.”

Just unlikely.

“It’s been a stressful day. We’re both wrecked. Let’s relax, ignore the future for tonight.” She stood, leaning into his warmth and love.

~ * ~

Halfway down the hall Tanner halted. He wanted to punch himself in the face. “I’m such an asshole. I didn’t even ask. How did the meeting go with the record label?”

“Oh, great. They still want us. Being a local label, they’d read the stupid article—I swear if I ever see Jayce, I’m going to castrate the shithead.”

Stand in line.

“Did my no-show cause a problem?”

She shrugged. “I was able to assure them you’d be in the studio to sing our duet together, so they were fine. The bigger hurdle was our missing bass. But Scarlett was there, told them she’d play lead and you the bass until we found a replacement. One of their guys was at our last show. Heard you playing bass, saw you could handle it.”

Tanner’s remorse swelled, almost choking him. “I’m sorry.” He stopped, cupping her face and kissing her softly. “I didn’t think. I was too busy having a pity party for one.”

“Forget it.”

The silent house registered. “Where’s everyone?”

“Celebrating.”

“Without you?”

“I told them I wanted to find you first.”

It’s official. Drowning in one’s guilt is a real thing.

“Do you want to leave? Meet with them, so we can all celebrate together.”

“Later. What I want to do right now doesn’t include them. Only you.” She ran her tongue along his neck, stopping to kiss the corner of his mouth. Her touch shot straight south. Within seconds he was harder than granite.

He gripped her ass, eliminating all space between them. Her hot desire made him damn near feral.

He needed this, her body, her touch. It stopped the worries racing and chasing each other around in his brain.

They stumbled against the nearest wall, tearing at each other's clothes. He helped her yank off his shirt, made quick work of her top, possibly popping a button or two in haste. Next came her bra.

He hoisted her up, and she wrapped her legs around his waist as he pressed her against the hallway wall. Bending slightly, he kissed her breast, laving it with his tongue while teasing the other with his hand.

"Tanner, please," she pleaded.

He stepped back, planning to carry her to the bedroom. She had other plans. She unwrapped her legs and wiggled. He was forced to release her.

She shoved him on the chest, catching him off guard. He staggered, falling against the wall. Before he could get his bearings, she unzipped and freed his erection. Wrapping her hands around him, she stroked from base to head before releasing him. He grunted at the absence of her touch but was too turned on to do more than lock his stance to keep from sliding to the floor.

Lowering to her knees, she worked on removing his jeans. On her way back up, she stopped at his waist, taking his length into her mouth.

"Fuck, Maggie," he hissed between clenched teeth. Her wet heat was nirvana. He tried his damnedest not to push himself too far into the warm depths of her mouth.

When she began a tight, euphoric rhythm, his climax built way too fast. "Stop," he warned.

She ignored him, and everything in his body tightened. Right before he went over, she stopped. The groan he released sounded like a wounded animal.

"Why?" she asked.

He couldn't see the details of her expression in the windowless hallway. However, the desire and playfulness in her voice was crystal-clear. She ran her palms up his thigh, wrapped a fist around him. She didn't move, but he couldn't stop himself from thrusting in her hand.

"Tease," he murmured.

Her sexy chuckle stirred him further. Then her mouth was back on him. He growled her name as he teetered on the edge. He warned her, but she only took him deeper. He came so hard he caught a glimpse of heaven.

After, she released him and slithered up his body. He placed an arm behind her knees, the other around her shoulders. When her feet left the ground, she gave a startled yelp.

"We're not finished yet." He carried her to their unmade bed.

He unbuttoned her skinny jeans. She lifted, allowing him to remove them and her panties. The curtains from the window were open and lights from the street filtered in, allowing him to admire her beauty.

She was gorgeous, all curves and strength. However, what he found the sexiest was her confidence. She enjoyed being on display for him and smiled without an ounce of inhibition. His woman was all sin and seduction.

He was already growing hard again.

Kneeling on the bed, he crawled to her, dipping to place kisses on her knees, then thighs, finally stopping at her stomach. Laying on his front, he ran his tongue around her bellybutton before dipping lower, burying his mouth in her curls and heat.

She arched, rocking over his tongue. "Please, Tanner, like that."

Her need was palpable and amplified his own. His fingers dug into her thighs, spreading her wider. He used his mouth, teeth, and tongue to work her into a frenzy.

Her legs went rigid, seconds later she shouted his name, coming apart around him. She begged for mercy. He didn't give it. Refusing to stop until he'd rung all the pleasure from her orgasm.

When she collapsed in satisfaction, moved to kiss the underside of her breasts, then her neck. He settled between her legs and slid inside her warmth, causing her to gasp.

Leaning back, he studied her face. "Are you okay with this?"

"Oh yes. I'm a little sensitive, but I want this." To prove it, she hooked a leg under his ass, pushing him in deeper. He began with slow, lazy thrusts, his eyes never leaving hers.

"This is what I want more than anything. More than any career. More than music. I want you and me. Together," he whispered before kissing her.

He switched to the rhythm that never failed to ignite her. He wanted her lost in sensations, unable to respond to his words with lies. Where she told him they'd be together even if he left ThreePence.

Her shallow pants became frantic as she edged closer to another orgasm. She met each of his thrusts with equal force. His worries crumbled away, overtaken by their mutual pleasure.

His growing orgasm coiled. Her nails raked down his back as her climax pulsed around him, causing his to explode like shockwaves through his body.

After they'd rung every ounce of pleasure from each other, he collapsed onto his side, keeping her in his arms. She wrapped herself around his body, burying her face in his neck.

"I love you," she breathed.

Chapter Twenty-Six

Maggie's phone chimed. It sat on the table between her and Tanner, they both checked it. He snorted. "Is it Zia again, *from upstairs*?"

Maggie smirked. "Yes. Our next guy is running late. He texted, said he should be here in ten minutes."

"Let's hope he's less of an asshole than the last one." Tanner grunted.

Lincoln and Maggie nodded. The jerk had the balls to ask if he made it into the band would he get a chance at Maggie.

Fucking D-Note article.

Although, watching Maggie emasculate the guy with her sharp tongue was entertaining. By the time she finished with him, his balls had probably crawled up inside his stomach. His smugness evaporated, and he meekly apologized.

The top basement door swung open, and two sets of feet clumped down the stairs. So much for a ten-minute reprieve.

Zia appeared seconds later with a hulk of a man standing behind her. He was medium height and wide as the damn door. All muscles. His short buzzcut and granite brown eyes made him look more like a bouncer than a musician. Hell, if he weren't carrying an Ibanez Bass, Tanner would've thought they'd hired a bodyguard.

Zia focused briefly on each band member. "Guys, this is Amel Toma." She told him everyone's name, and their job in the band, which seemed unnecessary given Tanner was holding his guitar, and Lincoln was behind his drums.

They responded with less than enthusiastic greetings. It reminded Tanner of his audition. He bit back a smile, deciding he'd try to be friendlier to the guy, even if exhaustion was eating at him.

Amel tipped his head in greeting, taking in ThreePence. His gaze skimmed past Tanner and Lincoln, resting on Maggie. He stepped to her, offering his hand. She shook it, asking if he had a song in mind to play.

He held up a palm. "Whatever you want, I'll do." His voice was like broken gravel, with a slight non-accent people got when they grew up speaking multiple languages.

Tanner handed Amel the sheet music for *Money* by Pink Floyd. The song was great to test the guy's abilities while also showing how well he played with the group.

"I don't need it," Amel rumbled.

He broke into a flawless performance with his bass. Even when Tanner joined, periodically speeding up and slowing the tempo, Amel didn't have a problem shifting his playing to match. Halfway through Tanner switched to *Joker* by the Steve Miller Band. Again, Amel made the switch with barely a stutter.

Tanner was able to get by on the bass. This guy blew apart his talent. Jayce's too. They needed someone who'd be able to connect Lincoln's drums with the front guitar and Maggie's vocals. This guy was it. He could tell they were thinking the same thing.

Surprise flooded him. He didn't have to talk to his bandmates to know their opinions. Tanner met them a little over a year ago, yet at times like this, it felt like he'd known them his whole life. Would this change when Scarlett returned?

The time they'd agreed on back when he joined ThreePence expired months ago. Something everyone was happy to ignore, yet sooner or later she'd be back.

Right?

Amel finished the final cords of the song. Silence filled the basement. During those beats, everyone's smiles widened, and Tanner guessed each internally celebrated finding their next bassist.

Maggie spoke first. "We have one more stopping by tonight, though I'm tempted to tell her not to bother." After a pause, she furrowed her brows. "Do you sing?"

"I've done some backup singing. Why?"

Yeah, why?

"Would you be willing to try a few duets with me?"

Amel scratched his nose, peering from her to Tanner. "Doesn't he sing those with you?"

"I do." Tanner sounded sharp, his annoyance clear.

He didn't have a right to it since he wasn't willing to fully commit to the band. Maggie was smart to consider a replacement. Yet, he couldn't deny jealousy was rearing its ugly green head.

"He does," she agreed. "But I need a backup plan for when Tanner leaves."

"Leave? Why?" Amel gaped at Tanner, confused fascination oozing from him.

"Because Scarlett might return. And Tanner is getting ready to take his CPA test."

"CPA," Amel parroted.

"Certified Public—," Tanner began.

"I know what a CPA is," Amel cut in. "Why would you give up this, for that?"

It would've been funny if this was the first or even the hundredth time someone in the rock world asked him this question. To them, nothing else mattered. There was no room for anything but the music.

Doesn't stability matter? Or family, a home, permanency?

"Because I like it," Tanner replied, trying to keep the annoyance from his voice. "You don't like what you're doing when you're not playing the bass?"

"Fuck no," the other man scoffed. "I help manage a Lebanese restaurant with my family."

A bark of surprised laughter escaped from Tanner. "Yeah. Working with family sucks." Remembering the days he helped set up, play, and break down sets alongside his mother made him shudder.

"Man, you have no idea," Amel said with easy humor. He turned to Maggie, asking, "You want to hear me sing something now, or wait until after your other audition?"

"If you have the time, do it now. If your voice works, I'll cancel the other one."

"In that case, I've got all the time in the world."

~ * ~

"Maggie isn't going to be happy."

Hearing her name, she set aside her book, tilting her head toward Lincoln's voice. He was in the kitchen with Tanner, and she couldn't hear his response.

Wanting to know, she scooted to the other end of the couch. Right next to the entrance to the kitchen.

Lincoln's voice drifted easily to her. "Amel can't make it to tonight's practice. Two of his brothers are sick, and it's Ramadan. There's no way he can get away from the restaurant until after ten."

Shit. Nice timing, Amel.

They were working on new material. She needed the bass to pull it all together.

"It's Amel. I'm sure Maggie will be fine with it." Tanner sounded downright petulant.

What the hell was his problem? Amel was great on the bass and never caused trouble.

"Aren't you two friends?" Lincoln sounded perplexed.

It matched Maggie's confusion. She leaned so far over the edge of the couch her fingers touched the floor. She needed to hear his response.

After a slight pause, Tanner answered, "Shit. Yeah, we are. I'm just irritable right now. Earlier, I'd decided to upload some pictures to ThreePence's Twitter and Instagram accounts… I made the mistake of reading the comments."

"Dude. Always a bad idea."

A chair scraped across the linoleum floor, and footsteps came closer. Maggie hastily shuffled farther down the couch, straining to hear. Yes, eavesdropping was wrong, but she wanted to know what was going on inside his head.

Seconds later Tanner said, "The hot topic amongst our fans is when Maggie will toss me aside for Amel. Most give it four months."

"Speculation and rumors don't make something real, man. If it were, I'm Cobain in hiding."

"I knew it," Tanner shouted with glee, and Maggie swallowed her laughter.

"And," Lincoln continued over Tanner's mirth, "you broke off your engagement to some woman named Jane to be with Maggie."

"Seriously? I went on two dates with her. Back when I first joined. Where did you read that?"

"Doesn't matter. It's not the point. What is, is don't read the gossip shit. It'll do your head in."

Someone drummed a staccato beat on the counter closest to her, then Tanner said, "Yeah, you're right. This crap normally doesn't bother me. I think the stress is getting to me. Next week I take the CPA exam. If I pass, I'll have to make a choice. It's messing with me. I don't want to let you guys down. I also don't want to abandon everything I've worked my ass off for." Something clinked, glass hitting a surface and ice tinkled. "That reminds me. I need to check my email. I'm waiting to hear back from my old boss at the accounting firm I interned at. He's supposed to write me a letter of recommendation."

Tanner's footsteps started in her direction. Maggie set her book on her lap and closed her eyes, pretending to sleep. She didn't want to talk to him. He'd know she'd overheard, and she was at a loss as what to say.

She was at war with two conflicting feelings.

One was to comfort him. Tell him they'd be fine. The other was to demand he stay, to forget about his old life. She'd worked too hard to get the band where it was, and he might screw it all up by leaving.

Not to mention what it'd do to her heart.

Chapter Twenty-Seven

"Are you ready?" Tanner asked Maggie, rapping on the bathroom door.

The shower shut off, and Maggie called, "Is your mom here?"

"Yes. Got here about ten minutes ago."

"Okay, give me five minutes."

He came into the living room, sitting next to his mom on the couch. "I don't know why we have to do this anyway. So what, I passed the exam. Big deal."

Okay, he was lying. Holding the letter that stated he passed was an excellent feeling. Better than Christmas morning as a kid.

Still, a big dinner at a fancy restaurant and a party was too much.

"Maggie loves you. She's proud of you, wants to show her support." His mom tapped his knee, gaining his full attention. "I'm proud, too."

Surprise and delight filled him.

"Well I am," she said defiantly. "I dropped out of high school yet managed to raise a fine, college educated man."

He hugged her. "Thanks."

Hearing Maggie's steps, Tanner pulled away. His breath caught. She was a fifties pin-up dream in a poke-a-dot halter dress, tight at the waist and flaring from there, ending right above her knees.

"Wow," was all he could manage.

She offered him a radiant smile before saying, "Ready to eat?"

He wanted to say he was ready to eat her but managed to keep that to himself. Though by the way Maggie's smile turned wicked, she might have guessed it.

She hauled him from the couch. "My parents phoned when I was getting dressed. They are almost to the restaurant. If we leave now, we should arrive at the same time."

"Are they coming to the party after?" his mom asked.

"Not my parents, although Levi and my sisters are coming."

"Will I be the only one there over fifty?" his mother huffed.

He bit back a smile. She wasn't really bothered. They both knew she could fit in with any crowd, no matter the age demographic. She was always ready to let loose.

"The Grimms will be there. Including his dad. Colton also said he was going to mention it to his family, so his parents might stop by the house." Tanner faced his mom, putting a teasing smirk on full display. "So, don't worry, there'll be some AARP members for you to hang with."

His mom slapped him lightly on the shoulder, amusement dancing in her eyes. "My son, ever careful with his mother's feelings. And hey, if Jacob's dad is part of the senior group, sign me up for my card. That man is *hot*."

"Ah. No. Stop!" He did not want to think about his mom hooking up with his friend's dad.

Maggie took his hand and his mother's, moving them toward the door. "Come on. If we don't leave soon, traffic will be a bitch. You two can finish this topic in the car."

"No thanks. We're finished," Tanner muttered.

~ * ~

Maggie hung up her cell, slipping her phone into the pocket of her vintage dress. She tried to suppress her frustration, knowing it wasn't Lydia's fault she needed someone to pick her up.

On the weekends she worked at a deli within walking distance from the house. Her shift ended after their family already left for the party.

Maggie grabbed Lincoln's truck keys from the bowl on a small vestibule table next to the door. "Lincoln," she shouted.

His head popped from around the kitchen entrance. "What?"

"I'm going to borrow your truck. I need to get my sister."

He gestured in the direction of the garage. "Sure, if you can move the two cars blocking me in."

"Well, shit."

"I'll do it," Tanner yelled from somewhere in the kitchen. Seconds later, his broad frame filled the hallway. "I can get around the cars with the bike. Would she mind riding on the back?"

"No, she wouldn't. That isn't the problem. Today is your day. You stay. Visit. Catch up with friends."

"It's no big deal. It'll take less than an hour, roundtrip. I'll be back before people start arriving." He sauntered closer. "It's not like you can ride wearing that dress."

"I could change." Guilt ate at her. He shouldn't have to chauffeur around her sister.

"No way," he growled in a low voice. "I will be the one to remove your dress. And I don't want to be rushed. I will start with those big white buttons." He ran a finger over four of them decorating the top of the dress. "Then I'm going to untie the material around your neck, letting the dress fall to your waist. After, I'll either lift the dress and take you from behind, while caressing your freed breasts. Or," he slid his palms along her sides, "I'll strip off everything except those thigh-high stockings and heels. The only question remaining is if I should take you slow or fast."

"Jesus, Tanner," she said in a shaky voice. "The sinful way you talk, the things you say… Why do you have to work me up without offering any relief?"

"Good. I don't like being the only one counting the minutes until I have you alone and under me. Or over me. Whatever you prefer."

"I like your idea, leaning me over something…"

Tanner stepped back. "Yup. I'm going to get Lydia. Now."

"Um, why?" His sudden need to leave confused her.

"Because if I don't leave now. Right now. I'm going to drag you into our bed and have you screaming my name so loud the neighbors six blocks away will hear you."

She swallowed. "Later."

"Later," he agreed, with a sharp dip of his chin and quick, heated kiss.

Letting him go wasn't easy. What made it possible was the anticipation. The hot build-up was going to make for one helluva night.

Chapter Twenty-Eight

Maggie made another pointless trip around the outside of the house. There was no sign of Tanner's bike. People were asking if he was blowing off his own party. He should've returned with Lydia a while ago, yet no motorcycle was parked outside, and neither were answering their phones.

Her worry had Maggie pacing. When she circled to the back patio for the fifth time, she fell into the plastic seats across from Carleen. She tilted her head in a silent question. Her fear matched Maggie's.

She shook her head, trying her sister's number again. This time she answered.

"Where the hell are you?" Maggie asked, her anxiety making her voice sharp. "Why haven't you answered your damn phone?"

"It was shoved in my purse with the ringer off. I took it out to call Tanner when you rang," Lydia huffed. "Where is he?"

Maggie's gut churned. Tanner wasn't the type to blow off someone, let alone skip his party.

Something's wrong.

"I don't know, Lydia. He left to get you right after we got off the phone."

"Shit." The worry in Lydia's voice, amped Maggie's.

She stood, needing to walk off her nervous energy. When she reached the tree on the far corner of the property her other lined beeped. She didn't recognize the number. "I gotta go, someone's calling. Ring me when he arrives." She disconnected without waiting for a response. "Hello?"

There was an eternal silence. She was about to check to see if the call was dropped when Tanner spoke. "Hey, babe, it's me."

His words sounded slurred, almost impossible to understand. Did he beg off from his own party to get drunk at some bar?

No, of course not.

"Where are you?"

"I'm here."

Holding in her exasperation, she asked, "Where's here?"

"On the phone." He giggled. Yes, an actual giggle. The man

must be high. "I'm here on the phone."

"I get that. *Where* are you? Why haven't you picked up my sister?"

"Sorry. Sorry. I didn't want you to worry. I talked the nurse into dialing your number. Shit, these meds are making me a loopy."

Nurse? Meds?

"What the hell happened?" she cried, catching Carleen's worried gaze from across the yard. She stood, moving fast in Maggie's direction.

"Shit. I'm all wrong. I mean, doing this all wrong." He was struggling to get his words in order. "I don't want you to worry. I'm fine. I was in a slight, small accident. Some asshole swerved into my lane. I wasn't going fast, but I dumped the bike."

"If it's 'small' why'd the hospital give you drugs?"

Carleen stopped in front of Maggie, her face contorted, pinched with fear. Maggie hit the speaker button.

"Ah, well I'm a little beat up…"

"Again, what's a little, Tanner? Explain." She twisted and yanked at a strand of her hair. "You know, never mind. What hospital are you at? We're leaving now."

"Hospital?" Carleen mouthed, placing a shaking hand over her mouth.

There was a shuffling noise, and Tanner asked someone the name of the hospital. He didn't even know where he was—damn that wasn't good. He gave her the name, and she hung up after promising to be there in less than a half-hour.

Thankfully Carleen's car wasn't blocked in. They arrived at the small, local hospital in less than fifteen minutes. After giving Tanner's name, they were directed to his room.

It was on the left at the end of the hallway. The decor was the usual bland, pastel hospital colors. The ones meant to either soothe or bore the patients into submission. There were two occupied beds. The one closest to the door held a middle-aged man with an unkempt beard. He gave them a tired smile before returning to his TV.

Maggie moved to the other bed. Tanner lay there, flat on his back, his eyes closed. The first thing she noticed was the splint on his left arm. He was covered by a blanket from the waist down, nothing else appeared broken.

She whimpered with relief. He turned at the sound, then gave them an exhausted smile.

Rushing to his bed, she pulled him into a hug. He yelped, and she jerked back so fast she almost fell onto her butt.

Tanner winced. “Sorry. I have some cracked ribs.”

Fast, heavy tears flooded Maggie’s eyes, and she heard Carleen stifle a sob.

He limply waved his good arm. “I’m fine.”

“You’re not fine.” Maggie made a fist, her short nails digging into her palms. “I should’ve gone. Or told Lydia to catch a ride with Levi. Now look at you.”

He glanced at his cast, then back at her. “I’m sorry.”

“What are you talking about?” She peered at Carleen from over his bed, wondering if she knew.

She ran a gentle hand through his short hair, giving Maggie a helpless shrug. She was clearly just as mystified.

“I fucked everything up.” He lifted his injured arm. “How am I supposed to play a guitar like this?”

Shit. He’s right.

Figures. They find a replacement for Jayce, and now need one for Tanner. Frustration made her want to shout and stomp her feet.

She peered into his eyes. The worries of the band faded. Here he was laying in the hospital, bruised and bloodied, worried about her.

Wrapping her arms gently around his neck, she made sure not to put any pressure on his ribs. “Stop. All that matters is you’re okay. You’ll heal, and everything will go back to normal.”

She meant every word but feared the last part was a lie.

Chapter Twenty-Nine

Tanner's cellphone began vibrating on his desk, and he answered it, noticing Colton's name flash on the screen. "Hey, what's up?"

"You at work?"

"Yup."

"It's past six on Friday night. You going to spend the night there?"

Tanner sat back, stretching his legs. "Yeah, probably. I swear, I've been at these financials all day, and I'm not even halfway through them."

"Take a break, man. You keep working at this pace you'll have carpal tunnel in your only working wrist. I will *not* be wiping your ass." Colton's smart-ass laugh carried through the line.

Tanner chuckled, leaning back in his chair, trying to massage the kink in his neck. "Thanks for your support, man. Still, I'm risking it. I don't want to fall behind."

He was fortunate. Right after the accident, an old friend from college contacted him about a position at his accounting firm. The job was temporary, with the option of becoming permanent.

It came at the right time. Tutoring and ThreePence brought in a good deal of cash. However, neither offered insurance, and he had a hefty bill from the hospital.

He'd broken bones in his forearm, and the break was bad. He'd needed surgery, where the doctor had to insert some plates and screws to help fuse the bones back together. He'd be in a cast anywhere from three to six months, leaving him without the added income from ThreePence.

Both Zia and Maggie insisted he take his usual cut from the shows. He refused. They were already paying Scarlett to cover for him and using their profits to market their EP.

"Are you going to at least meet with your woman later?" Colton asked, cutting into Tanner's musings.

He shook his head, trying to bury his frustration at his slow recovery and the disappointment at not seeing Maggie. Again. "No. They have a show tonight. I'll stop over her place sometime tomorrow."

"Then come with me. Take a break. I'm going to Mark's. He's having a couple guys over for cards and beer."

Sounded like fun, and he was going cross-eyed from staring at numbers. Still, kind of was a dick move. He told Maggie he wasn't going to ThreePence's show tonight because he was buried in work.

Though in truth, it'd mostly been a lie.

He did have a ton to do, but he skipped because going made him miserable. He missed playing, and watching from backstage depressed the hell out of him. Trying to get lost in the masses was even worse. All the people pressing too close, jostling him. It hurt and made him claustrophobic. Plus, ThreePence fan base was strong. Sooner or later, he was always recognized.

He loved the fans, their passion and loyalty. However, some were a tad too enthusiastic, grabbing on to him when he'd rather they didn't. And the hugs hurt his healing ribs.

"No, I better not," he told Colton.

The other man's sigh carried through the phone. "Listen, Tanner. I know things suck right now, but you can't stay holed up like a hermit. Get out, laugh a little, have some fun. It will do you some good. Stop you from turning into an old man at the tender age of twenty-nine—"

"Fine," Tanner said, cutting off his friend. "I'll think about it. When are you leaving?"

"I'm going to head to his place around nine."

"Fine, I'll go. Let me finish the one I'm working on, then I'll unchain myself from this damn desk."

Colton chuckled. "Okay. Now hurry your ass up and finish. You're on my team for poker."

"Yeah, yeah." Tanner disconnected, guilt eating at the corners of his mind. He pushed it aside. Maggie always did what she wanted, why couldn't he for once?

~ * ~

Maggie laid on the doorbell to Tanner's townhouse, stepped back, peering at the windows. Every single one was dark.

What the hell?

He'd told her he was staying home to finish some work crap. It wasn't even ten-thirty. He couldn't already be sleeping.

Sliding her cell from her back pocket, she scrolled through her contacts. Finding his number, she rang him. He answered, offering a distracted greeting.

"Where are you?" she snapped, her voice brittle.

"I stopped by Mark's. Colton invited me to play poker. Why? Where are you?"

"Standing outside your door," she hissed, her anger beginning to simmer low and dangerous.

She was a fool. After singing her ass off for hours, she'd been exhausted, ready to crash and sleep for twelve hours or more. Instead, she left the club, rushing to Tanner's place, all because he complained they were growing apart.

She'd dragged her ass to his place. To prove him wrong.

To show she'd make concessions. He couldn't come to ThreePence's show because his workload was too heavy, so she'd gone to him.

Raucous laughter and male voices filtered through the phone. The sound jolted Maggie from her internal pity-party and back to reality. The one in which Tanner wasn't at home slogging through work, wishing he was with his girlfriend, but he was partying with his bros.

Shit. Scarlett was hinting that staying in ThreePence long-term wasn't for her. When Maggie asked Tanner if he'd given any thought to returning, he kept saying nothing could be decided until his cast came off since the doctors didn't know how his arm would heal. How well his fingers would work.

Then, to top off her personal shit-storm, Motown liked Amel's voice but loved Tanner's. Made sense. He was the one on the EP. They want him if they decide to record more songs.

My life is ripping at the seams, and he's playing fucking cards.

Anger slithered through her body, making her pulse thump loudly in her ears.

The noise suddenly cut out. "Maggie, give me five minutes. I'm on my way. Knock on the house on the right. She has a key to my place. Tell her you're my girlfriend. She'll let you in."

"I don't give a shit about standing outside. I want to know why you were too busy to visit me tonight yet found time to hang out at some guy's house with Colton."

She could hear him pounding down the stairs. "Oh, come on, Maggie, be fair. Going to your shows isn't visiting you. It's watching you."

"Fine. Whatever. Then be man enough to admit you have no interest in going. Don't lie to me."

"Why can't you be considerate enough to remember I hate crowds? No. You make it the only way to see you. Two, I didn't lie," Tanner growled, his annoyance vibrating through the line. "I have been working all day. Colton convinced me to take a break. Should I have instead stayed home and mooned over my girlfriend who doesn't have time for me now that I'm not in her band?"

"Don't be ridiculous. I'm trying. I'm here now. Though not anymore." She disconnected, heading back to the parking lot.

Screw this. Screw him.

Sitting on her bike, she inserted the key in the ignition. Tanner shouted to her from across the parking lot. She ignored him, starting the engine.

"Maggie, wait!"

He caught up to her as she was pushing back the kickstand. Straddling the front tire, he gripped the handlebars with his one uninjured hand.

"What?" She shouted over the hum of her bike.

He rested his head against the handlebar, taking in a lung full of air. "I'm sorry," he panted, standing. "Please shut it off."

Seeing his tired eyes, she softened. "Fine. Whatever." She shut off her bike.

He held open his arm not in a cast. "Come here."

Again, she listened

Drawing her closer, he said, "I shouldn't have lashed out. I miss you. I'm frustrated." He hugged her, kissing along her hairline. "I'm terrified I'm losing you. Please don't leave. I want you here. I need you here."

Her fury melted like cotton candy on the tongue. She caressed the back of his neck, taking in his scent and warmth. "I'm sorry, too."

There was more to say, yet his lips were on hers, and she was more than willing to share his breath, instead of words. She wanted his body to soothe her aching heart, well aware it was a temporary fix to the growing gulf between them.

She cupped his ass, bringing him closer. He sucked in a quick breath. Maggie stilled. "Your ribs still hurt?"

"A little."

Trying to hide her aggravation, she weaved her fingers with his, leading him back to his house. He couldn't help his cracked ribs made sex a delicate process. They'd only managed it once.

However, it wasn't just their unrestrained lovemaking she craved. Even more, was having him in her bed. His warm body entangled with hers. The comfort offered from his physical love.

They hadn't slept in the same bed in more than a month. She was a restless sleeper, moved around too much, making it dangerous for his healing ribs. She hoped it wouldn't take another four weeks for them to heal.

He tugged her back to him. “Why did you stop?”

“I don’t want to hurt you.”

He nuzzled her neck. “The abuse is when you’re not close to me. I want you to stay tonight. Make love to me.”

The heat and demand in his voice melted all but a sliver of her self-restraint. “We can’t. Your ribs are healing. I don’t want to take the chance of hurting you.”

“I’ve healed enough to risk spending the night with you.” She felt his smile against her skin. “As for sex, you’re going to do all the work. You’re in charge.”

“Oh. I like that.” She slid a hand between them, stroking him through his jeans.

He hissed in a breath. “Inside. Now,” he commanded.

“Hey, you said I was in charge,” she teased.

“Okay. Get inside. Take charge.”

She shifted, taking his uninjured hand. “Come on. Get moving.”

“Yes, ma’am,” he laughed. It sounded lighthearted. His earlier misery seemed to have vanished.

She idly wondered if he was also using sex to ignore the fact their foundation seemed to be crumbling away beneath them. Peering at him from over her shoulder, she saw the relief in his eyes. Was it because they’d be okay for now, or because he’d convinced her to stay?

She didn’t ask.

Chapter Thirty

Tanner parked behind the old white van the band used for carrying their equipment to shows. He wondered why it was in the driveway with all its doors open. Maggie told him ThreePence had the weekend off.

He wanted to take her out of town for the weekend. He couldn't remember the last time they were alone or spent more than a few hours together.

Maybe they were using the free time to organize or clean the van.

Denial is a lovely, cruel bitch.

He stepped from his car as Maggie appeared from inside the van. She saw him, and broke into a huge grin, hurrying in his direction.

"What are you doing here? Why aren't you at work?" Her eyes widened and her smile grew. "Your arm! It's cast free."

He stretched both arms, flexing his fingers. "Yup, left work early today for my doctor's appointment. They removed it. I'm finally free. Feels weird, looks nasty."

She lifted his left arm, turning it gently. "It's so much thinner. Are you stiff? Will you be able to play your guitar any time soon?"

Annoyance bloomed in his chest. "Thanks for your concern," he said sarcastically. No surprise her first worry would be for the band, not him.

"Sorry," she winced, dropping his wrist. "Scarlett told me last night she doesn't want to stay with the band full time. It's been eating me alive. Then you show with your arm cast-free, I was so relieved for the band, I forgot to be a girlfriend for a second. I'm sorry. Of course, I'm worried about you."

For a second, my ass. When did I ever come before ThreePence?

He swallowed his irritation and plastered on a smile. He needed to talk, not fight with her. "You guys cleaning the van? Please tell me you still have the weekend free. I was hoping we could take off. Colton's family has a cabin in the Irish Hills, and he told me we could use it for the weekend."

He caught sight of Lincoln over Maggie's shoulder, and his

voice trailed away. He was carrying his snare and bass pedal. Tanner's shoulders slumped, good mood fading.

"I would love to leave with you," she said, leaning into him, "but Zia called this morning asking if we wanted to play at The Cherry in Traverse City. There was a last-minute cancellation and its high season. The club was willing to pay top dollar."

She played with the buttons on his shirt. "Come with us. I'll play at night, but the days will be ours."

"Aren't you heading out soon?"

"In an hour. That's enough time for you to go back to your place and throw some stuff into a bag."

If she wanted him to go, she'd have phoned him earlier. She was offering it now because he arrived unannounced at her doorstep. No thanks. "I don't want to be in the way. I'll use the extra time to get ahead at work."

"Come on. You won't be in the way. Hell, you could even come to a show and sing. You know the fans would love it. They miss you."

Bitterness destroyed the last of his good mood. When he first arrived, he wanted nothing more than to spend his weekend with Maggie. Now he wanted to get away from her.

Maybe he was being unfair, but he was pissed. She was taking off, he didn't know for how many days, and hadn't even bothered to tell him. Only asked him now because he was standing right in front of her.

He was damn tired of being her afterthought. He shook his head, rejecting the offer to join them.

"Fine. Whatever," Maggie bit out. "Can you at least be here on Monday?"

"For what?"

"We have an interview with a popular YouTube channel. I'd like you to be there for it."

"Why?"

"Damn it, Tanner! Why are you acting like this?" Her lips pressed into a thin line. "I want you there because you helped write half the new songs. It might not be you playing the guitar, but it's your voice singing with me on our EP. Remember? The one we're promoting? Or have you stopped giving a shit about ThreePence? Is your other news, you're officially quitting?"

"No—"

"Hey, Tanner," Amel cut in, walking from the garage, carrying his bass. "Are you coming with us? I'm more than happy to give the vocals back to you."

"Sorry, man. Not this time," Tanner answered.

"No. Not this time or anytime. Right, Tanner?" Maggie challenged, irritation etched on her every feature.

"I'll get out of your way. Have a good show." He stomped to his car, yanking on the door handle at the same time she yelled, "Wait. Are you going to come by on Monday? After work?"

His first impulse was to say no. However, that'd be a shit move. To let down the band because he was pissed at Maggie was juvenile. He nodded. He'd be there.

She called after him again. This time he ignored it, opening his door. He slid into the driver's seat. She probably just wanted to ask if he was coming back. He wasn't ready to discuss it.

A year ago, it would have been a simple choice. He'd have wanted the safe, stable career. Accounting.

Now, however, the choice was incredibly difficult. He missed the band and working with Maggie. He couldn't decide which would be better for him in the long run. Or the real reason he wanted to return to ThreePence.

Was it for her, or because he genuinely wanted to be a full-time musician? What if they didn't stay together? Would they be able to continue working together? Or worse, time passed, and he grew to hate her, for his decision to leave behind his old, practical life?

Shit, he didn't want to be like his dad. On the road all time, partying and forgetting his family. His kids. Dreaming that one day he'd make it big, believing it'd fix everything.

So caught up in his downward spiral, Tanner was almost back home before realizing he hadn't even kissed Maggie goodbye.

Chapter Thirty-One

Greg's heavy frame blurred before settling into a chair next to his vlogging partner, Sam, asking, "Is everyone there?"

The two men peered expectedly at the group through their computer.

"No," Maggie answered. "Tanner texted me. He's running late. He hopes to be here soon. Until then we can start without him."

She was lying.

She hadn't spoken to him since Friday. The weekend was super busy, and to be honest, she wasn't eager to talk with him. He'd stomped off without a backward glance all because she couldn't drop everything to spend a weekend with him.

Jerk.

Then when she tried to talk to him on Sunday, he didn't bother to answer his phone. Or call back.

She tried again this morning to remind him about the interview. Nothing. No response.

He was slipping away. In the quiet times, it ate at her, leaving her hollow. However, right now, with him blowing off the interview, burying her sadness under anger was easy. It was one thing to be mad and snub her; it was another to blow off a commitment to the band. That was unacceptable.

That was the problem with dating someone not committed to music. Tanner, and others like him, didn't understand. This wasn't a hobby. Music was her air.

Damn it! Tanner should understand.

He'd seen how hard everyone in ThreePence worked. Until his accident, he was the same. He'd shown up to every show, postponed his exam for the East Coast tour, helped write some of their best songs. Hell, he even swallowed his anxiety and sang with her.

However, she also couldn't deny the fact in all those months he'd never given her a straight answer about his plans *after* he passed his CPA test. He always told her they'd have to wait and see what happened after Scarlett returned. Almost like he hoped the problem would solve itself.

Lincoln elbowed Maggie, and she jolted from her dark

thoughts. The room was quiet. Everyone was waiting, eyeing her.

Oops.

She focused on the computer screen. “Um. Sorry, Greg. What was your question?”

“Oh, I thought maybe you didn’t want to answer. It’s somewhat personal…”

Maggie held in the need to groan. She understood fans wanted to know them, not just the music, but this part wasn’t easy for her. She hated sharing her private life, even with her closest friends. Sharing with strangers was painful.

However, a certain level was expected, and she gave Greg the go-ahead motion.

“There’s been speculation on whether you and Tanner are still together. Want to settle the rumors once and for all?”

What she wanted to do was laugh, though what he asked was far from funny. Simply put: she didn’t know the answer.

She opened her mouth, not sure what to say, when footsteps pounding down the basement stairs snagged everyone’s attention. Relief, anxiety, and longing flooded her, almost drowning her.

Tanner appeared seconds later, shoving a tie into his back pocket. Taking the empty seat next to Scarlett, he mouthed an apology in the general direction of the group. They were in a tight row, grouped around Amel’s large computer monitor.

Facing the screen, Tanner said, “I apologize for being late,” he told Greg and Sam. “I had an unavoidable delay.”

Greg waved off the apology and began bombarding Tanner with questions. “No worries. Maggie told us you’d be late. I see you have the cast off. We’re glad you’re on the mend. What does it mean for the band? Will you and Scarlett be trading off, or will you guys be adding more guitars to the music?”

“I wish I could give you a straight answer to your questions.” Tanner shrugged. “There are too many unknowns. The cast was removed four days ago, the same time ThreePence left for an out of town show. We never got a chance to talk. Plus, it’s too early to know how well my fingers will work.”

He lifted his left hand, flexing stiff fingers. Even with three people between them, Maggie saw him wince.

She recalled her reaction on Friday. The way she jumped on him about returning, coming off like she didn’t care if he was even fully healed. Or in pain. All that mattered was how he could benefit her.

Guilt crawled along the edges of her heart.

"Does this mean you might not make the upcoming tour?" Greg asked.

Shit.

Tanner's forehead bunched, his brows slamming together. "What tour?"

Shit.

She'd wanted to talk to him about it. There was just never enough time. Now he was going to be pissed, say they excluded him. That *she* left him out.

"Zia and our new label want us to promote the new EP. Tour locally and visit the venues that wanted us to return on the East Coast. This time ThreePence will be the main act," Maggie quickly explained. "It's still in the works. I'll tell you the rest later."

"Uh, oh. Trouble in paradise?" quipped Sam.

Now the little asshole wants to speak?

She sneered at the computer, zoning in on Sam. "We learned about all this recently. Neither Zia nor I have had a chance to talk with Tanner. Since his accident, he's been working another job. We don't see each other often as we'd like."

Sam licked his thin lips like he could taste the juicy gossip, ready to pounce on his next tasty meal. Thankfully Greg made a shushing motion and spoke over the other man. "I'm willing to bet even if you aren't completely healed many fans would love you there to sing." His gaze shifted to Amel. "No offense to you, but it's his voice on the EP."

He shrugged. "None taken. I'd have no problem giving the mic back to Tanner. I like being in the background with my bass."

"What do you say, Tanner? Ready to re-enter the spotlight with Maggie?" Greg persisted.

He didn't bother her like his beady-eyed partner, but she wished he would drop the question. They needed to discuss this when not doing a live interview.

Tanner shifted in his seat, his unease filling the room. Dread fell heavy, sitting like wet cement in her stomach.

"I don't know. This is news to me. I need to talk to our manager, Zia. With the entire band. It would affect both Scarlett and Amel. Then I have to consider my other job."

Greg read something, then said, "Yes, right. You're working at Lakeshore Associate. Isn't it a temporary position? Something to do while healing?"

"Not necessarily. When the accident happened, Scarlett was undecided if she wanted to come back."

Bullshit. We all knew she didn't want to come back.

"Anyway," Tanner continued. "I'm not sure I want to come back. Lakeshore is a great place to work."

Maggie gasped. How could he blurt that during an interview? And why hadn't he told her how much he liked his new job?

Lincoln leaned closed, whispering in her ear. "Are we losing him?"

She shot him a not-now glare and leaned forward, pushing down the heavy weight starting to travel from her stomach to her throat. "Greg, I'm sorry, you might have noticed, you've caught us at a chaotic time. You're better off asking us something in our past or future. The present is a bit muddled. Though don't worry, we'll have it settled before the tour."

Sam spoke. "How come you don't know, Maggie? Isn't Tanner *your* boyfriend? Or are the rumors true? Have you two split because you want to date Amel?"

"No," Maggie and Amel answered at the same time. She gritted her teeth, her tight smile probably more of a grimace. Sam would fit in well at TMZ.

"Maggie's a great friend. That's all," Amel said with his usual unflappable calm. "Besides I have a girlfriend. And no, Sam I'm not telling you her name. We'd rather keep it private."

Greg nodded. "Fair enough."

Thankfully he seemed more interested in the music than gossip and was running the interview. He reined in his annoying partner, and the rest of their questions were innocuous enough. Maggie was able to answer the ones directed at her on autopilot.

Good thing because her mind was frozen in shock. The day of reckoning had arrived. Time to choose: the music and her, or his nine to five dream.

~ * ~

The instant Greg disconnected, Maggie whirled on Tanner. "Seriously! You never planned on coming back. You couldn't have mentioned it before we were doing a fucking interview?"

His anger swelled, ready to burst like an overinflated balloon. He stood but didn't move closer to Maggie. He needed the distance. "Oh, we share stuff, do we? You're leaving on tour. You didn't bother to mention it?"

"I was waiting to see how you healed. We," she motioned to the rapidly retreating backs of their bandmates, "didn't want to burden you with it until you knew if you'd be able to play again."

Tanner's patience evaporated. "I understand *them* not telling me," he shouted. "For them it's a business decision. For you, it should've been personal. Any normal girlfriend would've mentioned she might be leaving for months."

"Says the career accountant," Maggie spat. "Were you going to tell me you weren't coming back until after you made partner?"

He released a harsh breath. "I haven't made a decision yet. I wanted to talk to you last weekend, but you didn't have the time. As usual."

"Excuse me?" Her voice was razor sharp and her body tense. "Should I have canceled the show because you needed to talk? Put my life on hold because my man needed me?"

"Jesus Christ, Maggie. I'm not asking you to give up anything. Not every man believes his needs come first, just like every woman isn't a selfless caregiver. Hell. You're proof of that."

Maggie reared back, eyes full of fire. "What the hell are you saying exactly?"

"You're the most selfish woman I know," he stated flatly.

She inhaled sharply. It occurred to him it'd be best if he shut his mouth. Cool off. At this point, he wasn't even trying to fix what was breaking between them. Instead, he was throwing gasoline on an already raging fire.

The problem was hurt and frustration washed away his good sense. "Your needs come before everyone else. Everything else —"

"It's not all for me. It's for the band," she interrupted.

"Bullshit," he barked. "You don't give two shits about Lincoln, Scarlett—any of us. We're only important as far as we help support your climb to fame. If I assist you in writing and get my ass on stage, I'm allowed in. Once I stepped away from your dream," he snapped his fingers, "I'm standing alone in the biting cold. Music and success are the only things you're capable of loving."

She jabbed him in the chest, baring her teeth. "What the hell would you know about love? Huh? You want safety. Security. Not the chaos and passion that comes with love. It's why you hold back with me. And why you won't commit to ThreePence."

"Damnit, Maggie! When have I ever held back from you? Maybe I should have. I should've trusted my gut." He spun away, pacing the room before returning to her. His heart ached and broke. "I didn't commit to the band because I have something else. Did you expect me to abandon the career *I've* been working toward all these years because it's what you wanted?"

"No," she stuttered, licking her lips, looking to the left.

Bullshit!

"Yes, you did." His heart emptied, replaced with liquid rage. "Is that why you're sleeping with me? Hoping it'll keep me around?"

She stumbled back like he'd pushed her. He wanted to take back his dirty accusations. She cared for him. This was him hurting, lashing out.

Tanner made to take her in his arms, to apologize. Maggie stepped away.

"You should leave," she said.

His heart stopped. "ThreePence or you?"

"Definitely me." She gave him her back. "As for the band, it's your decision. Leave us and go back to your *Pleasant Valley Sunday* life, or stay with us part-time or full, I don't care. Talk to Zia, not me. We're finished talking."

He wanted to yell. Tell her they were far from done.

What was the point? They both feared this would eventually happen. It was inevitable. "So that's it?"

"I don't want to be with someone who believes I'm some conniving, selfish harlot."

"I didn't mean it. I was angry."

Yes, she was selfish. However, he never doubted her love. His pride and worry had him attacking her like an asshole.

"Either deep down you do believe it or you think your anger gives you the right to speak so damn hurtful to me. Whichever it is, I don't want it."

"Bullshit," he said to her back. "I was wrong, but you're using it as an excuse to end things. We can work this out. You just don't want to put effort into it." Shaking his head, he said, "I'm not going to beg you to stay with me."

She didn't face him, instead she went to the table and shuffled through some papers. He was being dismissed.

Tanner heaved a heavy sigh, feeling like Atlas carrying the world on his shoulders. He gathered the shattered remains of his heart, silently leaving. Not daring to look back. If he did, he might lose all his self-respect and plead for any small piece of her love.

When he reached the top of the stairs, he wanted to make a right and push through the back door. However, he considered everyone in ThreePence his friend. Leaving without saying goodbye was wrong. He took a fortifying breath before trudging through the empty kitchen and into the living room.

In other circumstances, he'd laugh. They were staring fixedly at the TV trying to appear engrossed like they hadn't heard everything between him and Maggie.

"So, um." He cleared his throat. A lump had grown there, and talking around it proved difficult. "I will probably take the CPA job. It doesn't mean I want to end my friendship with any of you." He directed his gaze between Zia and Scarlett. "If you need me to cover a show, let me know. I'll do my best to comply. Still depends on how well I heal."

Zia stepped in Tanner's path. She placed a gentle hand on his arm. "Don't leave it like this," she whispered.

"It's for the best. We want different things, and I don't want our problems to affect the band." He cleared his throat. "So, um, good luck with everything. And I'm serious, if you need anything, let me know."

Walking away was difficult, nearly impossible. Something Tanner wouldn't have believed a year ago. It didn't matter. He needed to move on, start his real life.

Chapter Thirty-Two

"Are you leaving with us or going out?" Amel asked Maggie.

Passing Lincoln the snare drum she just removed, she said. "No, I'm meeting Kim at a bar down the street. Muddy Water, I think is its name." Maggie jerked her head in the direction of the exit. "Want to come with us?"

Amel shook his head. "Nah. I'm good."

The guy had infinite patience and never judged. She needed that right now. With her short fuse lately, having him and Lincoln was a godsend. Both men were so mellow, letting her attitude roll off them.

Scarlett was quietly replacing a broken string on her guitar, apparently eavesdropping. "Really. Again, Mags?" Disapproval seemed to drip off every syllable.

Amel might not judge. Scarlett didn't have the same compunction.

Maggie chose to ignore her friend and picked up the night's set list. She gave it to Lincoln before heading for the door. "I'll catch up with you guys later." She gave a quick wave, jumping from the stage.

Heading home to face her empty bed and hollow heart held no appeal.

"Wait," Scarlett yelled.

Maggie stuck with the ignoring routine, pushing through the door leading into the alleyway of Adam's theater. Scarlett moved fast, catching Maggie's elbow.

"What?" she huffed. "Don't start, okay? I'm not in the mood for a lecture. There's no reason I shouldn't go. It's not like I have a husband and a kid at home. No one's waiting for me." Shit, she sounded pitiful. "I want to have some fun."

Damnit. Stop rambling.

"Maggie, are you having fun? Tell me, honestly."

She shrugged. Hell if she knew. At least it kept her distracted.

"You're going to burn out," Scarlett persisted. "You can't keep going on like this."

There was no anger in Scarlett's voice, only concern. That was worse.

"I'm fine," Maggie snapped, jerking from her friend's grasp.

"I'll see you at tomorrow's practice. Bye."

Scarlett tried another tactic. "It's an early practice. Why not head back. Get some sleep?"

"No, thanks." Maggie started down the sidewalk, her strides trying to outrun her misery.

She didn't want Scarlett's pity. What Maggie needed was to lose herself in the noise of strangers. Spending time with close friends wasn't an option. While they never outright blamed her for Tanner leaving, she didn't miss the condemnation in their eyes and whispered conversations. The combination was strangling her.

It's why Kim was perfect. A drummer in a band who ran in the same circles as ThreePence, but didn't know Tanner or much about Maggie. The best part, Kim asked no questions. She only required a body willing to club hop with her.

This suited Maggie; all she needed was someone willing to keep her surrounded in noise. In distractions.

The silence was dangerous. It left her tumbling into a pit of regret.

Sure, the emotion was great for writing angsty love songs. The ones that used to give her trouble, now flowed from her like a broken faucet. However, she could only dwell there for so long before losing her mind.

She saw the red glow from Kim's cigarette farther down the sidewalk. She was a silhouette against the corner edge of a brick building. Spotting Maggie at the same time, she flicked her filter to the ground and sauntered toward her.

"Ready?" she asked, moving into the light. Even under the harsh streetlamp, Kim was gorgeous. Her wavy toffee tresses and darker shaved sides showed off her beautiful caramel skin and model cheekbones.

Maggie motioned for Kim to lead the way. The bar was a block from the theater. They talked shop—songs they'd written, the best venues, and such. Nothing deep or personal.

When Muddy Waters came into view, Kim smiled in a way that made her hesitate. Her grin said there was more on her mind than dancing to loud music.

"I forgot to mention I met a couple of hot guys during intermission. They're waiting for us here."

Maggie wasn't the least bit interested. "Great," she replied without enthusiasm.

Hooking up held no appeal. She didn't bar hop with Kim for the men. No, she craved the loud music and throngs of people. It helped with losing herself, her pain.

They stopped at the bar's entrance to pay the cover charge to a huge guy who could've been Amel's cousin.

Once inside she shouted over the music, "I hope once you meet them you'll dial up the excitement a bit more. At least for their sake. The blond one, Tony I think his name is, can't wait to meet you. He's been to your shows. He's a bit lovestruck."

"I'm sure it's more like lust-struck," Maggie muttered.

Somehow Kim managed to hear and laughed, shrugging. "Maybe. Does it matter? The guy is hot as hell, and you're single. You're not with the guy who used to be in your band, right? The one who looked like Theo James."

At times like this, Maggie wished Kim knew her better. If she did, she wouldn't mention Tanner. Unfortunately, Kim didn't and kept right on talking. "If you are, I get it. I wouldn't toss him. He's fine and has a voice that makes my panties wet."

"No, I'm not," Maggie said, both amused and pained listening to Kim's babbling.

Her hurt must've shown because Kim snapped her jaw shut, her focus no longer divided between the crowded club and Maggie. It was all on her now.

Dammit. Next will come the questions.

"Were you two more than casual?"

Maggie shrugged. No way was she going to discuss Tanner. So, instead of meeting Kim's gaze, Maggie checked out the bar.

They stood by a wall with a floor-to-ceiling window. To their left was a simple bar, with the walls behind lined with all types of liquor. Two bartenders managed the tipsy, demanding customers. Directly in front was somewhere around ten standing tables, each filled to capacity. Behind the tables was a large dance floor. In the center was the DJ, and around her were gyrating bodies.

Just what she needed. "Where are your guys? I'm ready to dance."

She didn't give two shits but didn't want Kim to ask any more questions about Tanner. Or tell her how his voice made her wet.

"Hell if I know." Kim swayed her hips to the beat. "They'll find us or they won't. Who cares? Let's go dance."

They cut through the tables, making their way to the dancefloor. Maggie let her anxiety, sadness, and pain flow from her body to be carried away on the sound waves. She closed her eyes, lifting her arms above her head, swaying to the sultry beat.

For a few songs, she found peace. Her mind was empty to

everything except the rhythm and the dancing bodies moving around her.

Then a tall, male body pressed in close behind her, swaying with her. For a moment, she let herself imagine he was Tanner. The stranger ruined it by sliding his hands around her waist. The man's hands were too thick and boxy, nothing like Tanner's exquisite, talented fingers.

His were perfect for strumming the guitar. Or her.

The fantasy shattered. Along with her sliver of contentment.

She twisted around, hoping this would be the guy who'd make her forget Tanner.

The man was attractive with blond hair, shaved on the sides and longish on the top. His neat, close-cropped beard framed a nice mouth. Yet her heart didn't race or even flutter. There was only mild curiosity. She wondered if he was the guy Kim was talking about earlier.

A cocky grin spread across his face as he moved closer. She let him, even tried to enjoy it. She really did, but it made no difference. He was all wrong.

Not his dancing. Hell, he was smoother than Tanner, yet she didn't enjoy it. The man's touch, his smile held nothing but false promises and empty lust.

The song ended, and she headed to the bar. She hoped he was smart enough not to follow. Politeness wouldn't be offered.

She motioned to the bartender.

Chapter Thirty-Three

Tanner's cell began vibrating on his desk. He ignored it, continuing to stare out the window of his tiny office. Not that he saw the view, he was too lost in his head.

Two weeks.

Two weeks and no word from Maggie. Lincoln and Amel texted a few times, but nothing from Maggie. In the beginning, he'd been delusional enough to believe she'd come back. She'd realize they were more than their differences, that they were worth saving.

Guess he was wrong. They held nothing of true value.

Tanner exhaled. It sounded hollow as his heart.

Damn it! He needed to stop pining for Maggie and start focusing on his future, his career. His heart might be empty, but his brain was overflowing with choices. Even with her brush off, he didn't know what to do; stay at his current job or chase the music?

Accounting had its positives. Having a steady income and hours was really nice. Plus, he liked his boss and his coworkers.

However, it didn't thrill him, didn't set his heart racing. He'd have a secure job, health insurance, and regular working hours, yet all the enthusiasm for it deserted him.

He kept trying to remember what he hated about ThreePence. None of it seemed monumental. Sure, sometimes the travel was a pain. Maggie's constant practices wore thin at times. However, he missed writing songs and watching them come together. To his complete surprise, he even missed playing for a crowd.

Someone knocked on the frame of his door, shaking him from his thoughts. Sandy Delft, a partner at the firm, stood just inside his office. "Bob wants to know if you've finished the Brighton file."

"Almost. Five more minutes."

Sandy nodded, but instead of leaving, she came closer. "I can wait. When you've finished, I'll take it to him."

Tanner gave an inward groan, knowing what was coming next. For weeks, she'd invited him out after work, making subtle hints she was interested in more than a working relationship. She was around his age, pretty in the conventional way he used to like. Now he wasn't even mildly interested.

ThreePence had ruined his career contentment. Its lead singer destroyed his old notions of what, or more accurately, *who* he found attractive.

"It has been crazy around here, despite tax season way off in the distance." Sandy ran her nails lightly across his desk. "Want to—"

His phone vibrated again, and they both looked at it. Zia's face appeared on the screen. Anticipation and anxiety shot through his veins.

"I better get this."

Sandy seemed like she wanted to stay and finish what she was about to say. Thankfully, she changed her mind, saying, "I'll give you privacy." She gave an awkward wave before leaving.

He answered his phone. "Hey, Zia. How are you?"

"I've been better," she said, jumping straight to the point. "I hate to ask you this. Scarlett's daughter is sick, and her husband is out of town for work. She's not comfortable leaving Noella with a sitter. You said to contact you if we ever needed you, so, um, is it possible for you to cover for her this Saturday?"

Tanner figured she was calling to ask him to fill in for someone in ThreePence. Still, even knowing this, his heart thudded so damn hard he was sure it'd bust through his breastbone. He tried not to think about Maggie and failed, though it cooled some of his anticipation. It shifted to anger, with a dose of deep longing. He wanted to see her like a junky wanted his next fix.

I'm pathetic.

Zia cleared her throat. "I know I'm asking a lot…"

"No. No. I'll do it. I want to." To his surprise, his hunger to be on stage nearly matched his craving for Maggie.

When did the shift begin?

Was it after he first stepped on stage with ThreePence? Or when he wrote that first song with Maggie or when they sang it together?

"Great! Let me give you the info," Zia breathed, her relief traveling through the phone line.

He grabbed a pen. "Hit me with it."

Chapter Thirty-Four

From her spot sprawled on the couch in the greenroom at the Heartbreaker, Maggie heard someone enter but couldn't see who it was. She didn't bother finding out who arrived. She was too busy feigning relaxation.

The person spoke, and her fake calm became real. It was a club employee, asking Lincoln where he wanted his drums.

Maggie pressed her palm flat against her chest, where her heart was thrumming. Pretending her adrenaline didn't spike every damn time the door opened was a challenge. She was beginning to fear it'd pound right out of her chest, landing on the dirty, gray concrete floor.

Seconds later, the freaking thing squeaked open again. She cursed her disgusting uncontrollable emotions. When nothing was said, she figured it was the employee leaving.

Get a fucking grip.

Who gave a shit Tanner was due to arrive any minute? She didn't need to act like some melodramatic teenager with her emotions all a tither. It usually took her less than a week to get over a man. A month had passed, and she was still a mess. Ridiculous.

The rusty hinges grated, yet again, against her heart and nerves. This time she willed her body to remain calm. Ingrained stubbornness along with convincing herself it was Lincoln or Amel, allowed her to stay relaxed.

Lasted three seconds.

Tanner's smooth, deep baritone filled the small room, asking Zia if he was late.

Maggie's body betrayed her, going on high alert. The simple question held nothing provocative, yet his voice wrapped around her, caressing her now feverish skin. She sat up from her reclined position to spy on him from the back of the couch.

So much for keeping it cool.

Whatever.

She was gifted with the sight of his broad back. He was facing Zia and Amel, setting his case on top of a multi-guitar stand. Maggie's gaze slid lower. The man always did know how to wear jeans. It hurt like a knife to her heart knowing he wasn't hers to touch anymore.

Zia cleared her throat, snagging Maggie's attention. Her friend was smirking.

Maggie gave a what-can-say-I half shrug. The man did have a fine ass.

Tanner turned, following Zia's gaze.

There was no denying it. He was even more handsome than the version visiting her almost every night in her fantasies.

His hair was a little shaggier than normal. His jawline wore a thick stubble, a day or two away from a beard. The facial hair softened his features. However, there was no missing the strain etched around his mouth and eyes. Or the exhausted set of his shoulders.

She wondered if the weariness was from his job, or if he was finding their breakup difficult. Did the what-ifs and regrets keep him awake late into the night, or was that just her?

Zia coughed. Maggie realized she and Tanner were staring at each other. In dead silence.

An oppressive quiet filled the space between them like California smog, blocking the light and making it difficult to breathe. Maggie stood, needing to move. To get her head on straight.

If she went on stage in her current mood, she'd fuck up the show.

Moving closer to the group of three, she snagged the setlist from the end table. "We have less than an hour before we have to be on stage. Tanner, we won't throw any new songs at you tonight. You and Amel discuss who sings the dude parts."

Handing Tanner the list, she forced herself to meet his eyes. She inhaled deeply, hoping it would calm her racing pulse.

Huge mistake.

She got a lungful of his intoxicating scent, one that always reminded her of sex and adventure. It kicked her in the heart and libido.

"Thanks," he said without any inflection.

He stepped back like he wanted more space between them. Then he shifted his attention to Amel, and they started discussing who'd sing.

His cold demeanor morphed into a sharp spike, stabbing her.

She looked to see if blood was oozing from her chest.

Huh, nope.

Maggie snatched up her laptop, noticing it trembled. "Zia, can we talk about the next show?" She needed something, anything, to distract her divided heart.

Half belonged to music. The other half to Tanner.

That terrified her. What if she couldn't get over him? Would her constant ache take away from her desire to perform and write? Lately, she'd struggled with both.

She tucked the laptop under her arm, wanting to ignore the way it trembled from her overflowing emotions. Gripping her friend by the elbow, Maggie guided her out. When Zia protested, Maggie leaned in, "We have almost an hour. We need to talk."

"Yeah, I gathered from the computer you're carrying. Why do we have to leave? Where are we going?"

"I don't know. Somewhere private. A broom closet for all I care," Maggie muttered.

Zia snorted. "I heard rumors about you and janitor closets. I'd heard the kinky fun started after the show."

They both glanced back at the greenroom, to Tanner. Memories Maggie would rather not remember flooded her.

"Shut up, Zia," she hissed. "I don't want to fuck you. Or talk about work..."

Zia halted in her tracks. "Oh. My. God. You need girl talk." She peered around frantically. "I need to find a window."

Maggie huffed. "The sky isn't falling, asshole. You know what, forget it. I'm going to get Lincoln." She swiveled around. "He'd be better at this than you, anyway."

"Aww, come one." Zia caught up, grabbing Maggie's arm. "I'll listen. No more smart-ass remarks." She placed her hand over her heart. "Promise."

Maggie slumped against the wall. "The show. It's going to be torture. I don't want to fuck up on stage."

"Why? Because of Tanner?"

"Yes, Tanner. I swear, Zia, it hurts to look at him. How am I supposed to remember lyrics or sing past the nerves lodged in my throat?" She leaned against the cool cinderblocks, glaring at her friend, though the anger was for herself. "I knew from the beginning hooking up with him was a mistake."

Zia scowled, but her tone was gentle. "Tanner was never a simple fling. Not even in the beginning."

She was right. "Whatever."

"And," Zia continued, "your problem wasn't starting something with him. It was ending it."

"What the hell are you talking about? He basically called me a cold-hearted bitch who only slept with him to keep him in the band."

"I'm not saying he was right. I'm saying, you were no better. You didn't mention the tour to him. Your excuse was lame, saying he only needed to know if he was going to be there to play his damn guitar. Talk about cold. As his girlfriend, it was sub-zero cold. Plus, he didn't just walk out. I recall he wanted to work on things. You told him to leave."

"Shit," Maggie coughed on an exhale. "The freaking basement was supposed to be soundproofed. Did you guys enjoy the show?"

Zia laughed. "If you don't want the sound to carry, close the doors at the bottom *and* top of the stairs. Hell no, we didn't enjoy listening. We love both you idiots. Hearing you two screwing up a good thing was painful. *And* as your manager, I wasn't pleased to know another member was quitting. One, I might add," she said, pointing to her chest, "I found, and told you not to mess around with."

Maggie stiffened. "Don't blame him leaving ThreePence on me. He knew the day he'd shown up for the interview he was going to quit. Remember. His job offer."

"Yeah, maybe. Who knows, maybe if we'd discussed it, the whole group, he might have changed his mind," Zia sighed. "One thing I do know is he didn't plan on ending things with you."

The knife of regret began stabbing her again. She ignored the pain. "It wouldn't have lasted. Things were rough when he was recovering from the accident. How could we survive like that on a permanent basis?"

Zia shrugged. "I don't know. Maybe you wouldn't have. How would you know? You didn't even try."

Her remark hit Maggie in the solar plexus. Tanner had essentially said the same thing.

They're right.

Before she could respond, a stagehand came rushing in from the hall, stopping in front of them. "You guys need to gather your stuff. The opening act is finishing a little earlier than expected."

"Go ahead," Zia told Maggie. "I'll get the rest of the band."

She nodded, starting for the stage. Before she rounded the corner, Zia shouted after her. Maggie stopped, waiting.

"Right now, channel the pain into the music. After the show maybe, you should talk to Tanner. I've never seen you this torn up over a guy." She came closer and rested a hand on Maggie's shoulder. "I think this one is worth the effort."

Maggie gave a bitter laugh. "Even if you're right, I lost my chance. You saw how he was with me tonight."

She turned from her friend, hoping like hell she could focus on the music. On the fans. She'd lost her heart to Tanner. Hopefully it hadn't stopped beating for the music.

~ * ~

Tanner twisted the cold tap on and leaned over the sink, splashing water on his face and neck. He stood, water dripped on to his sweaty shirt, down to his still pounding heart. He'd forgotten the thrill of being on stage. Adrenaline was pumping through him like he'd run a marathon or just had spectacular sex.

Which, reminded him how he and Maggie used to work off their excess energy after shows. He halted that line of thinking.

Recalling their naked after show ritual wasn't wise. He needed his wits for when he convinced Maggie to come home with him.

He missed ThreePence, and he wanted her. He couldn't lose both.

He wasn't sure if she wanted him back as either a lover or a band member, but he was determined to find out. Tonight.

Getting back with the band wouldn't be a problem. After the show, Zia asked him if he was interested in covering for Scarlett during an upcoming West Coast tour. She didn't want to be far from her infant daughter for so many weeks. Even knowing it meant she wouldn't be a permanent member of ThreePence.

For him, it would mean leaving his job. Something changed within him over the last year, and this didn't bother him.

Sure, he still loved accounting. There was something soothing about the process. However, never composing, practicing, and performing with ThreePence hurt something deep within him.

The real problem was he wasn't sure if he could take being near Maggie every day. Knowing he'd never make love to her or listen to her husky laughter in the middle of the night as they lay wrapped in each other's arms. Those memories left him wanting to run back to his old life. The one before he'd met her.

Those days now seemed gray, but at least they didn't fucking hurt.

He wadded his dirty shirt in one hand, with the other, he opened the bathroom door. He was done contemplating and staring at his stupid reflection. They had to talk. Make some decisions.

He wanted to know if his anger and her stubbornness wrecked the love between them.

The greenroom wasn't far. He arrived at the same time Amel and Lincoln were leaving. He stopped, peering past them.

Everyone was gone.

"Where's Maggie?"

"She left with Zia, shortly after the show. They said some shit about 'girl time.'" Lincoln used his drumsticks to make air quotes.

Tanner's shoulders slumped. His gaze fell to his feet,

wondering if he'd find his hopes puddled down around his scuffed leather boots.

"We're going to an all-night diner around the corner with the opening band. Want to go with us?" Amel asked.

Tanner saw the pity reflected in his friend's eyes. He hated it.

"Nah, I'll pass. Thanks," He shuffled backward. "It's late, and I'm staying with a friend. I better head over to his place. With the new job, it's been a while since I've seen him." He was babbling and stopped, gave a halfhearted wave before turning to go.

Lincoln stopped him. "Hey, man, great having you back tonight."

Amel nodded. "I know we didn't work together very long, but you were first-rate then, and tonight as well."

"You're saying that because you want him to stay. Then you don't have to sing anymore." Lincoln laughed, thumping the other man on the shoulder. Amel was such a mountain of a man he probably didn't even feel it.

Amel grinned. "Yup. Caught me."

"I don't mind. Glad to give you a break from it tonight," Tanner said with a shrug. "Anyway, I gotta go."

Pushing through the exit door, he quickened his pace. The urge to run was strong. Not to get away from Amel or Lincoln, it was more he needed distance from ThreePence. In the span of one night, the pendulum swung from the ecstasy at being back, to the aching anguish at having Maggie close physically but far emotionally.

Reaching his bike, he slung a leg over, then readjusted his guitar before starting it. The engine roared to life, temporarily blocking the night sounds, but doing nothing to quiet his chaotic mind.

Chapter Thirty-Five

Tanner closed the front door quietly, then toed off his shoes. Stepping from the foyer into the living room, he caught sight of Jacob sitting in his dining room. Parts were scattered across every free inch of his table.

He trudged toward his friend, his legs tired as his heart. "Why are you awake, and what is that mess?"

Jacob scanned the disaster surrounding him, pushing his black hair from his eyes. "Hey, man. I wondered when you'd roll in. How was the show?"

"Euphoric bliss and gut-wrenching misery." Tanner surveyed the destruction. There was a black box, ivory keys, and silver pieces everywhere. "What the hell happened here?"

Jacob leaned back, setting aside a thin pair of pliers. "It's a typewriter from the late 1800s. A big accounting firm in Birmingham hired me to fix it. They want it to look brand new, and for some reason, they also want it to work." He paused, filling a tumbler with an amber liquid. "I hope they aren't going to make some poor soul use it."

"Yeah," Tanner shuddered at the thought. "No one wants to go back to the days of whiteout and jammed keys."

"You want some?" Jacob asked, indicating the bourbon sitting amongst the tools and strewn pieces.

Now that he mentioned a little bit of liquid oblivion would be perfect.

"Fuck yes," Tanner exhaled, shoving back his chair. "Where are your glasses?"

"Cupboard to the left of the stove."

He found one and returned, filling it almost to the brim before dropping in the chair across from Jacob. He quirked his brow but didn't comment when Tanner downed half the glass.

The heavy liquid burned his throat, landing like a warm cascade into his stomach. He hoped its effects reached his brain soon.

"I'm thinking the night was more torture than bliss," Jacob said wryly.

"Yeah, okay. Though being with the group and playing was sweet."

Jacob shook his head. "I still can't believe it. Back when we were kids, you used to complain all the time about working the shows. Now it's your 'happy place.'"

"I was a teen. It's what they do, complain. In truth, I made good money. Plus, playing with different bands pushed me to become a better musician. I didn't realize how much I missed it until joining with ThreePence."

"So, was the problem tonight with Maggie?"

Tanner slumped in his seat, defeat mixing with his drink. "I can't figure her out. When I first spotted her tonight, I swear I saw something. Regret, sadness…*something*. On stage, I'd caught a flash of it again." He swallowed another healthy swig of his drink, craving the burn. Rolling the empty tumbler between his palms, he continued, "Then the show ended, and she was gone. Not even a wave goodbye."

Jacob played with the letter Q, then let it fall to the table. Tanner didn't have a clue what the other man was thinking. He was difficult to read. His thoughts could be on what Tanner told him, or he could be wondering how to fix the typewriter carcass before him.

Before his fiancé Greta, Jacob had been a machine. After his mom died all that mattered was taking care of his father and brother, and building his antique repair business, Rework. His only desire was becoming a successful businessman.

Until she came along, his complete opposite. Then it was like cupid shot him with an arrow. Twice. He couldn't stay away from the woman, no matter the roadblocks. And there were plenty.

"Did I ever tell you Greta pegged you and Maggie as a couple way before you two ever became one? At the barbeque last year. I told her she was way off base." Jacob paused, before muttering, "You know she was also right about Macy, too…"

Tanner was confused. "Wasn't Macy the lady who used to work for you?"

"Yeah. Anyway, it's not important." Jacob waved away the thread of the conversation. "What I was saying was Greta took one look at you two, saw the connection. And she was right. A blind person could see the sparks between you and Maggie."

He's going with relationship advice. This should be interesting.

Tanner motioned for Jacob to pass him the bourbon. He complied, and Tanner filled his glass. After a healthy sip, he said, "Could she also see we wouldn't last?"

He hated the bitterness in his voice.

"You sure it's really over?"

"Well, before tonight I haven't seen her in almost a month.

When I did, she ignored me. Plus, I'm here, getting drunk with you instead in her bed. So, yeah, I'd say we're finished."

"Hey, man, for the record you're the only one getting sloshed." Jacob chuckled. When he spoke again, his tone was serious. "Maybe she left because it'd shaken her, seeing you again?"

Tanner tried to absorb what his friend said, but he didn't drink often, and the bourbon was strong. Things were starting grow fuzzy.

While he sat, trying to decide if he should finish off his second glass or truly consider Jacob's words, someone came pounding down the steps from the loft. The footfalls were too heavy to be Greta's.

Tanner turned in his seat. Jacob's brother, Will, came striding toward them. He was the older sibling by two years, a lighter version of Jacob, with brown eyes and hair. When they were neighbors, the three of them were thick as thieves.

Will stopped, gripping the rounded arch. "Damn, Tanner, you look like shit." His gaze jumped between Tanner and the empty liquor glass.

Self-reproach flooded him. The last person who needed to be around someone halfway in the bottle was Will. "What are you doing here? Didn't you move out?"

"I did. Months ago. I stopped by after work for a visit, got roped into helping him," Will pointed to his brother, "with wedding planning and some work he's behind on."

He sat next to Tanner, then waved a hand in front of him. "Damn. Did you dive into the bottle?"

Tanner slumped. "Sorry, man."

"Chill," he chuckled. "You drunk isn't going send me on a bender. I do work in a restaurant. They serve alcohol."

"Whatever, shit's not helping anyway." Tanner pushed away his glass.

He didn't care what Will said, or the fact he'd been clean for more than three years. Tanner knew the fight hadn't been easy and the struggle with addiction was truly never over.

"You and Greta decided to have the wedding next summer, right?" Tanner asked, wanting to change the subject.

"Yes," Will exhaled dramatically. "Everything is on hold until Princess Cinderella returns from her sojourn."

Tanner was confused. "Who's Princess Cinderella?"

"Greta's sister Cindy," Jacob answered, sighing. "Will's never met her but has decided he doesn't like her."

Will opened his mouth, but Jacob waved him off. "Anyway, back to you and your problems."

"No, thanks, I'm golden. Let's talk about wedding plans instead."

They sat in silence for three seconds before bursting into ruckus laughter.

When Tanner could take a full breath again, he sat forward, elbows on the table. "Oh, shit that felt good. Anyway, I'll leave you to your work. I'm beat." He stood slowly, the alcohol playing with his limbs, making him a little unsteady.

Will stopped him with a hand on his shoulder. "Is it work or women? The problem."

Tanner sat back down heavily. "Both."

"Spill, man."

"Yeah," agreed Jacob. "Spill. Will practically has a vagina. He's perfect for these heart to hearts."

Will flipped his brother off, smiling. "Ignore the caveman. It wasn't long ago he was a miserable sack of man, needing his big brother's advice."

Jacob scoffed, but didn't disagree.

Will stood, moving to the kitchen, saying, "Okay, let's start with the easier of the two, the career." He opened a cupboard, grabbing a cup. After filling it with water he returned, giving the glass to Tanner. "Would ThreePence take you back? And is it difficult to get a CPA job?"

"Yes. No."

"So, if you left where you work to follow the music and down the road you decide being a musician isn't for you, could you get another job?"

"I suppose I could," Tanner answered, after drinking some water.

This option didn't sit well with him. He wasn't sure if it was because he wanted it, or because it bothered him to let a childhood fantasy die. The one where he lived a quiet, structured life.

He was too drunk to choose. "Okay, Dr. Grimm, let's shelve that for now. Tell me how to solve women."

Will flopped into a chair. "My first advice would be, don't get in too deep. Though I'd say it's too late for you."

Tanner shrugged.

"Do you love her?"

"Yeah."

"Did she cheat? Kill your puppy?"

Tanner's inebriated brain shuttered. "I don't have a dog."

"Dude, drink more water, you're drunk. I mean, has she done

something unforgivable?"

"No."

"Work it out. It's that simple. Not difficult."

"Man, I can't wait until you fall," Jacob cut in. "Then you'll understand the difficult part."

"I understand it," Will said simply. He didn't elaborate, but the silence whispered much.

Tanner dimly remembered Will dating the same girl through high school and after. Jolene was her name. They did everything together, including getting high. It hadn't ended well for either of them.

After a couple ticks of silence, Will leaned his chair back on two legs and smirked at his brother. "Now shut up, douchebag. Let the man hear my many pearls of wisdom."

"Pearls of wisdom," Jacob repeated in a mocking tone, but rolled his hand, in the go-ahead gesture.

"Don't fuck around," Will continued. "You love her, tell her. Fix it."

"Oh, it's that easy?" Tanner grunted.

"I never said it was, but if you love her, it's worth it. Don't waste time. It's not infinite. And I'm not even talking about all my shit. Have you ever met Lucas?"

"Poor bastard." Jacob muttered.

Tanner wasn't sure he wanted to know.

"That's right. We'd become friends with him after you left the neighborhood. Anyway, after being married less than two years, someone from his wife's work calls, telling him she'd fainted and was rushed to the hospital. She never woke. Passed away two days later. The doctors said it was some coronary artery problem. She was three days shy of her thirty-first birthday when she died." Will snapped his fingers. "Gone."

"Damn, Will," Tanner said after a deep swallow of water. "Is that an argument for or against love? The guy must be devastated."

"Well, yeah. Although he doesn't regret being with her. Falling in love and marriage. No, he told me his regrets lay in the time he wasted without her."

Tanner gave a shaky laugh. "You're telling me I should make up with Maggie because one of us might die tomorrow?"

"No, asshole. Man, you're dense as my brother," Will grumbled. Jacob tossed a fistful of typewriter keys at his brother. He ducked, then looked back at Tanner. "I meant, if you love her, don't waste time on stupid shit. Stop drowning your sorrows or using some other dumb, idiotic tactic. Go to her. Talk to her, even if it's to find out she doesn’t feel the same. If she doesn’t, it’ll help you get over her. Believe me.”

“Maybe.” Tanner wasn’t sure if he honestly agreed. Pain, confusion, and bourbon crowded his brain. He shook his head. “Enough. It’s late. My mind is fucked. Tell me what’s going on with you guys.”

Chapter Thirty-Six

Maggie pressed the doorbell to Tanner's townhouse, noticing the slight tremble in her hand. She focused on the ugly green paint on the door, instead of picking apart her whirling and chipped emotions.

Sounds from the TV drifted through the door. Good.

She'd been too nervous to call before coming to his place. She was afraid he'd see her number and wouldn't answer his phone. Or worse, tell her to leave him alone.

Standing at Tanner's door was like being at the top of a metaphorical rollercoaster. She wasn't sure if she was prepared for the fall.

Would it end in delight or devastation?

She'd never put herself out for rejection. Sure, many times for her music, for her band, but never for a man.

Never for love.

I can't do this. It's bullshit what people say. Rejection is worse than not knowing.

She was one heartbeat away from bailing when the door swung open. Colton's tall, muscular frame stood before her.

If he was surprised at her unexpected arrival, he hid it. "Come in."

He moved aside, opening the door wider. She left the porch, stepping directly into the small living room.

Tanner was dozing on the couch. He was flat on his back. One long leg stretched out, the other slid off the sofa, his barefoot resting on the wood floor. There was a small pile of papers resting on his chest.

Colton closed the door and bellowed, "Hey, Tanner! You've got company."

His booming voice bounced around the confined space, startling her. Tanner shot up, spilling papers all over the floor.

He looked slightly wild, eyes blurry from sleep, with his hair sticking up in odd places. He was quite adorable.

Reaching down, he gathered the papers into a pile, setting them on a coffee table. "Asshole," Tanner croaked over Colton's laughter. "I swear you do that one more time—"

Whatever else he was going to say died when his eyes met her.

His gaze seemed to swallow her.

"What are you doing here?" He sounded curious, not angry.

"I need to talk to you," she said.

He didn't answer, only studied her. It unnerved her, making her shuffle from foot to foot, like an anxious kindergartener

"I'm leaving. I need to get some, um, milk," Colton said, cutting into the increasingly awkward silence. He waved at Maggie, before slipping past her, pulling the door shut behind him.

"Milk?"

Tanner snorted. "Dude's lactose intolerant. He's not real good with silence and tension. He'll say anything to escape it." His smile fell. "Who'd you talk to? Zia or Scarlett?"

What do they have to do with anything?

"Neither." She almost asked why. Telling him what she'd come to say before losing her nerve was more important. "Can we talk?"

He nodded, motioning for her to sit. More than anything, she wanted to crawl onto his lap. To curl up and wrap her arms around his neck, cuddling into his warm, strong chest.

Resisting temptation, she sat at the farthest end from him.

"I miss you," she stated bluntly, opening her heart, offering it to him to caress or cut.

Something seemed to soften in him for half a second before his lips thinned, and the muscle in his jaw twitched. "I miss you, too, but you've made it clear, you're done with me."

"I was angry. And scared. I didn't mean it."

"It took you, what, a month to decide you didn't mean it?" He sounded cold, uncaring.

Dread made her words freeze behind her lips. She was too late

Swallowing her nerves and second-guesses, she began talking. "I've never been in love. I don't know how to do this." She shrugged, helpless when facing her mistakes. "I messed up."

He rubbed his eyes, studying her. He wore an expression of pure exhaustion. "What made you come here tonight? Really?"

He was acting like she had an ulterior motive. She didn't understand it and tried again. "I'm here because I love you. I'll never be done with you. I don't care that you don't want to be in the band. I want to be with you."

"Don't want to be with the band," he echoed her words, sounding confused. He studied her, seeming confused. "Have you talked to anyone in ThreePence recently? I gave work my two weeks' notice. I'm going on tour with you."

~ * ~

Maggie gaped at him, one hand resting on her neck. Did she not know?

She'd been careless with his heart countless times, but never deceitful. Not once. Not with him.

Tanner wasn't sure what to believe. He wanted more than anything for her words and motives to be true. For her to have come to him wanting to repair things between them not because he was back with ThreePence but because she missed him.

He wanted it to be true so bad he ached.

How could she not know?

She huffed out a laugh. "I wondered why none of those assholes were answering or returning my calls." She leaned back into the couch, covering her face. "Shitheads."

Tanner broke into a grin that reached his freaking soul. Maggie clearly was aggravated and confused, but he wanted to dance.

It was after ten at night, yet it felt like the summer sun was shining on him.

"I went to Scarlett first," he said, "wanting to know if she liked being back. She told me she doesn't want to leave the band altogether but working full-time sucked. She wants to sub. We went to Zia, and she was fine with the change if the rest of you were cool with it. Lincoln agreed, and Amel was more than happy with me taking over the vocals again." Tanner chuckled, recalling Amel's happy dance at the prospect. No joke, the guy hated the limelight.

Tanner waited for Maggie's response. Her brow furrowed, and her bottom lip was caught between her teeth.

Did he misunderstand her earlier? Maybe she wanted him back as a boyfriend but not in her band.

His heart skipped a beat when he asked, "The only one left to ask is you. Do you want me back? In ThreePence?"

She blinked, and her anger seemed to pop. In the next second, she was catapulting into his arms. "What? Are you crazy? Yes, I want you back."

He didn't realize the tide of misery he'd was drowning in until her lips were on his. Then he was like a drowning man taking his first breath of air.

Twining his finger through her short hair, he deepened the kiss, parting her lips and making up for the weeks they were apart. She moaned, and he reveled in the exquisite sound.

When they broke for a moment, he rested his forehead against hers. "Did any of them know you were coming here?"

"Zia did." Maggie's brows furrowed. "Why didn't she say

anything?"

"Because she was being a friend. Not manager." He kissed the crease between Maggie's brows, then the tip of her nose. "You came here believing I wasn't coming back to ThreePence. Knowing it would be difficult. You didn't care. You were willing to try. Do you know what that means to me?"

Tanner was positive, winning the lottery wouldn't feel this damn good. He'd won his heart, his Maggie.

He loved his stubborn, strong and fierce woman.

"When you walked through my door," he continued, "I'd have taken any piece you were willing to give. Pissed me off. And in the end, it might have ruined us. Instead, Zia let you come here as my girlfriend, not a band member."

"You want me? Do you love me?" she whispered, her breath mingling with his.

"God, yes" He kissed her, quick and firm. "I've wanted you since I first laid eyes on you. The only difference now is I also want ThreePence."

"For me, or yourself?"

"Both. Being a CPA is great but isn't for me anymore. I'm not going to lie; the unstable life ahead is terrifying. However, without music, my days have become gray and dull. A huge part was losing you. Though, just as much, I missed the thrill of performing. I missed creating. Writing lyrics and working with everyone to turn it into a melody, a song."

He studied her, considering. "Do you want me back with the band, or just you? You seemed upset that I'm rejoining the band. Does it bother you we don't have an expiration date? Are you worried us working together and dating will be too much? If so, I don't want to lose you. I'll find another band."

Maggie pushed him playfully. "Don't you dare."

He fell back into the couch with her on top of him. His arm wrapped securely around her waist. She kissed his neck, jawline, and finally, his lips.

Between kisses, she said, "You're mine. And you're ThreePence's."

"I wouldn't have it any other way."

Chapter Thirty-Seven

Tanner trailed his tongue between her breasts, moving to the center of her body, nipping and kissing a sensual path. He reached the apex of her legs and paused, inches from her heat.

Maggie whimpered, arching up. He kissed her. Then nothing more. She shifted on her elbows, looking down the length of her body at him.

His gaze flickered to hers, eyes hungry, unfocused. He didn't move.

Was he trying to drive her insane with need? Make her beg? Fine. She would.

"Tanner, please..."

"Pleading voices." He ran his fingertips along the inner side of her thigh, making her shiver and her skin rise as if greeting him.

"Begging skin," he whispered, his hot breath a ghost caress. His almost touch had everything female in her pleading for more.

"Jesus, Tanner." She sounded desperate and didn't care. "Don't compose a song. Make love to me."

"If your body isn't worth a song, I don't know what is..."

She gave a cocky smile. "I didn't say it wasn't, just not now. Now I want you to do other things with your perfectly sinful mouth."

And, oh heaven above, he did.

Later, Tanner lay flat on his back. Maggie snuggled into the warmth of his chest, his heartbeat a wild staccato against her ear. She sat up, grinning. "My, my, honey, your heart is racing. Are you going to be okay?"

"If my heart gives out right now, I'd die a happy man." He ran a hand over the back of her head, resting at her neck. "Where in the hell did you learn to do that thing with your tongue? And why haven't you done it before?"

"Came to me today. I guess I inspire your lyrical side. You inspire my lascivious side."

Multiple fists pounded on their hotel door, and they both jumped. Lincoln's voice carried through, muffled but understandable. "Are you two ever going to leave your room? We're supposed to do a meet and greet before the show."

"Oh damn. Right. I forgot." Tanner headed for the shower while shouting to the guys, "We'll be there in twenty."

Lincoln knocked again, with less force. "You better be, or I'm going to have Amel break down the damn door and drag you two lovebirds out, naked or not."

"Dude, you're getting Tanner, I'll get Maggie," came Amel's deep rumbling voice.

"Assholes." Maggie laughed, then shouted, "It'd make for interesting press."

Their laughter filtered through the metal door. Seconds later, she heard their retreating footfalls.

Tanner peered at her from the bathroom door, steam billowing around him. "Don't even think about it, Maggie. We don't need the media attention that bad. Hell, we're playing at the Red Rock."

Fireworks of euphoria burst through her body at the mention of her favorite amphitheater. She flung back the covers and sprinted toward him. He stepped around the door, catching her. Damn, she loved the way his warm, firm body fit against hers.

"I know!" She said gleefully, happiness rushing through her veins. "I still can't believe it. We're the opening act, and I bet by next year we'll be the headliner."

"With you as the driving force behind us, I'm sure it'll come true." He kissed her ear. "Now let's conserve water. Get in the shower with me."

She slid her legs over the side of the bed till her toes touched the floor. "Last time we took one together we stayed in there until the water ran cold."

"I promise to be good this time." He smirked, bringing her close. "Or at least quick. I can have us clean and satisfied in less than ten minutes. I'll even have time to check on my clients."

"Do you need help?"

"No. I woke up early this morning. Finished what I needed and emailed it back to them. I'll check later to see if they have any questions."

He'd decided to take on a few finance clients, to keep him up-to-date in the accounting world. A backup plan, in case he ever decided to go back full time.

Tanner had been right. Their shower was fast. And incredibly satisfying. They even managed two minutes to spare before the meet and greet started.

Waiting for the elevator, Maggie entwined their fingers. He smiled at her. The love in his eyes stole her breath.

Before Tanner, she believed selfless love didn't exist. She'd been dead wrong.

The need to put her career before Tanner didn't exist because she knew he'd never ask. He supported her driven nature, not wanting to be the person holding her back.

Now that she didn't fear choosing one or the other, she craved a balance between love and passion. So far, they'd found it.

Their fame would grow or recede. They might want to start a family. Whatever they decided, they'd adjust. Together.

Apart, they were an incomplete melody. Together, they were a unique, wondrous love song.

About the Author

DK Marie loves to indulge in all things hot. Men, writing, reading, and coffee. The order of importance depends on the day.

Like characters in her books, she lives in Michigan, enjoying her happily-ever-after with her husband and kids. When not indulging in all things hot, she loves theater, concerts, and to travel.

DK loves to hear from readers. You can find and connect with her at the links below.

Website: www.dkmarie.com
Twitter: https://twitter.com/dkmarie2216s
Facebook: http://facebook.com/dkanso
Pinterest: https://www.pinterest.de/DKmarie/
Instagram: http://instagram.com/dkmarie2216
Goodreads: https://goodreads.com/user/show/52007413-dk-marie

~ * ~

We hope you enjoyed *Love Songs,* book 2 in the *Opposites Attract* contemporary romance series. If you did, please write a review, tell your friends, or check out the other offerings at Champagne Book Group.

Now turn the page for a peek into *Fairy Tale* Lies, book 1 of the *Opposites Attract* series.

Fairy Tale Lies

Opposites Attract, Book 1
By DK Marie

Greta and Jacob aren't looking for love, but when they meet, their attraction is white hot, melting away all self-restraint.

Both times.

The first is a stormy spring afternoon, spent indulging in each other's bodies. When they're abruptly interrupted, they part ways convinced they're nothing more than an erotic chapter in the other's life.
However, when they unexpectedly meet again, Jacob isn't willing to let Greta slip away. He convinces her to give them a chance.

Lust turns to love, but resentments fester. Jacob's convinced Greta will never see him as anything more than a blue-collar nobody. A temporary indulgence. Greta fears she isn't strong enough to stand against both her family's scorn and Jacob's growing anger.

As tempers flare and passions deepen, they have to decide if their love is strong enough to shatter the cynicism and misconceptions of what it means to be each other's fairytale ending.

Chapter One

Greta Meier dashed down the carpeted hallway of Swift Financial, ignoring the agony of power walking in three-inch heels. That pain was minuscule compared to the dread pooling in her stomach. She'd lost track of time. Again.

Sure, she'd managed to fix the in-house software issue but, meanwhile, had forgotten the new client meeting. Glancing at her tiny gold Rolex, she groaned. Less than five minutes to make it to the other end of the building.

She could picture her boss's disappointed face, made all the more stressful because it was her father. The image had Greta quickening her pace to a near sprint.

Rounding the final corner, she sighed. The large glass doors were propped open. Relief calmed some of her anxiety. She wasn't late.

Inside the conference room, her assistant Rae motioned to the empty seat next to her. Greta nodded and skated alongside the outermost edges of the table, wishing she were smaller, invisible. She hoped no one would notice her near tardy arrival. The last thing she wanted was to come across as the empty-headed daughter of the boss. Someone who'd gotten the internship through nepotism. Therefore, any misstep ate at her confidence like termites to wood.

She took her seat next to Rae and tried to squash her rampant doubts. Running a shaky hand over her chignon, she made sure every hair was in place.

"Where's Allen?" Greta glanced around the table while needlessly straightening the collar of her pale, pink blouse. Realizing she was fidgeting, putting her anxiety on full display, she stilled and met Rae's gaze.

She handed the client folder Greta hadn't had time to open and sighed. "Another virus was detected on Blake's computer. He demanded we fix it, like yesterday. Allen's working on it."

Greta accepted the portfolio, her worry shifting to annoyance. She didn't want to talk about her ex-fiancé, much less be reminded he was in-house counsel. Before their breakup, they hardly ran into each other at work. Now Blake kept inventing problems with his PC and contacting the IT department. Rae and Allen found it hilarious, but Greta despised the drama. It made her and Blake appear unprofessional.

Refusing to meet Rae's playful smile, Greta peered down the table at her father. His back was to a large window with its blinds pulled. The leaves from the giant elm and oak trees swayed in a lazy breeze, helping to block Michigan's hot summer sun from the room. She'd love to be out there, relaxing in the shade, enjoying her summer and free of stress.

Her gaze zeroed back in on her father, and the usual mixture of pride and discontent filled her. She understood he only wanted the best for her, but sometimes his rigidness was stifling. Carrying her father's expectations, and his disappointment of her, was a heavy burden to shoulder.

Thankfully, he hadn't noticed her near-late arrival time. There'd be no displeased glances, no lectures concerning punctuality. He appeared distracted, deep in conversation with a man she assumed was a new client.

She gave an inward sigh of relief, allowing some of her distress to dissolve. Father's career talks turned back the clock, and suddenly she was closer to seven than twenty-seven. Enjoying the reprieve, she relaxed into her seat and studied the client. He sat sideways, elbow propped on the table, large hand covering most of his face as he talked with her father. There was something familiar in the set of the client's broad shoulders and his inky black hair.

Inexplicably, her heart began to race. Watching him filled her with trepidation and an unexpected yearning.

Her father faced the room, pulling her gaze from the stranger to the wall clock. Yup, ten on the dot. A meeting never started late.

She glanced back at the client and choked on an exhale, her heart plummeting. He'd dropped his hand and was facing forward.

It can't be him.

Her heart skipped with joy. Then promptly flooded with dread.

"You okay?" Rae whispered. Her voice sounded far away, wrapped in fog.

Greta couldn't answer because the client's familiar icy-blue gaze had locked on hers. His eyes widened in recognition.

He was clean-shaven, and today his hair was neat and combed back, but there was no mistaking him. *Jacob*. He had one of those striking faces, impossible to forget. The memories of the way those bedroom eyes had heated as he'd taken in her naked body, or how those full lips had ravished her, made him unforgettable.

However, she wished he'd slip from her memory and the conference room. Whatever his reason for being here wouldn't be good for her.

"Good morning. Let me introduce Mr. Jacob Grimm."

Hearing his name, he turned toward her father, allowing her to breathe.

Rae nudged Greta, probably waiting for an answer. Too bad. She was admitting nothing.

"He runs Rework, a business repairing and refurbishing antiques. We're taking it to the next level," continued her father. "He plans on opening a brick-and-mortar shop in Detroit and developing a better online presence."

Business owner? No, no, no.

There had been some mistake. He wasn't supposed to be sitting at her father's conference table. Jacob was a deliveryman. He worked for his uncle. It's what he told her at her mother and stepfather's home. So, why wasn't he lifting heavy things and breaking promises?

Greta flipped through the file Rae had given her. Successful was an understatement. His client base was impressive, as were the big names in the dossier. Stapled to the back of the folder was a copy of Jacob's license.

Foolish woman. Hadn't her father always told her to come to a meeting prepared? Had she even glanced at the file, she'd have recognized Jacob in an instant. Weeks had passed, but that foolish, impulsive afternoon was far from forgotten.

As her father addressed the room, Greta focused on Jacob's picture. She found it safer than facing the actual man.

They'd only spent a couple of hours together, but his wicked full mouth and penetrating gaze had been impossible to forget. Along with his magical ability to destroy all her restraints. Greta still couldn't quite believe how easily her inhibitions had fled in the company of a perfect stranger.

She closed the folder and rubbed her sweaty palms on her pleated linen skirt. She stared at her father and tried to concentrate on his words, though he could've been speaking another language and she wouldn't have noticed.

There was no way she could swallow her embarrassment and work with Jacob. Not even for a day, let alone a week or more.

Her pulse thudded in her ears. What if he bragged about his one-night-stand with the boss's daughter? Father would kill her. Not literally, but professionally. He wouldn't want the family name smeared with tawdry office gossip.

He'd promised, after she graduated with her Master's in Web Development, she'd take over Swift's websites and handle the clients needing web development help. Would the offer still stand if he learned of her history with Jacob?

So much for proving herself with a summer internship. Greta wanted to weep at the disappearance of her imagined stellar portfolio. Swift Financial would have been wonderful on her resume.

Focus. I need to focus and get control of the situation.

Leaning in, she whispered to Rae, "I need to go. Would you and Allen mind handling this account? I'll owe you one."

"What's wrong?" Rae's forehead furrowed in concern.

That question was too big to answer now. Later. "Will you do this for me?"

Rae bit her lip. "I'll try, but you know your father wants you in charge of web designing."

Yes, I know. Hopefully I'll come up with a stellar excuse to wiggle out of the Rework contract.

She'd worry about it later and mouthed a thank you and gathered her papers. When there was a pause in the main conversation, she addressed the room. "I'm sorry. There's been a mistake. Allen Carnaby will handle this account with Mrs. Caitlin." She stood. "I'll find him."

Her father's stern voice stopped her. "No, Ms. Meier, the account is yours and Mrs. Caitlin's. I have another project in mind for Mr. Carnaby." His tone brooked no argument.

Darn it. There went her quick and painless getaway.

She nodded. To argue was pointless and would only anger her father. Returning to her seat, she glanced covertly at Jacob. He'd lost most of his color and looked like he'd been poked with a cattle prod.

Replaying the exchange, she realized she'd been addressed by her last name. Jacob must have caught it, grasped its significance. He appeared rattled.

Good.

Maybe he didn't want to share their secret any more than she did. Thank goodness. It would save her from her father's wrath.

Next challenge—squashing her lingering thrill at seeing Jacob again.

Chapter Two

Her, of all people!

Jacob blinked. Nope, she hadn't disappeared back into his fantasies. Her!

He tried not to stare but found it difficult to accept the rapid-fire shocks. The most nerve-racking item of the day was supposed to be signing his financial dream on the dotted line. Instead, he sat face to face with the woman who haunted an entirely different set of dreams.

He'd strived to banish the memory of their spring afternoon together. He wanted to forget the way her laughter had made him lighter, more alive. He'd tried to forget those soulful hazel eyes and sexy, full lips. Lips made for kissing.

He sure as hell hadn't forgotten the way she'd barely given him time to dress before shoving him out the back door. Confused and insulted, he'd returned to the grand salon, or whatever rich people called those extra useless rooms, to help his uncle finish the job. She'd disappeared, obviously embarrassed by him and what they'd done.

Going by her current reaction, things hadn't changed. She still saw him as a weed in her impeccably manicured life.

Not that he wanted to make their past known. A Meier, not a Silverstone!

The delivery order had clearly stated the items were for a Silverstone residence. Hadn't she made the comment the home was her parents'?

Shit. Was she Charles Meier's niece, daughter, or young wife? Each one of those options landed like a brick in his gut.

Seriously, of all the women in the world, why did it have to be her? Here? Now?

His life revolved around building Rework. His focus so complete, he couldn't remember the last time he'd been on a date or even noticed a pretty woman.

Then two months ago, his uncle Marty called, asking if he'd help deliver and install an antique chandelier. Jacob agreed, expecting nothing more than a little extra cash.

Instead, he'd been knocked on his ass at the mere sight of the woman who answered the door. Her jewel-like amber eyes, accented with those full lips, was captivating. What's more, after they'd left for lunch and talked, her confident reserve and quiet ferocity seduced him. To his surprise, she was as drawn to him as he to her. Watching her struggle between virtue and wickedness, and letting her wild side win, had been the hottest thing he'd ever experienced.

"Mr. Grimm?"

He gave a mental shake and focused on Charles. Freaking Charles *Meier*. "Sorry, what did you say?" Jacob was proud at how calm he sounded.

A Meier, not a Silverstone...

"Would you please accompany Mrs. Caitlin and Ms. Meier to their office," her father or uncle or husband repeated.

Jacob suspected Charles made this request a few times.

"They'll need your insight for the new webpage and additional information to upgrade your accounts."

"Okay. No problem," Jacob replied.

The two men stood and shook hands. Jacob's was trembling, but at least he'd been able to talk past the anxiety trying to claw its way out of his throat.

He followed the two women from the conference room, wondering if he'd jeopardized years of hard work with one impulsive and incredibly hot afternoon. He couldn't lose his contract with Swift Financial. Every bank had turned him down, said his company was 'too niche', this was his last chance.

What was she to Charles Meier? Would she tell him how'd they met and what they'd done?

Sleeping with his wife or daughter might be enough to have the man searching for loopholes in the contract and dumping Rework.

Once in the corridor, Jacob moved next to the women. His focus shifted from the woman who used and dumped him, to the pretty African-American. She was watching him with open curiosity.

He didn't want to have this conversation with an audience. "Greta, can we talk... alone?"

She didn't even bother looking in his direction, answering in an imperious tone and sounding like the princess she thought she was. "No. There's no need, and please address me as Ms. Meier."

The other woman gasped, her gaze jumping between him and Greta. "You two know each other?"

"Yes," Jacob replied.

Greta spoke over him. "Not really."

The hell she didn't. Was she going to pretend they were

complete strangers?

"Mr. Grimm," came a man's voice from the conference room.

All three swung around at the unexpected interruption.

The guy stumbled back. Jacob could only imagine the expressions on their faces.

"We forgot to have you sign a couple of things. Will you please come back? I'll show you to the IT office after."

Jacob ran a hand down his face, peering at Greta. From the hard set of her jaw and defensive posture, her talking probably wasn't going to happen. He nodded to the man, moving away from the two women.

Before returning to the conference room, he stopped and faced Greta. "We aren't finished. We have to talk."

The prospect didn't seem to please her but screw it, he needed answers. And to set things straight. There was no way she was going to ruin this for him. After years at a standstill, his business was moving forward.

~ * ~

Before Jacob's large frame had retreated inside the conference room, Rae twisted around and seized Greta's shoulders. "Spill, woman. Please tell me you've had sex with him."

"Rae!" Greta whisper-shouted, checking the hallway. Thankfully, they were alone.

"What?" Rae's tone was pure innocence. Her smile was pure wickedness. "That guy was created for sensual nights."

Or stormy afternoons.

"Geez, Rae. You're married."

Rae's smile widened, and she looped an arm through Greta's, leading them back to their office. "Yes, and happily. But I'm not blind. Now, tell me, how do you know our newest hotter-than-hell client?"

Rae's petite frame and dainty features hid an oversized personality, one that was opinionated and outspoken. She was the complete opposite of Greta. Despite this, or maybe because of it, they'd become fast friends. However, it didn't mean Rae wasn't always shocking Greta.

Like now, with her blunt assessment of Swift's newest client.

"I'd rather not say," she clipped. "Just know this. He's a problem I don't need right now."

"Honey, life's full of problems. At least he appears to be an interesting one. Heck, sometimes problems turn into answers you didn't even know you were searching for."

Greta was in no mood for whimsical notions. "Doubtful. I'm

back under my father's roof for the summer, trying to prove my worth as a web developer, while also in the final stretch of my master's program. I have enough stress. I don't need to add man-drama to the mix."

"Me thinks the lady doth protest too much."

"Not so, Shakespeare." Greta laughed lightly, though her smile faded when they reached the IT department, reminding her she'd be stuck here with Jacob for at least a week, maybe more, depending on what he needed. "There has to be a way out. I can't work with him."

Once inside, Rae closed the door then pulled her chair next to Greta's. From her friend's tenacious expression she wouldn't rest until the whole story was told.

She laid a gentle hand on Greta's arm. "Did something bad happen with him?"

Touched by Rae's concern, some of Greta's embarrassment slid away. "No. Nothing like you're imagining."

She had no desire to reveal her sexual escapades. At the same time, she didn't want Rae to think Jacob was some deviant. He might be careless with another's emotions; however, she wouldn't risk the small possibility of sabotaging his career with false gossip.

Time to fess up. "I behaved shamelessly with him, and now I'll be reminded of it daily."

Rae frowned, perhaps in confusion.

Greta sighed. "I'll tell you, if you promise me two things."

"Sure. What do you need?"

"One," Greta ticked off her conditions on the tips of her fingers, "don't judge. Two, could you talk to my father about covering the Rework account?"

"The first one's easy. We've all made mistakes, and, like I've said before, he looks like a fun one." Rae winked. "And I'll do my best with the second."

The woman was incorrigible. Greta couldn't help smiling. "Okay." She took in a deep breath. "Around two months back, my mother and stepfather were out of town, and their housekeeper was on vacation. My mother needed me at their place."

"The estate?" Rae asked.

"Yes. They needed me there to accept a delivery…"

Chapter Three

Two months earlier, midmorning.

Greta twisted her key in the lock of the large oak double door to her mother and stepfather's house and peered over her shoulder at the sky. Wind whipped through the trees and angry clouds gathered, promising a wicked May storm. The air gave off a vibe of rowdy danger.

Trepidation ran down her spine, and goosebumps rose on her arms. Even as an adult, she disliked thunderstorms. The violent beauty and chaos unsettled her. She preferred things calm and safe.

Stepping inside, she dropped her purse and keys on the vestibule's delicate antique table. After heaving the heavy door closed, she disengaged the alarm then headed for the kitchen, passing the circular stairway on the long trek to the back of the house.

Her t-strap sandals clicked along the marble floor and echoed off the walls. The sound was desolate and usually bothered her. Not today. Right now, her sole focus was on getting that first cup of coffee.

Striding through the high-arched entrance of the kitchen, Greta made a beeline for the coffeemaker. After starting it, she leaned against the counter and yawned, wishing she'd stayed the night instead of getting up early to make the drive from her father's place.

Her mother wasn't home, waiting to dissect Greta's life, pointing out the ways she was lacking. Guilt fused with frustration. Her attitude was ungrateful, but her mother's overbearing ways chafed.

She'd hoped after moving away for college, the dynamics between them would change. No such luck. Whenever she visited during school breaks, her mother ran her life like a drill sergeant. Paraded her around to every boring social event in Petite Bois, and making sure everyone knew Greta was dating Blake, the most eligible bachelor.

After the breakup, Mother berated Greta privately for leaving Blake and insisted she give him another chance. If she spent too much time with her mother, she might wear her down. Not because she loved or wanted Blake, more from pure exhaustion. Mother was relentless.

That fear kept visits brief and infrequent.

They'd begun dating her last year of high school. Blake's family was longtime friends with both her mother and father and her family adored, heck still adored, him.

She had too, in the beginning. His confidence and cockiness made her feel sheltered and protected. Though, after a time, his arrogance and vanity ate at her admiration. The final offense was his wandering eye…and body.

Recalling the image of him kissing the curvy blonde, his hands under her skirt was no longer a punch in the gut. Instead, the overwhelming sensation was relief. Marrying Blake would have been a disaster.

It ate at her, all she'd given him. Three years of her life, her virginity, and for a while, her dignity. There was also the colossal mistake she made when they were together. The one in which she suggested he work for Swift. Even hinted to her father that Blake would be a perfect fit and put his resume on the top of the pile. That last blunder was coming back to haunt her this summer.

The coffee machine dinged, bringing Greta to the present. She stifled another yawn and grabbed a mug. The deliverymen were supposed to arrive between ten and one. The way these things worked, they'd probably turn up fifteen minutes after one.

Before the thought was even fully formed, the eerie chime of the doorbell echoed through the silent house, startling her. So much for the theory of late arrivals. The bell rang seconds later. She set her empty cup on the counter and made her way back to the front.

Impatient people. I mean, give me a minute to make it to the door.

"I'm coming," she called pointlessly; the trek from the kitchen to the front of the house wasn't a couple of steps. No one would hear her.

When she reached for the enormous handle, the bell chimed yet again. "Hold your horses," she muttered, yanking open the door.

A reprimand hung from the tip of her tongue, and there it froze.

A tall, hulking man stood before her. She wasn't frightened.

No, she was mesmerized.

A clap of thunder chased a strong gust of wind. It whipped around him as if trying to caress him with greedy, invisible hands, pushing midnight-black hair into his face. He thrust a free hand through the wild wavy locks, revealing stormy blue eyes.

His gaze bored straight into her like he could read every single one of her thoughts. Knew her deepest desires.

Her heart skipped a beat, and she tore her eyes from his. Not knowing where to look, her gaze skittered over his face and shoulders, taking in the light stubble on his strong jaw. Her focus rested briefly on a full, generous mouth before moving to his open collar. There the barest hint of ink from a tattoo showed. She shifted back to his thick disheveled hair and had to resist the urge to run her hands through the unruly locks.

These unwelcome thoughts surprised her. He wasn't anything like the perfectly coiffed men in her life, yet she liked what she saw. Maybe because she'd been thinking of Blake, and this man was clearly his opposite.

The man cleared his throat, his Adam's apple fascinating her for a couple of beats before she made her way back to his stunning eyes.

"Um, I'm Jacob Grimm with Careful Moves."

Jacob. A strong and masculine name. It suited him.

"We're delivering a living room Baroque set and installing a Lobmeyr chandelier." He glanced at the clipboard then back at her. "Is this the Silverstone residence?"

"Oh, yes. Sorry. Come in." Greta stepped aside, hoping he didn't notice the heat creeping up her neck and cheeks. She'd been gawking at him like an idiot. He was probably wondering if she was a mental case. "Let me show you the room."

The hallway was wide enough for them to walk side-by-side, even as they moved past the main double stairs. Silence fell between, not uncomfortable, but it made her aware of his warmth and the unexplainable pull toward him. She studied him surreptitiously, noting his height. She was five ten, yet her chin didn't reach his broad shoulders. He had incredible biceps, muscular with a light dusting of hair. Ink peeked from his shirtsleeve, and she wondered if it was a continuation of the tattoo at his collar.

She gave a mental shake.

Why was he so fascinating? He wasn't her type. At all.

A deliveryman.

She didn't have anything against them. She'd just never noticed before. At least not like this.

Was it the brewing storm or the man himself, giving the air an electric charge?

Stopping at the threshold of the great room, she explained the layout her mother and stepfather wanted for the set. Also pointed to the light fixture they wanted removed and replaced with the antique chandelier Jacob delivered.

The room was enormous, but he told her they'd need to take

apart the double doors and possibly the frame. He asked where they were to put the old stuff. Greta tried to remember where her parents wanted the original set stored. She was finding it difficult to concentrate. Jacob stood close, and all she could focus on was how good he smelled. It took every single ounce of her willpower not to lean in and inhale him.

A charged silence filled the room as her gaze drifted from his tantalizing neck to focus on his face. She was startled to find him studying her with more than a hint of polite curiosity.

"Sorry," he muttered hoarsely, breaking eye contact and moving back. "I'm gonna let the other men know we might have to break down the door and frame before they begin unloading." He started down the hallway.

As he moved farther away, she wondered about his apology. Was it for their close proximity or the brief heat she'd seen flicker in his eyes?

Either way, distance between them was a good thing. She breathed through her nose and let it out her mouth, running her fingertips along the V-neck of her sundress. Her minds-eye flashed to his hands taking the place of hers and dipping in past the cotton neckline.

Get yourself together, Greta.

She distanced herself from Jacob, from her unsettling desires. Once in the kitchen, she leaned against the counter, letting relief and disappointment flow through her. She couldn't understand her sudden and visceral reaction toward a complete stranger.

Shoving her agitation aside, she grabbed the mug she'd discarded earlier and poured her much-needed coffee while vowing to stay away from the movers. Particularly the one with sexy, volatile, hunger-filled eyes.

Clutching the cup as if it were a buoy keeping her safe from treacherous waters during an approaching storm, she left the kitchen and kept her gaze locked straight ahead and away from the great room. Needing a quiet sanctuary, she climbed the main stairs to her stepfather's library. Books always had a calming effect on her.

Gripping the railing, she slowed her pace, denying the urge to dash up the final steps like a child trying to outrun messy emotions. Reaching the top, she crossed to her stepfather's overly masculine and stuffy room.

She'd never cared for the leather furniture, dark paneling, or the ostentatious desk. However, the papery smell of books was heaven on her frayed nerves. Running her fingertips along the nearest shelf, she picked a couple different titles and sat on the couch. Settling into the supple leather cushion, she opened the book on the top of her pile and prepared to lose herself inside it.

And failed miserably.

By twelve she quit. She'd enough of reading the same page over and over. Her mind kept wandering from the book to a particular man in the great room.

Restless and hungry, she left in search of food. When she made her way to the stairs, the movers' voices floated to her.

"I parked us under a large tree near the front of the driveway. Let's eat there," came a man's voice she didn't recognize."

"I didn't bring anything but saw a few restaurants within walking distance. I'm going to see what I can find."

Greta recognized the deep timber of Jacob's voice. It sent a shiver of pleasure down her spine. She stopped at the bottom of the stairs as the three men came into view, moving past her and toward the front double doors.

Without thinking too much about her motives, she interrupted them. "Sorry. I didn't mean to eavesdrop. I overheard your lunch dilemma." She inclined her head in Jacob's direction. "There's a great carry-out close by. I was going to walk there. You're welcome to join me."

The three men eyed her in varying stages of surprise. Jacob opened his mouth, but a guy with a gray beard answered first. "Thank you, ma'am. We don't want to be a bother. I'm going to share my lunch with him."

Jacob and a tall, rail-thin guy standing next to him broke into raucous laughter.

"What?" Gray beard asked, sounding offended.

"Marty, you eat like a horse," replied the other worker through his laughter. "I can't picture you sharing an apple, let alone half your lunch."

"Besides," Jacob said, his gaze locking on her. "I'm starving. I want everything."

His words sent a wicked buzz of anticipation zinging through her. She dropped his gaze, afraid her desire was painted on her.

"Jacob..." Disapproval dripped from the older man, the one Jacob had called Marty.

"Sorry. I didn't mean to cause a problem." Greta turned away, embarrassed.

Was her little infatuation with Jacob so obvious his boss felt like he needed to protect his employee from her?

"I'd like to go with you," Jacob called after her, his heavy footfalls coming closer. "Are you leaving now?"

She stopped and faced him, refusing to meet the other men's eyes. "Yes, I'm ready now. Are you?"

His long legs ate up the rest of the space between them, and he stood in front of her. "Like you wouldn't believe."

His words sounded like a whispered promise. A thrill shivered through her, growing and spreading. Her whole body throbbed, keeping in time with her quickening pulse.

Take a breath; he's just a man.

She led him through the living room and to a short hallway to the back patio. They passed the inground pool and cabana, stepping to a tree-covered pathway.

"This is a shortcut. It will take us to the back gate and straight on to the main street," she told him.

His gaze met hers, moving briefly to her mouth before studying the path.

Flowers bloomed everywhere. Roses, lilacs, and other plants she couldn't name. The sight took her back to her childhood when she'd pretended the courtyard was a fairy tale forest. Even now, it hasn't lost its magical appeal. After living in a college town apartment, on and off for the last six years, she'd forgotten its beauty.

Greta ran her fingertips over the different flowers and leaves, very aware of Jacob. He was the type of man any woman would have a hard time overlooking, yet her usual need to fill the silence was absent. Her ease around him was unexpected and wonderful.

Reaching the back gate, he unlatched it and held it open for her, stretching his sea green polo a crossed his muscular chest. She tried not to stare.

Needing a distraction, she asked the first question that popped in her mind. "Is Marty your boss?"

Not real stimulating. Still, it was better than asking some of her other questions. Such as, was he willing to take off his shirt?

Sure, way more interesting, but not appropriate. *At all.*

He nodded. "Yeah, he owns Careful Moves."

She pointed to her left, indicating their direction. "He didn't seem pleased with you leaving. Is he afraid you won't come back?"

"I might not. He's been a real ass. Sorry." Jacob winced before smiling. "But no, he doesn't like his men hanging around the clients. Doesn't want anyone claiming we're unprofessional."

Greta held in a laugh. If his boss knew half of the crazy, improper thoughts she had this afternoon regarding one of his employees, he'd worry more about his client's actions than those of his employees.

"Sounds like my father. He's a real stickler for that kind of stuff."

"Oh, yeah, what's he do?"

"Business owner—" She stopped mid-sentence. A huge gust of wind swirled around them, blowing her unbound hair into her eyes before diving under her dress and lifting it.

She gasped, clutching the cotton material and glancing at Jacob, catching him eyeing her legs.

He averted his gaze to the roiling clouds. "Think the storm will pass?"

"Who knows?" The weather. A nice, safe topic, though another part of her mind was dissecting the hungry way he'd eaten up the sight of her legs. "It's been looming, so far nothing except wind and heavy clouds."

He turned his attention from the sky. "Find anything interesting in your library?"

The sudden topic change threw her, but she rolled with it. "No. I skimmed through *Gatsby* and reread my favorite scenes."

Reading was stretching the truth. What she'd really been doing was staring without comprehension, too busy straining to hear Jacob's voice and footsteps, and wondering why she cared.

"*Great Gatsby*. I love it, even if the ending's depressing as hell."

She cut a sideways glance. Was he serious?

He must've caught her skepticism, because he chuckled. "I know, amazing. I can lift heavy stuff *and* read."

"Not what I was thinking," she lied, knowing the heat flooding her cheeks gave her away.

"Uh-huh, sure. Believe it or not, I can read books without pictures. Just last summer I graduated from Dr. Seuss levels. My family's proud."

"Ha, very funny." Greta was horrified to hear herself giggle. She wasn't a gigglier. "What do you like to read? And please, don't give me the names of children's authors…unless, of course, it's the Grimm brothers."

He groaned, a smile tugging at the corners of his mouth. "God, no. I had enough of those when I was a kid. My mom was obsessed with those stories."

"In what way?"

"Let's see. She read all of their stuff, both in English and

German. Married a man with the last name Grimm and named her boys Jacob and Wilhelm…"

"Oh my God. You're a Grimm brother. I love it!"

"Glad you love it." He gave a wry smile. "But if you ever happen to run into my brother, Will, whatever you do, don't call him Wilhelm."

With difficulty, she held in another atrocious giggle. She loved his dry humor. "Duly noted."

They rounded the corner, and her favorite sandwich shop came into view. "There it is, Mattie's Deli. Best lunches in Petite Bois."

"Good thing." He frowned at the darkening sky. "The storm might break open any second."

"Maybe, still this is Michigan. You never know, it might pass us by."

Facts and desires were churning within her violently as the clouds above; she couldn't tell truth from fiction. Only knew she didn't want to rush her time with him.

Jacob was a stranger she wouldn't see after today. It didn't matter; she wasn't quite ready to give him up. She was too sensible to ever act on her attraction. However, it sure was fun standing close to the flame.

They crossed the street, and he held open the door to the deli. Stepping past, she brushed against him. The slight contact had her insides tightening in keen awareness, and she had to force herself to keep moving.

The heat might be fun, but a single flame could become an inferno and consume everything in its path.

He'd come in close behind her. All she had to do was lean back to press against his delectable chest.

Resisting the urge was difficult, making it nearly impossible to concentrate on the menu posted above the counter. She didn't try and ordered the first thing her eyes focused on: a turkey sandwich with homemade sauce.

Turning, she studied him while he read the menu. The impulse to run the pads of her fingers along his jaw was hard to resist. It made her heart beat a little faster.

"If I order the large fruit salad, will you have some?" he asked, seeming oblivious to her ogling. *Thank God.*

She nodded, and he added it to his order. The teen-aged boy behind the counter handed them a ticket, and they moved off to the side to wait.

Jacob leaned against the wall, crossing his feet at the ankles and shoving his hands into his front pockets. “Thanks for bringing me here. Left to my own devices, I’d probably have spent my lunchbreak wandering around trying to find food. Or worse…sharing lunch with Marty.”

She laughed at his dire tone. “I don’t mind. I needed to eat, and I like talking with you.”

“Yeah, it’s been nice.” He sounded shocked.

Greta opened her mouth, licking her lips, planning to tease him. His gaze zeroed in on her mouth, making her playfulness evaporate. Uncrossing his feet, he shifted closer.

She didn’t step back, and he advanced. Jacob’s gaze jumped to her eyes then back to her mouth, teeth capturing his beautiful full bottom lip briefly before letting go.

She wanted to lick the moisture left behind.

We hope you enjoyed this bit of *Fairy Tale Lies*. Both books are now available at all major retailers.

~ * ~

Interested in getting advance notice of great new books, author contests and giveaways, and only-to-subscriber goodies? Join https://www.facebook.com/groups/ChampagneBookClub/.